# IMMORTAL CELLS

## TYROLIN PUXTY

IMMORTAL WORKS
SALT LAKE CITY

Immortal Works LLC
1505 Glenrose Drive
Salt Lake City, Utah 84104
Tel: (385) 202-0116



Cover Art by Ashley Literski
http://strangedevotion.wixsite.com/strangedesigns



This book is a work of fiction. Names, characters, businesses, organizations, places, events and incidents either are the product of the author's imagination or are used fictitiously. Any resemblance to actual persons, living or dead, events, or locales is entirely coincidental.

ISBN 978-1-953491-50-3 (Paperback)
ASIN B0BSSTY3YM (Kindle Edition)

*To my son-shine.*
*To my mother.*
*To my husband.*
*To my grandmother.*
*To every cat in existence.*
*There are never enough words to express my love and gratitude.*
*So I'll just start with these six.*
*I love you. Thank you.*
*Always.*

# CHAPTER 1

Running on an empty stomach proves difficult, but it is far better than the alternative. Exposed in an expansive field, I'm left to contend with wild animals and frost because the guards chased me out of town. My cramped home, damp and falling in on itself, provides more safety from the elements.

The cold night air stings with each inhale, my bare feet calloused and bruised from days spent fleeing.

It doesn't make any sense. Not *once* have I broken the law. Not *once* have I hurt somebody. My only crime is existing, which is the biggest felony of all.

Utterly exhausted, I focus on the shrubbery ahead and wonder if it's safe to rest, but I'm left with little choice. I can't keep running like this, and if I slip in the mud again, I might twist an ankle.

My heart pounds in my ears as I reach the bushes. I crouch down and pull back the greenery, checking for wild animals. The burnaprays are particularly nasty critters, hunting in packs and digging through live prey's flesh until they reach their favorite part of the body—the bone.

Fortunately, I find no evidence of their nest or waste about. Twigs poke and scrape at my face as I step into the bush, the stinging nettle brushing against my calves. As best as I can manage, I curl into a tiny ball in the mud. It's times like this I wish I wasn't so ridiculously tall. In my homeland many years ago, six foot eight was considered average height. Civilians in these parts cower at the one-foot height discrepancy, so I've become more reclusive than usual.

I laugh at the thought, most likely due to long-term sleep

deprivation. *Reclusive.* Can't get much more reclusive than sleeping in a bush in the middle of the wilderness.

The wind picks up and the branches batter my body. Perhaps prison wouldn't be much worse than this. After all, I've reduced myself to nothing as a protest for my freedom. But surely *this* isn't freedom.

Homeless and friendless, I no longer have an identity, a purpose, or a hope in the world. I live on faith; deciding to believe that one day something *will* change so that I can thrive instead of survive.

Hugging myself, I close my eyes and shiver. *Imagine a warm fire, Malin. A roasty, toasty fire. That's it, girl. Imagine it's there.*

My robe's material is thin and barely covers my gangly arms. I'm naked beneath the fabric, having had no time to grab clothing before the guards came knocking on my door. It's like they waited until I was most vulnerable before they confronted me. But surely, they couldn't have known.

How did they even find out? I kept to myself. I barely visited the market. I told nobody who I was. Unless they've been tracking me this entire time...

My mind races with useless thoughts, barely distracting my body from the bitter air. I'm too cold and too alert to sleep normally—something I've long forgotten how to do, anyway.

A deep slumber could fix everything, but it's been years since I've had the opportunity to rest. Every night begins with my back against the wall, watching. Just watching. And waiting.

Despite my better judgment, I close one eye. Then, without permission, my second eye droops as my chin nuzzles into my chest.

I may not be able to sleep, but it's a relief to rest. My stubborn lids feel glued shut, oblivious to the reality beyond.

And for the first time in years, my mind succumbs to the darkness...and a scream echoes in the distance...

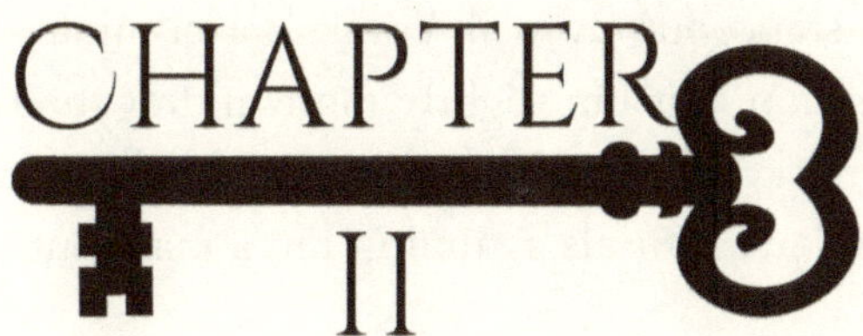

# CHAPTER II

I haven't stopped trembling since the night the guards captured me because I fell asleep. At first, I thought it was from fear, but I'm instead considering that it's fury; fury at the situation, fury at my life and fury at the chastising screams in my mind.

*You idiot. For years, you've remained on high alert. And the one time you desperately needed to keep your eyes open, you go and do the opposite! What's wrong with you? Did you want to get caught? How could you? Do you regret it now?*

It's an ongoing barrage of rhetorical questions.

*You're mortal now. How do you expect to survive this? Mortals need warmth – the right amount. They need food, water, sleep. These are all things you've gone without for months, or even years at a time. You don't even know how to take care of a body properly!*

There's no turning back now. Once you're sent to the Immortal Cells, you're there for eternity. Or if you're a mortal who has regrettably been mistaken for an immortal, then you're there until you die.

Like me.

I screwed up.

Squished between two guards who are a head shorter than me, we rock back and forth in sway with the carriage. The clip-clopping of the horses is a nice distraction from my gurgling stomach, which only garners negative attention from the guards and the prisoner across from me.

He fits in with the guards better than I do. Surely this man was born around here. The mousy-brown hair, the petite build, and pale skin are markers for the central-landers.

Me? I stand out, even if I wasn't a criminal. My height alone draws attention, but I'm slightly more androgynous than the others. The long neck, the broad shoulders, and golden hair that hangs by my jawline have mortals assuming I'm a man, but that's just not the case.

Not that it matters. I no longer have an identity. My name, gender, race, and ideals are unimportant when I already have to conceal every facet of my being.

The man across from me has dark rings beneath his eyes, assumedly from lack of sleep. Is that how they caught him, too? He's dressed in beige overalls and work boots, heavily implying his role as a farmer. No doubt he was responsible for keeping his town fed, and yet, here he is. Sentenced to a life of torture and torment, simply because he is an immortal.

I clear my throat, uncomfortable from the lack of water. It's been at least a week since a drop has touched my dry, cracked lips.

"Got summin' to say?" The guard next to me spits, then tightens the cuffs on my wrists. They were tight enough as it was.

"No," I respond distantly. "Just thirsty."

The man across from me widens his eyes, as if I've spoken something taboo.

"Immor'als don' get firsty!" The guard snaps back, the barrel of his gun pressed threateningly into my side.

"Yes, they do," I say, careful not to make eye contact. "They feel everything a mortal feels. Sometimes much worse."

"You'll 'av your 'ead chopped for spoutin' nonsense like that!"

I shrug, trying to disassociate from the burning sensation in my wrists. I swear these cuffs are trying to slice into my bones.

"Makes me sick even sittin' next ta summin' so vulgar." The guard continues to vent, squirming restlessly next to me. "If it were up ta me, I'd fro you all in a big 'ole. Seal it up. Be done with you lot."

I notice the man across from me quickly wipe a smirk from his face. The problem with mortals is they fear what they don't understand, and propaganda only worsens any misconceived perception of us. We already live sad enough of an existence without the worry of being chased and abused.

"Almost 'ere," the other guard announces as the carriage slows down. "Least these ones didn't put up much of a fight. I like when they're resigned to their fate."

"I prefer a rumble, though!"

I struggle to believe this particular guard would fare well in a fight. He's well-fed, to put it nicely, and seems to enjoy the art of conjecture far too much to trade the speaking word for fists.

"You're in the wrong job," the more subdued guard mumbles.

I dig my feet into the wooden floor when the carriage rolls to an abrupt stop. The man across from me isn't as dexterous and almost face-plants, only regaining composure by scrambling in his cuffs while being pulled by his collar back into his seat.

"Al'ight, Stretch. To ya feet!"

I don't realize straight away that the guard is referring to me. Are we required to stretch our muscles before we stand? Is that some sort of procedural practice implemented to cope with the long ride?

"Me?" I clarify.

"Yeah, ya tall freak!"

Oh. *Stretch*. It's a cruel nickname. I suppose this sort of treatment is just a taste of what's coming.

Grimly, I stand and stoop over so as not to hit my head and patiently wait for the carriage doors to open. The man across from me doesn't need to hunch, coming up to my shoulder when we stand. He forces a smile and goes to shake my hand, then rolls his eyes at the cuffs.

"Name's Rune. They'll strip our identity soon, so I thought I'd introduce myself before I become a number."

The stout guard kicks Rune in the back of the knee so that he loses balances and almost collapses.

"None o' that! Silence ya immor'al!"

Rune stands back up, his mousy hair falling into his light eyes. He goes to say something, but notices the seriousness in the guard's expression and thinks better of it. I don't understand how he has the gall to act so nonchalant. Maybe he's a good actor. Maybe I am too. Perhaps I don't look nearly as terrified as I feel.

The doors to the carriage open, the stream of sunlight welcoming despite the gloomy sight before us.

I suck in the air and forget to exhale as I stare at the gray prison block. It's impenetrable from what I can see. Guards galore surround the building, the walls taller than anything I've come across before. Even the tower overlooking the prison is much grander than castles I've visited in the past.

"Get out!"

The guard pushes me, mud splattering up my calves when I step off. It was cold in the carriage, but at least I had the body warmth of the sweaty guards to keep me somewhat warm. The weather here is even more chilling than where they picked me up.

Rune jumps off and lands beside me, his shoulders tensing when he locks eyes with his new home.

"How old are you?" Rune whispers.

I shrug. "Does it matter? We're here forever."

"Just wanted to know if you lived a decent life before we arrived."

Rune looks like he's in his late twenties or early thirties. That's generally when immortals stop aging. His personality, however, has the zest of an older teenager, even despite the circumstances.

"No immortal life is decent," I respond coldly.

"It can be."

I don't get a chance to reply when we're pushed again towards the entrance. Together we trudge forward as a small door within the concrete walls opens, leading us to a narrow corridor.

For decades, I imagined the possibility of ending up in this earthly hell. I visualized the lack of color, the square blocks, the abusive guards. I just never considered the smell. The foul odor is overwhelming, a strange mix of dead fish and vulture vomit.

Fortunately, immortals don't need to breathe for survival purposes. It's merely a comfort thing. *Un*fortunately, I'm mortal, and the stench is so overpowering it still manages to sting my eyes and crawl its way into mouth.

"Yikes," Rune mutters, covering his nose. The guard hits him on the back of the head, instantly silencing him.

Terror truly hits when we're instructed to halt. Is this where the torture begins?

"Smoke signal." The guard says from behind. He motions towards the tower, a purple haze of smoke wafting from the arched windows. I desperately want to ask what it means, but that would mean severely overstepping my boundary.

"Understaffed and overcrowded *again!*"

I glance over my shoulder to find the stout guard throwing his hands up dramatically while the other remains still and stoic.

"These ones won' be able ta ge' their uniform today, then?"

"No. They'll need to bypass the infirmary and get their numbers assigned."

"Ugh! Why can't these blas'ed immor'als just *die?*"

Rune flinches at the harsh words, but I've often wondered the same thing. Through starvation, dehydration, hypothermia, and severe blood loss, immortals have persevered. Yes, the hunger pangs feel like acid burning the insides. Yes, dehydration leads to severe hallucination and fatigue that can take months to recuperate from. Yes, I met an immortal who never fully recovered from hypothermia and continued their day-to-day life either sleeping or shivering. The body doesn't like the mistreatment...but it just refuses to give up.

"We're getting close," the other guard says under his breath, but I'm not sure what he's referring to. "All right. Take a left."

With another customary push, Rune and I turn left down the corridor and are met by a muscular guard who barely fits his uniform. He nods, opens the door and leads us inside.

It's an empty, gray room except for an older woman in a brown suit who fills out forms behind a stone counter.

"Hurry, hurry," she says without looking up.

We're not pushed this time, the original guards having remained outside of the room. Instead, the muscular guard glares at us as a warning and I attempt to swallow the lump in my throat.

"What...what do we do?" I ask, unable to conceal the tremor in my voice.

"Come here," the woman says, snapping her fingers. "You're well overdue. Were other carriages outside with you?"

"I don't...no, it was just our carriage."

"And it was only the pair of you inside?" She peers over her glasses, raising her eyebrow at me. This woman looks ancient. Her hair is pinned back so tightly in a bun, I fear her face might slide off if she were to ever lose her hair band.

"Yes," Rune answers for me.

Huffing, she gathers a bunch of papers and crumbles them. "*Great.* Now we're *really* overdue. We anticipated seventeen other captures this week. Some of you must be getting better at hiding."

"Evidently not us," Rune tries to joke, but it falls flat. "I never tried to hide. The mortals in my village liked me, you know."

"Nobody likes you," the woman says dismissively, scribbling on a piece of paper. "We want every filthy immortal off our clean streets so mortals are protected. I keep telling them we need more cells. If you creatures could stop breeding out there, it would help immensely. Now come here and give me your arm." She snaps her fingers at Rune, who reluctantly steps closer and reveals his wrist.

Without hesitation, she reaches for a stamp and presses it into his skin. He winces and I can almost hear the steam rising from his scorched flesh as a sideways 8, an infinity sign, is forever imprinted.

"1-2-2-5-5," she addresses Rune. "You will be escorted to your cell."

Rune and I exchange concerned glances. It's not like we've bonded since our trip together, but there's something about farewelling a familiar face in an unfamiliar space.

The muscular guard leads Rune out of the room, closing the door behind them.

"You. Tallie. Wrist," the woman says. "Quick, quick. You know the drill."

Hesitantly, I give her my wrist and refrain from squealing at the burning sensation as she marks my skin with her stamp. Glancing down at the horizontal 8, I can't help but question it.

"Miss? What is this?"

"Infinite. To remind prisoners they're here forever. It's also your mark until we have someone available to give you your uniform."

It's difficult to concentrate on her words when the searing pain only worsens with each passing second. "Oh. Th-thank you for informing me."

The woman raises her eyebrow once more. "Odd to thank me. Hmm. All right. 1-2-2-5-6."

"Is that my cell?"

"That's your *name*."

I exhale, forgetting about the terrible odor. "But that's not my name."

Silence. An eerie, haunting silence. The woman leans in, her milky eyes filled with hatred. "That's your name *here*. And you're here *forever*."

I think of what Rune said earlier, about his prophecy of the prison stripping us of our identity. I spent years running from myself, hiding from myself, lying to myself. If this is the last person I shall ever be known as, then I've at least earned the right to be called by my name.

"My name is Malin," I say defiantly, my chin lifting as I speak. "I understand the premise of my imprisonment. But my name is Malin."

"Your name is 1-2-2-5-6."

"My name is M-Malin."

The muscular guard returns, his forehead crinkled at the standoff between myself and the older woman. His boots slam against the floor as he approaches me, wraps his giant hand around my wrist and twists until something pops.

Screaming in pain, I drop to my knees, trying to discern whether the searing skin or the dislocated bone is more painful.

They leave me to weep on the floor, mocking my position as they tower over me.

"The entitled coxcomb wanted to be called by its name."

The guard throws back his head with laughter. "Obnoxious thugs. The younger immortals are so much worse."

Nursing my wrist, I consider my words. "But I'm mortal."

The woman snorts. "No mortal has ever wound up here. There's no mistaking one of you. Especially once you get your uniform."

"I'm mortal," I repeat, wondering if there's a way to prove such an outlandish statement.

"If you're mortal, then you'll die a saint. Otherwise, you'll rot here in eternity. Either way is fine by me," she responds, growing tired of the conversation. She redirects her attention to the guard. "Please take it away from me."

"*She*," I correct, surprised by my sudden backbone. Talking back is just asking for punishment.

The built guard tugs on my elbow, nearly pulling my arm out of its socket. I swiftly stand so that I'm not painfully dragged along the floor, my cuffs clanging together.

Unable to wriggle out of the guard's grip, I find him much more intimidating than the others. Not because of his biceps or scowl, but because he's noticeably tall—around my height. I'm not accustomed to people in this area able to meet my eye level.

He leads me into a long block of cells. Hundreds, maybe thousands, of immortals press their faces into the bars in an attempt to get a good look at me.

I want to look at each and every one of them so that I can understand their reactions, but it's frightening to maintain eye contact. They're not criminals, but if they've lived here long enough, who knows what they've become?

"*Got ourselves a mortal! Look at that skin!*" someone from a cell on the second floor calls out, and people cheer. I don't understand how they've managed to assume that about me.

"*Tasty, tasty, tasty!*"

"*Where's their uniform? Huh? Why'd we have to be stuck with it?*"

I'm so confused. The guard only tightens his grip around my elbow as we continue down the line of cells. Is this how brides feel walking down the aisle? The fear of being judged, pained with the uncertainty of their future?

The ceiling lights flicker, which is bad news for the prisoners. The cells are not illuminated in any form—not a candle, not a generator. Inside is dark, and if the ceiling lights in the corridor fail, it'll be as black as night.

None of the immortals look healthy. They're pale, gaunt...with a strange shade of blue painted on their flesh...

Are they *that* sickly and mistreated? Are these bruises from constant beatings? Squinting my eyes in the dim light, I peer in closer at the immortals who hang by the bars; my arrival the only exciting thing to have happened all day.

But their bruised skin...

I feel woozy at the thought and stumble over my feet, which are suddenly heavy with dread. My misstep is enough to make the guard groan as he readjusts his grip around my elbow.

What have I *done*? How could I possibly be trapped here? The immortals aren't living; they're barely existing!

"You killed them..." I say, my eyes darting from one prisoner to the other.

"They've tried," the guard admits. "An underfunded, growing prison needs fewer inmates."

"But the blue skin..."

"In the unlikely event of an escape, we can track you down easier. Blue skin means they're slower, weaker. Win, win."

"When...when will..."

He waits for me to finish, but when I can't form the words, he responds. "You and the other one will get your uniform when our medic returns. Could be tonight. Could be next week. You can't plan life."

No... No, you certainly cannot plan life.

The door to my cell is already open, and sitting in the darkness on the bed is a very solemn looking Rune. His eyes light up when he sees me and honestly, I'm sure mine do, too.

A familiar face in an unfamiliar place.

The guard releases me and unlocks my cuffs. The relief is palpable and I instinctively rub my wrists, soothing the ache.

"Get in, please," the guard says.

"Thank you for saying please," I blurt, and we stare at one another awkwardly for a moment.

"Cells automatically open at 7am. Somebody will be by to give you your uniform at some point."

Without another word, he slides the cell door shut and leaves us in the grim solitude. Uncomfortably, I join Rune on the bed, dismayed to feel that it's as hard as the cement floors.

"Let me give you the grand tour!" Rune attempts to sound jovial, but there's no denying the defeat in his voice. "No toilet; I assume because they discourage immortals from that kind of thing. There's this bed and another plank in that dark corner. There's only one pillow which smells a little funny, but I'm happy to share it with you. We can implement a one night on, one night off system. And—as you can see—that's it, really. I'm hoping the longer we're here, we might get some privileges. Like a writing desk or a harmonica. I can't be sure, of course. But...there's always hope."

Tears sting my eyes, and a gentle hand rests on my shoulder. With that one kind touch, I allow myself to burst into hysterical sobs. "How did I end up here? I'm so stupid!"

"Not stupid. Just unlucky."

My vision blurs, and I want nothing more than to feel the warmth of another person. At first, I'm surprised by my forwardness, but quickly remind myself that prison isn't the place to feel shame for wanting basic human needs. So I nuzzle into Rune's chest as he wraps his arms around my body, stroking my hair while I choke on tears.

And in the brief intervals when I'm not howling...I hear Rune cry too.

# CHAPTER III

"So, what are you in for?" Rune jokes.

We sit cross-legged on the floor with the one frayed blanket resting on our legs. I give him an insincere smile, tired from my distraught display.

"Thank you for earlier."

He frowns. "For what?"

"For, you know, being there when I cried. It's been a long time since...since I've had someone there for me."

A smile quickly replaces his befuddled expression, and he waves the compliment away. "Don't mention it."

"I never told you my name," I say, my raspy voice echoing down the cell block. Rune doesn't seem to mind his louder volume, only having one inflection. "It's Malin."

"Pretty. Don't hear names like that."

"It's northern. I'm assuming the name Rune means you're from the east, but you're not...how people from the east usually look."

Rune points to his hair, then to his smaller frame. "Mother fraternized with the enemy, let's say. But technically I'm from the central land. I'm a bit of a mutt, truth be told."

"Is Mother still alive?"

Rune shakes his head and I nod understandingly. It's not uncommon for immortals to have mortal mothers.

"If you don't mind me asking," I continue, "is your mother the reason why you never felt the need to hide from the mortals?"

Rune glances up at the stone ceiling, regaining emotional composure. "Yeah. Mother was a hard worker. My grandfather taught me how to work in the fields and grow food. Our village was laid-back, grateful, kind. A real community. At first, I didn't know why I looked so much younger than my peers. I thought it was the lifestyle. I was strong and athletic from daily physical work. It was only when I reached fifty and still looked twenty that people began to whisper."

"You didn't know you were immortal?"

"Not until my sixties. Mother explained everything on her deathbed. She assured me I'd be safe in the village and that as long as I kept the mortals fed, they couldn't harm me. That much was true until recently. Guards visited the village one morning. Just a routine check-in. A nervous villager must've let something slip, because the guards stalked my every move. They broke into the barn. They watched me through the night. They 'accidentally' shot me in the shoulder. When I didn't die from infection, they knew. That's how I ended up here."

My heart twinges for Rune. His experience is so forlorn, so tragic. He actually had a semblance of a life that was ripped away from him.

"Did your community protest? Or stand up for you?"

Rune glances down at the fresh scar on his wrist and nods. "Some did. One was shot when he stepped forward to vouch for my innocence. He was only nineteen."

"I'm so sorry." My apology means nothing when I can't fix it. It hangs in the air, heavy and silent, so I change the topic. "How old are you?"

"Ninety something."

I don't respond maturely. Instead, my jaw drops and I deny his answer. "That can't be. You're too young. How do you know you're not mortal? Immortals need to be at least two hundred to be sure."

"Trust me, I know." His smile is genuine, but the lowering of his gaze means he's concealing something he's perhaps not ready to share. "When you know, you know. I thought age was a touchy subject for you."

I rewind my memories, reliving my abrupt answer when Rune

asked me about my age. In an attempt to mimic his coy reaction, I smirk. "Don't you know that a lady never reveals her age?"

This time he laughs, raising his hands as if to surrender. "All right, all right. Hint received. What about you? Do you have a story?"

I consider the question, wondering whether now is the time to confide in my roommate. We have eternity to get to know one another, so maybe I needn't rush the bonding process. "There's not a lot to say. I'm from the north. As a child, we lived in peace. Immortals weren't hunted or loathed. But as I grew, there was a target on my head. So I ran. From county to county, town to town, alley to alley. I've not had a home, a family, or a companion for as long as I can remember. In a sick twist of fate, this cell is probably going to end up being much safer and comfortable than anywhere I've ever lived."

I'm relieved I didn't share my entire story, because Rune's face says it all. After telling him a brief and edited summary, our dynamics change. Polite listening turns to pity and he reaches for my hand and squeezes it gently.

Kind human touch is so uplifting. I'd forgotten.

"I know this isn't how we wanted our lives to end up," Rune says, lowering his voice for the first time this night, "but I will always be here for you. Whenever you need a laugh or an ear to bend, I'm your man. I promise you."

I tenderly squeeze his hand back, emotion bubbling in my chest. I can't bring myself to speak, but Rune doesn't seem to mind. To quell the quiet, he hums a lullaby, his baritone voice soothing.

We shift positions so that we curl into one another for body heat, our heads resting on the itchy pillow. Rune readjusts so that I can have the majority of the cushion, but pebbles would be a more comfortable option.

"I promise, Malin," he repeats tiredly between hums.

Once again, I don't verbally respond, keeping my back to him and sleepily moaning incoherent nonsense. It's the only way I know how to reply.

Rune doesn't know promises were meant to be broken.

$$\infty$$

*"WAKE UP!"*

The words are thrown at us like angry profanities, the commands repeating down the cell block. Batons are rattled against the bars, ringing in my ears.

Drearily, I pull myself into a sitting position and notice I've accidentally stolen the entire blanket for the night.

"Sorry," I mutter to Rune, who is rubbing his eyes and stretching out. He has a slight grin on his face. Has he forgotten where he is?

"It happens. How did you sleep?"

Distracted by the loud clang on our door, I don't answer. The guard storms by and our door automatically rolls open. Guess it's feeding time.

"How did you sleep?" Rune repeats, getting to his feet.

In the short time I've known him, I've learned that he struggles to accept unanswered questions. Maybe he's just persistent, or maybe it's a quirk he can't shake.

"Poorly," I say. It's a half-truth. Given my history of not sleeping for days, weeks, months at a time, any form of shut-eye fills me with gratitude. Even in the terrible conditions of the prison cell, there was something reassuring about having a roof over my head and someone next to me.

"Same," he admits. "But you don't snore, so that's a plus. Twitchy legs though."

Despite the open door, we're reluctant to move from the protection of our cell. I inch closer and watch hundreds of blue, gray, and purple immortals gather into the corridor outside. Their clothes are all torn and frayed, assumedly wearing the same thing they wore when they first arrived. It's scary to think how long some have endured the prison. One hundred, two hundred years? I've barely been here for twelve hours.

I have so many questions. Will they be kind? Have they turned into monsters? I've noticed several with scowls. Many with drooped faces. There's one across from us who doesn't leave their cell, sitting in the corner in the shadows. A grim reminder of my future. It's hard to discern the figure in the darkness, but I note a long beard. Presumably it'd be difficult to shave in here. Why hasn't he joined the others?

I step away from the door as prisoners pass our cell, zombie-eyed and compliant. It's as if they're on autopilot, not even stopping to peer in to check out the new inmates. Frightened, I press my back into the wall, far away from the entrance, and wonder why they don't look at us. Have they lost their humanity since being here? Curiosity? Intrigue? Is that all gone?

"Should we follow them?" Rune asks. "I bet there's breakfast."

"This isn't a holiday," I say through gritted teeth. "The guard said someone will collect us for our uniform assignment."

"Didn't he say something about being short-staffed? I doubt they're coming this morning. Come on. Let's follow the others. They'll show us the ropes."

I admire and resent his optimism. He steps outside of the cell once the crowd of prisoners disperse. Hesitantly, I stoop and follow a confident Rune down the corridor.

Just ahead, the immortals are forming stoic lines as they march through two large doors. Prison guards stand on either side, their arms crossed and their eyes narrowed. We join the end of the queue, keeping several feet behind the others. Rune fidgets, turning deathly pale when he focuses on the back of a woman's neck in front of us. I don't think he's had a chance to observe the other prisoners and absorb the severity of our position. The woman is visibly malnourished, bones poking through her bruised flesh. The back of her neck in particular is bluer than the rest of her body, skin practically sliding over what's left of her muscles. She is literally a rotting, functioning corpse.

Rune instinctively strokes his pale arm, as healthy blood travels through his veins. His wide eyes glance up at mine and all I can do is nod sadly. Many years from now, new immortals will look at his rotting flesh and react in exactly the same manner.

I feel so out of place here. Not only because of my skin, but the lack of urgency or even tension is unnerving. The prisoners have lost their will to live, nothing more than empty shells, destined to carry on whether they like it or not. I've resigned myself to my fate, but like Rune, there's still a spark, still fear, still hope...still *fight*.

...isn't there?

Step by step we continue until we enter the bland hall with no natural light. The immortals silently take their places at stone tables, crammed in tightly with one another.

"What is this place?" Rune whispers.

"I think it's a cafeteria." I motion at the tables, but I could be wrong. I can't smell food. Or hear pots clanging together.

It's only as everyone finds their seats that they finally lock eyes with Rune and I—the two outsiders. I expect backlash. I expect slanderous name calling. Instead they solemnly and almost in unison, clasps their hands together and stare at the empty tables.

The life has been sucked out of them.

Rune tugs on my elbow and leads me towards a table in the corner where three other immortals are sat.

"May we please join you?" Rune asks, his charisma overshadowed by nerves.

When they don't acknowledge us, we tentatively sit on the edge so as not to disturb their state.

My stomach churns, not just from hunger but from a deep sense of dread. Something doesn't feel right. *Nothing* feels right here, but there's electricity in the air. Imminent danger.

"Rune." I swallow hard as the prisoners take a deep breath in. Then they exhale. *Together*.

"Malin." As if taming a wild animal, Rune stands carefully, keeping his gaze locked on the immortals at the table. They don't blink. They only stare at their bony hands...and breathe.

I follow Rune's movements, backing away from the table as we navigate through the maze of a hall.

"To the cell?" Rune whispers.

For some reason, heading back to the cell seems like a smart way to trap ourselves as voluntary sitting ducks. I don't know what's coming, but after years on the run, I've become quite adept at sensing confrontation.

The hall is void of guards or any authority. It's like they've thrown us in here together to...

To...

Didn't that guard say they try to kill the immortals?

*Oh no.*

I start running through the hall, leaving Rune behind. My only focus is on the now closed doors and getting out of this room. There isn't a door handle and they're sealed shut. Desperately, I bang on the wall and scream for help.

Help that will never come.

"What? What is it?" Rune asks.

But the other prisoners have stopped breathing. They know.

"Hold your breath," I say, inhaling deeply. "The torture is coming."

Before Rune can even react, a forceful hiss explodes from the corners in the room. Harsh thuds come from inside the walls as shrill whistles sporadically sound like a siren. Rune and I press our backs into one another in an attempt to protect ourselves from what's to come.

"They don't care!" Rune must mean the prisoners, who all sit in a trance.

I want to tell him it's because they've been conditioned and are no doubt used to such treatment. But I won't risk breathing. I don't want to become one of them.

Green fog lifts from the ground, soon encompassing the entire hall. I almost scream when the fog dances in my eyes, completely burning my retinas. But like a strong protest, I keep my mouth shut and howl internally.

The bastards are gassing us.

Rune coughs from behind and I want to help, but can't risk damaging my body to defend his. Rune is not going to die. Be in discomfort? Of course. Potential permanent pain and scarring? Absolutely. But he won't die.

Through the haze, I notice the other prisoners sitting erectly with their eyes closed, as if desensitized to such treatment.

When I feel Rune collapse behind me, I drop to my knees and turn to face his writhing body.

"*Help!*" He yells in agony as his skin sizzles before my very eyes. I can't bring myself to check my limbs. Instead, I throw myself over his pained body, wrapping my legs with my tattered robe and frantically try to cover as much of our torsos as possible. Holding my breath, I close my eyes and do what everyone else does—I wait for the torture to subside.

I can't say how much time passes. It feels like hours. But it couldn't be more than two minutes at the most as the whirring stops. I desperately inhale air filtered through the meager sleeve of my robe as I hold it to my face.

It isn't clean. It isn't fresh. But it isn't toxic.

Too afraid to open my eyes, I remain on top of Rune, trembling violently. But we need to move. Opening my eyes, I assess the damage. When I realize our exposed skin is sticking to one another, I gag. Frozen, unsure as to what I should do, I only imagine our shared screams as our skin tears from our body. But the longer we wait, the worse it will get. Delicately, I pull my shin from his, wailing as our fresh wounds peel away with ease.

The prisoners, now satisfied that the process is complete, stand and gather by the closed doors, side stepping around the pair of us, having fallen in a heap in the middle of the hall.

"Rune?" I croak, my voice shredded despite keeping my mouth shut. I can't imagine what his insides must be experiencing.

He's quivering about as much as I am, but he slowly opens his bloodshot eyes, the long lashes on his lids waving like wheat. His face is red and moist, but faring better than I expected. He might just heal if he can take care of his skin.

"I want to go home, Malin," he says, blood trickling out of his mouth.

At least he has a home to return to. "That wasn't a nice induction, was it?"

"I don't know if I can stand. I feel sick."

"Me too. Maybe there's showers. That's what we need."

"We *need* a medic."

We *need* a lot of things; things they are deliberately depriving us off. They said it themselves—they're understaffed, underfunded and overcrowded. Immortals are evil and the less there are, the better.

I give Rune a few minutes to compose himself, and with many grunts, we manage to help each other to our feet.

Like the sheep we're slowly turning into, we join the end of the line once again as the doors to the cell block reopen.

"Malin, you're so burnt," Rune's voice is unpleasantly hoarse.

"We all are," I dismiss. Actually, the other prisoners don't look as bad as we do. Maybe it's the blue skin, or maybe it's something their bodies are accustomed to. Either way, their appearance remains virtually unchanged.

"I need water," Rune says.

"Stop talking. Rest your vocal cords. We'll find something."

Hobbling at the back of the prison line, we return to the cell block and watch as the majority of prisoners simply return to their cells.

Seriously? They obediently gather in a room that gasses them, then without so much as another word, they wander back to their cage?

Frustration takes control of every other emotion. I tell Rune to stay where he is to conserve energy then stumble towards the prisoners.

"Excuse me! Could somebody please direct us to the showers? Or a water source?"

My request goes unanswered. As each syllable dries my throat further, I seek help from every cell I pass. Weakly clinging to the cell bars, I approach every mindless immortal and beg for some sort of direction or advice.

I'm met with sad shrugs and vacant stares, which only aggravates me further.

"Come on, you lunatics! Speak to me! We need your help!"

"You won't get help from them." A smooth voice interjects, clear and precise. "They're all dead. They just don't know it yet."

I search for the voice, my burning eyes landing on the cell to my left. I recognize the dark outline as the bearded man, lying with his feet up on the bed. This was the immortal who didn't join the others in the hall.

I hang by the entrance of his open cell, every action wearing on my joints. "Will you help? Please? We're in so much pain."

The figure half-laughs, then throws his head back, resting it on the stone wall. "Nice to hear some fight in you. Wonder how long you'll hold on to that. All fight gets diminished."

He wants a fighter? I'll damn well show him a fighter.

I intrusively storm into the cell and tower over his bed. My menacing glare doesn't intimidate him the way I intend, but he finds my zest amusing.

At least from this angle, I can see him better. His skin has tinges of pale blue and purple, but he isn't as underfed as the others. All things considering, he's in pretty good shape. He even has a couple of abs.

Thankfully, he's wearing black trousers, but I can't see a shirt anywhere in his cell. His beard is dark, so I deduce he's most likely from the east. There are some creases beneath his eyes which means he's a lot older than most of the immortals. Pushing seven hundred, easy.

His cheeks are plump; nicely hydrated which means he has access to water.

"I'm not playing games," I say. "We need to clean the toxins from our skin."

We lock eyes for several moments, as he scrutinizes me from head to toe. Eventually, he claps his hands together and springs out of the bed.

"All right. I'll give you a go. Come with me."

His energy is contagious. When he stands, we are almost at eye level, which is a rare treat for me. But he isn't interested in locking gazes. He's already zoomed out of the cell, shouldering into any immortal who gets in his way.

I hurry to keep up with his long strides, waving at Rune to follow us down the corridor. This guy possesses a *move it or lose it* attitude and I don't want to miss my opportunity. I glance over my shoulder, watching as Rune blindly hobbles after us, barely managing to keep his eyes open. A pang of guilt strikes me.

"Excuse me? Can we wait for my friend to catch up?"

"*Friend?*" The man stops in his tracks and stares at me.

"My cellmate."

"Oh." As if somehow mollified, he laughs. "That's not a friend, mate! That's a one-way ticket to a murder-suicide pact that only ends in permanently mangled bodies. And insanity. Don't forget insanity! Get out of my way," he adds when an immortal accidentally bumps into him.

I don't know how I'm supposed to respond to that. His short monologue does however give Rune enough time to join us.

"This the future murder victim?" The man laughs at his own joke. "Name's Zain. The first gassing is the most agonizing. Once you get your uniform, you become numb to most of the torture. Good for us, but stupid if all they want is to inflict pain. Come on."

I don't know what to make of Zain. He's stereotypically how I imagined the inmates to behave. I thought they'd all be arrogant and push us around instead of behaving like mindless zombies.

As we follow him down the cell block, he leads us through a small alcove and into a dull room with drains and exposed pipes.

"Showers?" My tone is far too hopeful.

"Used to be," Zain says, folding his arms. "They turned off the water years ago, but poor maintenance means sometimes you're lucky to get a couple glasses worth. I mostly use this as my drinking source, but it wouldn't hurt to ration it to clean yourselves up."

Rune doesn't waste any time. He stumbles forward and lands on his knees next to a leaking tap. Frantically turning every handle, low-pressure water finally trickles out. He rolls onto his back and allows the water to run into his eyes and down his throat.

"Don't let him drink it all up," Zain warns. "You're in poor form, too."

He's right. Selflessness doesn't get you far in a place like this. I approach Rune and gently nudge him out of the way so I can splash water into my eyes. It stings like hell, but it definitely alleviates some of the burn. Using what's left, I rub water onto the limbs that took the brunt of the gassing. It's not enough to cleanse entirely, but it's better than nothing.

The water slows to a few drops. Rune and I stare at the tap like entertained toddlers, hoping that by some miracle, water will rush through the pin-sized holes.

"That's it for the day," Zain announces. "The water pressure will build up again in three to six days. You'll learn the schedule. Just don't let me catch you stealing any that's rightfully mine. I get first dibs. This is the only favor you'll get from me. Understand?"

"Thank you, Zain," I say.

Zain's shoulders relax. Through bleary vision, I check to see how Rune is going. He doesn't move from his position, still staring up at the tap.

"It's finished, Rune."

"I know," he rasps. "I'm just not ready to move yet. It hurts."

"You two have a long way to go," Zain mumbles. "Maybe next time don't go to the chow hall. Just a suggestion."

I don't know why his tone triggers me the way it does. "Your arrogance is unappreciated, Zain. It's our first day here. How were we supposed to know breakfast would entail gassing? The others didn't seem to know either."

"Oh, trust me, they knew." Zain runs his fingers through his unkempt hair, a signal of social discomfort. This guy is hard to pinpoint. But I'll learn. "It's fifty-fifty. Thing is, on a good day you will actually get some grub. It's not tasty, but it might be off chicken. Stale bread and rice. One time there was fruit, but that was before the prison was so underfunded. The more overcrowded we became, the more they'd slip in a few surprises. The soup would contain burnapray poison. A lot of people never quite recovered after that. Then they became less subtle in their attempts to kill us. They'd straight up offer the poison in cans."

This is enough to grab Rune's attention. Groaning, he sits up but keeps his eyes closed. "People drank it?"

"Yeah. A lot of prisoners tried to die. It was better than this, right? Thing is, we're immortal. That's the whole premise of this prison. So every time they drank poison or refused to eat, they only destroyed their mind and bodies to an extent that there's no recovery. The body's gotta be in good shape to regenerate. A lot of them are conditioned to do the same thing over and over again, on autopilot. Sometimes they get food and they eat. Mostly they get tortured."

"So the chow hall is not mandatory?" I ask before Rune opens his mouth again. I want him to rest his vocal cords.

"Short-staffed. Guards don't like us and don't implement much. If I don't eat, then they don't need to worry about it. Trust me, you're best staying far away from the chow hall. Not much good comes from it."

I point at his physique, only now noticing the various tattoos around his waist. "Then where are you getting your food from?"

"I didn't realize this was an interview," Zain says dryly. "My turn. What's your name?"

"Malin. This is Rune."

"I figured that when you called him Rune. So, Malin. Northern name?"

"Yes."

"Not a lot of your people left up there. Unless something's changed since I've been locked up."

My gaze drops to the pus weeping from my leg. I really don't need a reminder about my history, so I avoid his question by tending to my wound. I press my robe into it, wincing at the shooting pain.

"Right. Touchy subject. I get it," Zain raises his hands as if to surrender. "Answering your question about food is a sensitive topic for me, all right? I'm not proud of what I do, but I refuse to become a shell of a human being. I work out to keep fit, I do puzzles to keep mentally active. And if I need to catch rodents to keep my body alive, then I will. I'm also not averse to sneaking into the guard's quarters for bread and meat. And if you see any immortals without fingers, then you know that's when I got desperate." He wriggles his own fingers, a shameful expression swiftly masked by something much more threatening.

I glance at Rune, who has scrunched up his nose in response. He clears his throat, careful to word his next question. "But why do they want to kill us?"

"Because they don't want us here. We can't be out in the real world. We're here for eternity. It'd be much easier to get rid of us, wouldn't it? And the more compliant we become, the simpler the experiments become. There was only one incident that involved decapitation by guillotine about a century ago. Of course, the guy survived it. Was just a talking head."

A talking head? The concept baffled me. How could a head talk without lungs? If the body was still intact and the lungs were breathing elsewhere, did that somehow allow a quantum airflow? I suppose I shouldn't question it. I barely understand how any immortal body keeps pushing through impossible ailments. It is what it is.

"He slurred a lot and slept most of the day away, but he was still alive," he continues. "One of the immortals with a medical background begged to reattach his body. It worked, but he lost the use of his legs and arms. Eventually his head detached again without ongoing treatment. After that, we rioted. It was the last time I saw this place actually alive. We refused to allow such mistreatment. Life as a talking head? You can't get crueler than that. After we trashed the place and injured guards, they promised never to decapitate another immortal again. However, that was also when they became tougher with everything else. It was around that time the showers stopped working. And they never repaired the damage. The ultimate punishment."

The information is difficult to swallow. Nauseated from the concept of failed uprisings and beheadings, I sit against the wall, ignoring the various pipes and taps prodding my back.

"It's a lot," Zain confesses. "Sometimes I've thought about going rogue. Killing every guard in here and risking the bullet wounds to seek revenge and get out of here."

"What stops you?" I eventually ask, having zoned out for a couple of moments.

"Fear." He smiles, as if tormenting me. "What's for me outside of here? From one prison to another. You'd need an army to survive out there. And as you can see, there aren't many contenders in here to join my rebellion. Blasted zombies."

What a morbidly accurate sentiment. While I was on the run, I wondered whether it was worth turning myself in, if not for shelter and rest. Now that I'm here, I just want to escape. Is there no option for us that involves any variant of satisfaction?

Guards yell something in the distance. My ears prick at the curse words, having never appreciated such vulgar vocabulary.

"Get the kid up," Zain instructs. "Solitude time."

"What?"

"After the gassing, they lock you in your cell until the afternoon. It is their procedure."

"And then what?"

Zain shrugs. "Depends on their mood. Understaffed, so they might allow some free time and mingling. Everyone is so warped in the head that they know we won't cause any grief. Or they'll keep us locked up until tomorrow."

Rune is a deadweight, too exhausted to even lock on his core to help me lift. Zain doesn't offer to help either, so I'm caught awkwardly trying to pull Rune to his feet without knocking his burnt skin.

When I manage to prop him up against the wall, Rune mouths a thank you, breathing shallowly. He breathed a lot more poison gas than I did. I keep hold of his arm, careful to maintain his balance.

Zain steps closer, his head tilted. "When will you get your uniforms?"

"We don't know," I say. "What are they, exactly? Everybody is wearing something different."

"Must be nice to be so ignorant, Malin. The uniform *is* the pale blue skin. The purple bruises. The medic drains our blood."

My heart skips a beat.

The uniform isn't a fabric or material—it's a branding to prove their immortality. The prisoners are literally walking corpses, doomed to suffer forced anemia.

I fight the urge to purge once I understand why their skin looks so blue. It's not that they're cold or standing by poor lighting or have been beaten to a bloody pulp.

And they're waiting to drain my blood, too.

"You right?" Zain asks when I almost drop Rune.

"No..." I utter. "No..."

"It's not pleasant, but you'll cope. I've managed to regenerate most of my blood. I hit myself or keep to the cold whenever I know there will be interactions with the guards. Keeps my skin looking bruised. Better than suffering the ongoing draining."

I turn to Rune who looks as horrified as I feel. He steps forward, keen to run from such devastating news.

"Thanks for sharing the water source," I say as I guide Rune through the showers.

"Thanks for giving me someone to talk to," Zain responds. "Most inmates are either dead, jerks, or boring. They're useless. Oh, another tip. Don't go to the second floor. I confess to eating a few fingers here and there, but the inmates on two are proper cannibals. They keep to themselves most of the time, but will be on the prowl when they get too hungry. They're smart. You'll never see them gamble the chow hall. Instead, they'll cut open your full stomach."

Rune's eyes widen. "Are we safe if we stay inside our cell?"

"If your cell doesn't have any loose bricks or bendable bars, sure."

"We'll check them now," I assure Rune. "If the cannibals eat inmates, does that mean they kill the immortal?"

"Think again. It's impossible for a human to eat another human's bones, right? They only eat the meaty parts. It's a fate worse than death."

This is by far the most upsetting news I've heard all day, and I don't have the strength to process everything Zain is telling us.

When we leave the showers, most of the prisoners have returned to their cells and three guards are locking up.

Zain confidently approaches the muscular guard who led me to my cell last night. He shoots him a cheeky salute and smile. "Sorry for the delay. Was showing the newbies around. We locked up for the rest of the day?"

"Afraid so. Hurry up." The guard's eyes dart awkwardly to the side.

"Trying to remember my prisoner number?" A cheeky grin spreads across Zain's face. "Can't remember the last time you ever used it. You don't need to pretend in front of these guys."

I have trouble comprehending why this guard's tone is so noticeably softer than the others. Once we're out of earshot of the guards, Zain whispers to me.

"I've known him since he was a kid. His dad worked here and passed away a couple years ago. The prison is really all he's ever known, so he practically lives here. He's your go-to guard. He'll never beat you or treat you badly. Not with me around. I call him Mitty."

Mitty. I'll make sure to commit it to memory. "He twisted my arm pretty badly yesterday."

Zain's eyebrows raise. "Is that so? Hmm. I'm sure he only did it to look tough in front of the others. I'll chat to him about it. We can't have him hurting the two prisoners I can actually have a conversation with."

Zain's cell is across from ours and slightly to the left, so he bids us a farewell and returns to his shadowy home. A guard is not far behind him and slides the door shut.

Rune isn't as eager to get back inside. Instead, he spends a few seconds checking the strength of each bar and kicking at the stone wall between cells.

"What the 'ell are ya doin'? Ge' inside!" A gruff guard belts, pushing Rune and me forward. We land on the rock-hard bed, the door slamming behind us. I lower myself to the floor, much preferring the feel of it compared to the bed.

"I hate it here," Rune says, his voice still coarse.

"Shh," I instruct. "Let your voice heal."

He waves his hand dismissively. "My voice will be fine. I was stupid screaming in there. Be good as new tomorrow."

"Tomorrow when we may receive our uniform?" My shoulders roll forward at the glum thought. "I'm not so sure the color blue suits me."

Rune doesn't have a chance to respond to my distasteful joke. We hear the prisoners above us taunting and screeching manically.

"*Yum yum yum! Those new inmates look fleshy and healthy! What a feast!*"

"*We're coming for you, freakshow tallie. And the little farmer...bet he's full of flavor.*"

The guards on the second floor rattle the bars with their batons and curse several expletives in an attempt to shut them up.

Rune and I creep closer to one another, silently searching the cell for easy exits or weapons.

"There's nothing in here to defend ourselves with," Rune says, as if reading my mind. "I can't believe it. Cannibals. *Cannibals.* That was the last thing I thought about when I came here!"

"They can't reach us. Besides, we're strong at the moment. We can take care of ourselves."

"Can't believe that Zain guy was right about them. Guess that means he's right about the uniforms too."

I don't verbalize it, but I get the unfortunate feeling Zain is right about a lot of things.

# CHAPTER IV

The advantage to being stuck in a cell is the ability to catch up on years of missed sleep. Drowsy, I roll to my side, my joints aching from the horrible floor.

When my brain equalizes with my body, I see Rune sitting with his knees pulled to his chest, staring through the bars. Maybe it's my eyes, but his skin looks virtually healed. Any peeling or weeping has disappeared, and the rash is barely visible.

"What's wrong?" I whisper, unsettled by the eerie silence.

"The guards were talking. The medic is back."

A cold shiver runs down my spine. Time really wasn't on my side. I'd hoped the medic would be gone for days, weeks even. But back *tonight*? What if I don't survive the blood draining process? Scratch that. I *won't* survive the process. I've heard of mortals beating the odds in various near-death scenarios, but they're rare, right? But maybe, just maybe, I could be *special*?

*Maybe?*

"Your voice sounds better," I say in an attempt to distract from his news.

"I heal fast," he replies disinterestedly. He glimpses at me, then widens his eyes. "Oh jeez, not like you! Malin, you're red raw!"

I can't bring myself to look at my hands. I can already feel them crusting over, my wounded flesh sticking to the hard ground. "I bet. Is the medic coming to collect us?"

"Yes, soon." He crawls towards me, his eyes scanning my entire body. "Oh Malin. Don't you regenerate? I thought all immortals can, well to a point, so long as the body is in a relatively healthy condition."

"I don't think my body has been in a healthy condition for a long time," I say, thinking back to all the times I've been forced to mistreat it. "Look at everyone in here. They deliberately keep them sick so they can't heal. They're the walking dead."

"Good point. It's easy to forget how lucky I've been."

There's a loud slam, followed by harsh whispers. I can't pinpoint the words, but it sounds like they're bickering with one another.

I hold my breath so that I can hear better, but it's redundant when my heart thrums in my ears.

Heels thwack against the concrete, their strides long. They're in a rush, each step walked with purpose.

I'm not the slightest bit surprised when a petite woman casts her shadow over us, her forehead perpetually crinkled.

"Oh." She looks us up and down. "Experienced the gas today? Not a great introduction, is it? Come on. Time you became part of the family."

Fumbling with the keys, she slides open the cell door. She's dressed in a pale blue suit which contrasts with the rest of the prison. This woman is certainly not a guard, and she isn't dressed like a medic. If anything, she looks like a wealthy visitor who decided to drop by unannounced.

Rune and I don't move. Like stubborn little children, we remain seated.

The woman rolls her eyes and petulantly hunches forward when she groans. "Come on! I came back just to do this. The guards are complaining you look too human. This will only take a minute. Hurry."

It means nothing to her. Nothing to Rune. Nothing to the prisoners. Draining their blood is an inconvenience, an annoyance, an illness.

For me it could mean an execution.

My throat feels like sandpaper when I try to swallow. Reaching out for Rune's hand, I squeeze it tightly then cringe at our clamminess.

"If you don't come now," the woman articulates, "I'll let the cannibals have you. What's it going to be?"

Rune scrambles to his feet instinctively, offering to help me to my feet.

There are worse ways to die, and gradually passing out from blood loss seems like the better option. So unless I attempt to fight my way out of here, I'm left with no other choice.

I tug on Rune's arm, and when the woman is satisfied with our calm obedience, she turns on her heel and encourages us to follow.

We hang several paces back, ignoring the zombie-like gazes of the insomniacs who watch us through our cells.

"R-Rune..." My bottom lip quivers, unable to formulate a sentence. "Rune, there's something I need to tell you."

He pats my shoulder tenderly. "I don't like blood either. It's okay, we'll get through this."

"It's not that," I whisper. "It's...about..."

"Silence back there!" The woman claps her hands, but doesn't bother to face us. Instead, we continue down the endless corridor until we reach a spiral staircase that goes underground. "This is the infirmary. It's predominately for our mortal guards, but if your head happens to fall off, then we can reattach it. That's one of our main rules. Stupid things like headaches, rashes, or dehydration won't land you here. I'm far too busy and underpaid to deal with nonsense like that."

We follow her down the tiny stairs; I have to walk on my tiptoes just to ensure I don't fall off each step.

At the bottom of the staircase is a giant metal door and a sense of dread washes over me. So that room is the room where I'm going to die.

"Will you go first?" I ask Rune, pleading with my eyes. "Please?"

"Oh. Yeah, sure, whatever."

The metal door creaks as the petite woman yanks on it, then waves us in. "Come on. I only have an hour!"

I wish I had that long.

Just like the rest of the prison, the room is uncreative and undecorated. There's a steel slab in the center, and a table with various tools and equipment scattered across it.

"Boy. You first. Up you go." The woman shoots a confused look at me. "You, thing. Stand in the corner and wait."

Arms folded, I slump into the corner, chewing on my bottom lip. I've never needed to use the bathroom so urgently. Nor have I truly felt the frustration of thirst or the delirium from lack of sleep. In this moment, I've never felt more human.

Anxiety is an entirely unhelpful state.

Rune happily hops onto the slab, dangling his legs while he waits for the woman to connect the needle to a tube that leads to a bag.

"Arm out," the woman instructs. "Open and close your fist as quickly as possible. We need to pump fast."

Rune responds courteously to each and every command, remarkably casual considering the unpleasant scenario. I cringe as the needle enters his veins and almost immediately, his blood is drawn through the needle, down the tube and into the bag.

After ten minutes, his face begins to drain of color, but his expression remains the same. He's only a touch paler than usual; certainly not sporting the corpse-like appearance.

"Feels a bit gross," he admits, and the woman hushes him. "How much longer?"

"Just keep opening and closing your hand."

This time, Rune doesn't comply. We're too distracted by the hurried steps coming down the stairs. The door suddenly bursts open and a flushed Mitty enters out of breath. He leans over and rests his hands on his thighs, trying to find the air to support his dialogue.

"Angela...we...we need you."

The woman now known as Angela huffs. "Somebody always needs me! What could be so urgent that you dragged yourself down those stairs?"

Mitty glances at me, then back to Angela. "We should speak in private."

"No. I'm busy! Tell me now."

Breaths now shallow, Mitty stands upright in an attempt to reinstate his authoritative image. "Angela, they need you upstairs. An immortal has just died."

Rune doesn't notice Angela drop the syringe. He doesn't even flinch at the blood oozing through the small hole in his arm, nor does she do anything to aid him. We all stare at Mitty, awestruck by the revelation.

"That's...not possible," Angela finally says. "Is it...?"

"That's why we need a medic." Mitty scrunches his nose at the bag full of Rune's blood. "It's just uniforms. They don't need them tonight."

Despite the unprecedented news, I'm overcome with relief. If I were alone, I'd be dancing and rejoicing, arms flailing above my head. Instead, I allow my muscles to relax and thank imaginary entities for sparing me.

The initial shock wears off and Angela tends to Rune's arm, albeit hurriedly. "One bloody thing after another with you lot! A dead immortal? What a paradox. This ever happened in your time?"

She directs the question at Rune and me. Lost for words, I shrug and maintain my dumbfounded expression.

"Dunno," Rune says, taking the pressure off me. "I'm only ninety or so. Lived in a village with mortals my whole life so I don't know a lot about them. Us, I mean. We're not that different from you."

"Ninety?" Mitty repeats under his breath, his eyebrows whooshing upwards. "You're so young..."

"Not young enough to be down with the new music the kids are playing. All of these panpipes. What's up with that?"

Rune is confusingly spritely for a man who has just lost a couple pints of blood. His natural charm draws a smile out of both Angela and Mitty, but they wipe it the second they feel it clinging to their faces.

"You take the prisoners back to the cells," Angela instructs the guard. "As for you two, I'll be back once this nonsense is sorted. Until then, not a word is to be spoken to the other prisoners. Do you understand? This is highly confidential."

"The prisoners are either brain-dead or cannibals. Who are we going to tell?" Rune asks, the question obnoxious, but his tone sincere. Semi-satisfied by his roundabout way of agreeing to keep his lips zipped, Angela shoos us out of the infirmary as we follow Mitty back up the curved staircase.

Mitty has the decency to keep his footsteps quiet while the prisoners sleep, unlike Angela who almost deliberately made noise to assert her superiority. The large guard seems somewhat unnerved, lost in his own thoughts.

I recall Zain's perception of Mitty and how he was the only one who treated the immortals with a shred of decency. It contradicts my earlier encounter with him, but maybe that was all for show. Perhaps I can test Zain's theory.

"How did the immortal die?" I ask, barely able to hear my voice.

"Not allowed to say," Mitty replies almost automatically. "They weren't...they weren't sick or anything...at least, nobody thought so. They just..."

"Were they old?" Rune bravely jumps in. I pull a face at his eagerness, concerned that his inability to lower his voice will detract the guard from answering.

"Ancient," Mitty breathes, his hands trembling as he fumbles for the cell keys. "Rumor is four digits."

"Wow!" Rune exclaims with childlike wonder. "Maybe immortals *do* die of old age. It's just older than most."

"I honestly don't know." Mitty's gaze lands on his boots once he stops in front of our cell. He unlocks the door and rolls it back for us, motioning us in.

"Were they from the north?" I clear my throat. "Did they look like me?"

"Never have I seen a prisoner from the north until your arrival." He speaks with such clarity that I believe him. "Good...goodnight."

"Goodnight," I reply, biting my tongue when I go to call him by the nickname Zain gave me.

Sheepishly, Mitty closes the door and rushes down the cell block, assumedly back upstairs.

Rune lowers himself on the bed, careful not to knock his bruised arm. "This is wild. A dead immortal? We have to tell that guy we met today."

"Zain? We're sworn to secrecy."

"We owe him something. He helped us find water, warned us about the second-level cannibals. The least we can do is share juicy gossip."

I understand Rune's point of view, and the crazy thing is, I actually agree with him. But the fact an immortal died tonight, just minutes before my own death, has me shaken.

In the dim lighting, Rune looks nowhere near as pale as he did in the infirmary. Despite the upset and the long walk, he appears rather rejuvenated.

"How on earth do you have some color in your face? Don't you feel woozy?"

"Very. Nauseated. Headache. But that's how I get when my body rejuvenates. I doubt they'll be able to make my uniform stick, unless they keep draining me every couple of days. Give me another twenty minutes, hour tops, and I'll be feeling better."

I envy Rune. There were always rumors that immortals had powerful abilities, which is one of the reasons why they're so feared. From self-healing, to mind manipulation to incredible strength, immortals were allegedly fearmongering gods capable of pure destruction or glorious creation.

That's pure mythology though. Different corners of our land have certain perks stemming from evolution. Easterners can sell ice to a southerner—they're just that charismatic. Northerners...have a very destructive ability...but all these have been exaggerated purely to tell a good story.

Mind control and ease with words, for example, are two very different things.

Rune, whether he knows it or not, falls into a speedy regenerative category that is a direct link to his ethnicity. He certainly isn't superhuman; if he was, the needle wouldn't even had had the chance to penetrate his skin. Same with the gas; it wouldn't have affected him so severely if legends were true. But he *definitely* harnesses a useful ability...and I can't help but hate him for it.

"Malin?"

Why did he sound so concerned? He's on the edge of the bed, leaning in close to me. It's only now I realize I'm still standing by the door, staring at the 8 tattoo on my wrist. How long have I been in this state? Am I in shock?

"Malin?" Rune repeats. "Are you okay?"

"No," I say after a long pause. "No, I'm really not. I'm going to die here."

He snorts. "Hypochondria, much? Just because one immortal died doesn't mean it'll catch on. Unless it's an immortal disease the medics manufactured." His eyes widen at the thought. "No. No, I'm sure it's fine. You and me? We can't die. Like, we literally can't, no matter what we do."

Him? Of course not.

Me?

All mortals eventually die.

And the clock is ticking.

# CHAPTER V

The night creeps on, as the previous day's events bombard my sleep. I had been *this* close to divulging too much information that could ultimately get me killed. Luckily for me, Rune was impervious to my hysterical rants that the end was nigh, so I dropped it.

If I revealed my mortality, he would've asked how it was even plausible; and that's just not something I'm prepared to talk about. Not now. Maybe never. Perhaps as I age, Rune's suspicion might coerce me into talking. If I'm lucky enough *to* age. I'll most likely starve long before that.

I roll over, having bargained to use the blanket if Rune had possession of the pillow. My skin still burns from the gas, like an intense sunburn, and wrapping the blanket around my limbs is the only thing that eases the discomfort.

I've chosen the floor as my permanent bed so that I can stretch without my legs dangling off the edge of the bed. Rune is twisted like a pretzel, having barely used the pillow at all. It must be so nice to be fearless. Able to accept that pain is fleeting, and knowing permanent repercussions are easily reversed. I resent his ability to regenerate and wish I could do the same.

When Rune stirs, I pull myself into a sitting position. He soon mimics me, his hair sticking up like he's been electrocuted.

"Morning," I rasp. "Sleep okay?"

"I've been thinking," he says between yawns. "I'm going to work out why that immortal died. Not much else to do around here, so maybe I could be a detective of sorts. You could assist me if you wanted. We can interview anybody willing to cooperate!"

"Rune," I say carefully. "I think you're still drowsy. We're in prison. Not a playground. We can't investigate important matters like this."

"Why not? We'll tell that zany guy."

"Zain."

"Yes, him. He knows everything and everyone. We'll get to the bottom of it. We might even get rewarded for a job well done."

"Rewarded by who?" I say, exasperated. "Yes, it's a shock. But ultimately the guards, medics, and warden want us dead. We're a burden. They've said it themselves. If they managed to kill one, then you can bet they'll try to repeat such a feat. We've all got targets on us now."

Weary, Rune takes a little longer to comprehend my protest. Then he says something I didn't expect. "What makes you so scared?"

Damn it. Rune doesn't have the ability to move on from an unanswered question. He'll just keep repeating the same thing over and over until I reply.

"I guess in a scenario such as this, it's easy to doubt your immortality." I speak as carefully as humanly possible. Words are weapons. "I mean, one suddenly dies. The others are in a zombie-like state from mistreatment. Can you really *live* in this environment? I just don't want to do anything to provoke the officials. Nosing around in this business is only asking for trouble."

"I want a quality of life too, Malin. The difference is you seem suited to enduring the current conditions and learning to manage them. That hasn't worked for anyone in here. So what if I shook things up? There's nothing else to lose."

"That's youth talking!" I admonish. "If you remember, Zain said conditions worsened after the riot. We've been here a couple of days. We don't know the system yet. There's always something to lose."

The tension between us is palpable, a fierce glint in his eyes I've not yet had the misfortune of witnessing. We're clearly on two different pages and if he wants to play detective, then he better not get me involved. I have no idea who he expects to speak to. The guards? Nope. Brain-dead inmates? Unlikely. Cannibals? The man is unhinged.

"Are you the type of person to do what you want, even against the advice of others?" I ask solemnly. Even as young as ninety, he should at least have an understanding of his behaviors.

Pensive, Rune scratches at his rather healthy-looking skin. "No, I take things onboard. I'm only stubborn in the heat of the moment. You'll have a better chance of swaying me if I fail."

I snort, both frustrated and relieved by the confession. Emotions are tricky to tame, especially when they're not your own.

Eager to change the topic of conversation, we plan out our day as best we can, first deciding to never return to the chow hall. Like Zain, we would rather catch rats than undergo that painful experience again. Beyond that, the day is nothing more than a blur.

"WAKE UP!"

I jump at the sound of the cell bars rattling, as the doors automatically roll open one by one. Several guards pass us by, sticking their nose in our room and sniffing. For what, I'm unsure of, but my imagination certainly hasn't diminished.

Keeping to our cell, Rune and I watch as the lifeless inmates continue their daily routine and walk down the corridor towards the chow hall. Today might be another gassing. *Or* the odds may be in their favor and they could finally be served food. It doesn't seem to matter. A routine is a routine. I'm just relieved the guards don't care enough to enforce it. At least we know to remain here, and grab our daily drink from the leaking shower taps.

"Hey."

I'm surprised to find Zain peering into our cell, his hair wilder than yesterday. His eyes look drowned in sorrow, but there's an eagerness in his tone. Maybe he's just excited to have inmates he can intelligently converse with.

"Hey buddy," Rune says. "We didn't go to the chow hall. Not worth the gamble. You coming to the showers?"

Zain rests his forehead against the bar, seemingly listening to an internal monologue. "I found out something pretty terrifying. I don't know if it's true, but if it came from Mitty, then it's bound to have some clout."

"Dead immortal?" Rune blurts. "Yeah, we heard the same thing last night. This Mitty guy has a big mouth. Reckon we can pull some more information out of him?"

I shoot Rune a warning and study Zain's surprised expression. I guess there's a lot running through his mind. He's probably wondering how we could've possibly known before him and what implications that could present. No doubt he fancies himself the pod boss.

"We were supposed to get our uniform last night." It pours out of my mouth. There's something about Zain that makes him extremely difficult to lie to. "We were interrupted when Mitty requested that the medic tend to the dead immortal."

Instantly mollified by the explanation, Zain relaxes his body and breathes. "Right. So, obviously you know it's not good. And I can't seem to work out who the victim is. There's thousands of immortals trapped here. I've made an effort to get to know all of them over the years, but it's getting harder and harder to associate with any of them. I want to know if it was someone healthy or if a cannibal digested the deceased to the point of permanent death. Or are the medics experimenting on immortals underground? It's been driving me absolutely nuts." He pauses. "Want to get some fresh air?"

My heart flutters at the thought of fresh air. Is there such a thing here? Is there a place where I can inhale and not be overwhelmed by such pungent odors? Or is that wishful thinking?

Zain must read my expression. "Not used to the smells, eh?"

"They're awful," I admit. "Doesn't seem to get any easier."

Amused, Zain leads us out of the cell and down the corridor. He must feel like the cool kid on the playground who has no boundaries. I feel like I *should* be in the chow hall, despite not wanting to be severely burned again, and Zain is the rebellious jock reassuring us that it's okay to skip the morning routine.

Rune and I keep quiet, a little uncertain whether we should follow Zain at all. Could the guards beat us for leaving the cell block? He's taken us through at least three doors until we're out in a cemented courtyard where crumbling vines have overtaken the majority of gym equipment.

"Are we allowed to be here?" I ask.

"They're understaffed and we mean too little to make a fuss over. Trust me, it's fine. I come out here all the time. Don't work out much as you can see. These things were rusting long before I got here. It's just nice to get away."

He takes us to a steel bench which is losing its battle against the elements. It's filthy; practically camouflaged beneath dirt and vines.

The three of us sit and Zain stares up at the overcast sky, basking in the fresh air. "This is my favorite time of day. Especially when it rains. It's pure bliss. Keeps me sane. Relatively speaking, of course."

"You never tried to escape?" Rune eyes the impossibly high walls. I'm way ahead of him, having already scoped the area for an exit. Any opening, any weapon, any*thing* that could aid in a jailbreak.

Zain's smirk is partially covered by his bushy beard. "During the riot, a lot of us tried. Despite being understaffed, this place is genuinely well equipped when it comes to preventing inmates from escaping. I've designed a lot of theoretical breakouts. I've attempted seduction, manipulation, deception. Nothing works. Can't even scale these walls. See how smooth they are? Short of climbing on one another's shoulders...but you'd need a lot of immortals to try that before getting zapped by a guard. I can't remember the last time I even thought about escaping. I've considered every angle. This is my life, and I've come to accept it."

I hate that. I hate that this is what he's been forced to accept. I hate that he's going to be here forever and I hate that I'll be killed in the interim.

"There's no way out?" I ask, frustrated by the helplessness in my voice.

"Not without getting caught. There's always intense labor work which is outside of these walls. I've heard the conditions are much worse though. Theoretically there's a better chance of escape, but I haven't been game to risk it. Yet."

Worse conditions than inside the prison? Is that even possible?

"Is this where you find the rats?" I ask conversationally, although that's not a question I ever thought I'd ask.

"Rarely." Zain twists his neck, a satisfying crunch proceeding. "Rats tend to hang inside. This is where I get extra water when I can. Where I come to think. Sometimes I sing. Sometimes I punch the walls." He glances down at his knuckles and I notice the scars etched into his skin. "The other immortals stopped coming out here a long time ago."

"Why?"

"They're conditioned to do the same thing every day. Eat, torture, sleep, repeat."

"What about the cannibals?" I ask. "They seem pretty switched on."

"We made a deal. Morning is my time out here. I'm a better fighter than most of them. One on one, at least. They learned that the hard way." He grins at the memory. "The guards get suspicious when a lot of us come here. I can slink away, no worries. But a dozen cannibals strutting into the courtyard together? The guards would know something is up. Probably assume they're going to attempt an escape. Because of that, I'm safer out here than anywhere else."

His words bring me immense comfort. I feel as long as Zain is in my presence, I can't be harmed. He's my protector; something I've not had before.

"You seem to be making the best out of a bad situation," I say optimistically, wondering if I can alter my mindset the same way.

"What choice am I left with? Rot? Become a monster? I won't let them take my essence away."

"I respect that," I say with a slight bow of my head.

We enjoy the stillness for a moment, a hint of rain in the heavy clouds above. There's something eerily pleasing about the courtyard. Despite the abandonment, it's charming to see life finds a way. The various vines, albeit dead, and other shrubbery that have crept into such an impenetrable building gives me a glimmer of hope. Through persistence, life snuck into this hellhole and flourished for a period. That means I can find a way out.

"Rune is convinced he's going to find out what killed the immortal." The words fall out of my mouth and I cringe at my petulant urge to tattle.

"Is that so? Good on you, buddy," Zain says without the slightest tone of sarcasm. "Hey, let me know how I can help. It's important we figure these things out."

That was not what I expected.

I turn away from Rune when he shoots me a smug expression.

"I've already lined up Mitty. Leave it with me and I'll get as much out of him as I can. When I sneak into the guard's quarters for food, I might overhear something," Zain continues, practically inebriated with enthusiasm.

Maybe it's easier to be excited about such a morbid topic when you live for eternity.

"Speaking of food," I say, placing my hands over my stomach. It's almost beyond hunger; just an empty vessel of occasional cramps and nausea. "What would you recommend?"

Zain glances up at the gray sky. "Birds won't be out today. Rats might be an unpleasant way to introduce you to starvation. My guess is the guards will be gathering to discuss the dead immortal while the prisoners are in the chow hall. Now might be a good opportunity to sneak into their quarters."

A wide grin spreads across Rune's face, but I feel void of any emotion. I've only been locked up for a couple of days and already we're contemplating breaking into the guard's quarters?

"I don't know..." I mumble. "Sounds risky."

"There's very little risk if we go right now."

"I thought you said no more favors."

"This isn't a favor. I'm hungry and you two are an extra pair of eyes and ears. You in?"

Rune jumps to his feet, prepared to follow his new leader to the end. Not one to succumb to peer pressure, I remain seated and consider the options. Starve and die. Eat, get caught and die.

At least I'd have a full stomach.

Sighing, I stand. "Let's go before I change my mind."

ZAIN WALKS through the prison like he owns this place. Fast paced, chin held high and a confidence I could only ever dream of.

He leads us through a new part of the cell blocks, and as predicted, the guards are nowhere to be found.

"Where do the guards meet?" I whisper. "If they're not in the quarters, I mean?"

"There's business quarters and relaxation quarters. Business is where they discuss important matters and relaxation is where they go for their breaks or to eat."

"Right."

Some immortals are still bunkering down in their cells, but they're practically immobile skeletons. It's the saddest thing I've ever seen.

"Wait for my signal," Zain whispers once we reach a faded red door at the end of the corridor. In desperate need of oil, the door squeaks as he pushes on it. He pokes his head in, pauses, then motions for us to follow him through.

It's a small hallway, where another less-faded red door resides.

"These aren't locked?" I ask.

Zain pushes on the door and grins. "Sometimes. Evidently, not today. Why lock anything when your prisoners are mindless zombies? They've got a cushy job. Although I've come to wonder whether Mitty deliberately leaves these unlocked whenever he gets the chance...he knows what I get up to..."

For the sake of morality and humanity, I certainly hope that's the case.

I feel sick to my stomach once we're inside, my nervous bladder filling as I gaze at the room.

It's gray, like every other aspect of the half-stone, half-cement prison. The only difference is the worn red carpet and brown couches. A tiny fireplace keeps the room warm and in the corner is a buffet of food.

I almost salivate at the sight. We slink towards the food, dismayed to find a lot of empty plates and crumbs.

"Guards have already eaten breakfast," Zain mutters.

"Still!" Rune licks his lips. He reaches for a sliver of a muffin and moans at the taste.

Zain picks up charred toast, unfazed by the presumably awful texture and taste.

There are a lot of bones left over and fruit I've never seen before. But I find every piece of crumb, every stale pastry, every half-eaten fruit and shove it into my mouth.

I can't stomach most of it. Instinctively, I spit out the stale pastries and the acidic pale pink hexagon fruit.

Mouth full, Zain frowns. "Be careful with the fringle. A lot of people are allergic to them. They're native only to this part of the land."

Yep. My lips are tingling and I can feel tiny little bumps blistering on my lips. "What else can I eat?" I lament, scooping up every crumb I can.

"Burnt toast?" Zain suggests. "Hey, we're lucky today. Usually there's not so much food. And I'm not allergic to fringles, so don't mind if I do."

My stomach knows food is about and can't seem to accept the poor quality presented to it. It wants anything and everything. If I could just bypass my mouth, then it'd be fine.

But I can't eat the fruit. I can't get the pastries down when they're hard as rocks. Reluctantly, I scrape off the ash on the toast and eat the crust, relieved to have something to digest.

"Eventually, you'll learn to deal with the allergic reactions. Or you won't mind chipping a tooth to eat the stale pastries. Hunger always wins," Zain says, swallowing without chewing.

He might just have a point.

We freeze in place when the door squeaks.

Zain curses and drops the food scooped up in his hands. "Hide!"

Hide? I'm a giant compared to these people! How can I possibly hide?

It's every man for himself as Rune dives behind one of the brown couches. Zain is a little more creative and extinguishes the tiny flame in the fireplace with his foot and curls up inside.

Seeing no other option, I crouch beneath the buffet table, barely covered by the short cloth dangling over the edge.

Two guards walk in, one female, one male. Succumbing to the uncontrollable chattering teeth, I scramble into the corner and hold my breath. Rune is exposed from this angle. If the guards walk in this direction, he'll be caught.

"Beats me why the immortals got food. Spaghetti, pancakes, quiches. Half of them don't even know what they're shoveling into their pie holes." The male guard slips off his boots and throws himself onto the lounge, eyes closed. Rune flinches only inches away. "As long as I've been here, the chow hall has been specifically poison based. Why now would they waste resources on them?"

The woman hangs by the entrance, her eyes squinting as she checks the perimeters of the room. "This door wasn't locked."

"Yeah, that was me. Why bother? They're all in their cells."

"The cannibals don't go to the chow hall. They have free rein during that half hour."

Frustrated, the male sits up. "Look, it's fine. The cannibals either stay in their cells or hunt the others. What, you think they're going to sneak in and assault us? We've got weapons. They haven't got a chance. You're new here. Not a lot goes on."

The woman isn't buying it. "In the month I've been working in this prison, an immortal died, someone from the extinct line of northerners was brought in, and now the inmates are getting palatable food. Something is going on and you know it!"

Rune glances over at me, his forehead crinkling. Damn it. He's going to have a lot of questions after this.

"The guards are waiting for instructions, all right? We just do as we're told. Eventually they'll send someone to explain the situation. All we can do is wait." The male guard sighs and nuzzles back into the sofa. "Light the fire, would you? It's freezing."

I swallow the lump in my throat, fearful for the absolute pain Zain's about to endure.

This isn't the time to be heroic. I can distract them, but it will ensure my torture.

The woman approaches the fireplace and I suppress a whimper. I can only see her feet, but she stops, leans over and curses.

There's a grunting sound, followed by several shouts and thuds,

As much as I don't want to see, I can't help but poke my head out from under the cloth and gasp at the sight. The woman has Zain by his beard, while the male uses his baton to inflict severe gashes on Zain's bare chest.

"I told you to lock the door!" The woman hisses at the male guard.

"Why don't you hit him? Get some of that anger out?"

"Are you a cannibal?" The woman kicks Zain in the ribs with her boot.

"No, that's Mitty's little sidekick," the male says.

The woman grabs the man's baton and stops him mid swing. "So he's not brainless?"

"Brainless, yes. Zombie? No."

"Then why isn't he in labor? We need more of them."

"I told you, he's Mitty's little sidekick. He protects him from the gruesome chores."

Zain rolls onto his side, spitting up blood and nursing his abdomen.

*I hate this, I hate this, I hate this.*

"Well I don't respond well to nepotism or bias!" The woman grabs Zain by his hair and forces him onto his knees so she can bend over and lock eyes. "No more easy living for you. You're starting work tomorrow!"

"Do I get paid?" Zain manages to utter, which is met with a slap to the face.

"Come on." The woman tugs on his elbow, halting when Rune leaps out from his hiding place. "You! Where's your uniform?"

"I regenerate quickly," Rune says, jutting his chin out. He puffs his chest in an attempt to look bolder than what he is. "Zain shouldn't be punished. Not alone, anyway. We're...I'm his accomplice." Rune's eyes dart in my direction, as if expecting me to jump out and admit fault.

But I don't know if I can...

The man rubs his hands together as he towers over Rune. "Oh goodie. Fresh skin to pound on."

"Grab him," the woman says, boredom evident. "Torg will brand these slick thieves and send them into the fields. We need them out there. We're short on firewood."

It's my chance. My chance to reveal my hidden location and confess my sins.

But I can't do it.

Even as Zain and Rune are dragged literally kicking and screaming out of the guard's quarters, I keep still and silent, processing the sight before me.

Soon, I'm left in silence, the memories of their anguished cries replaying over and over in my mind.

I couldn't have left my hiding place. Zain said conditions in labor were worse than in here, and I'm barely surviving as it is!

I did the right thing...for myself...didn't I?
Damn it.
If I were immortal, things would be different.
Or maybe they wouldn't be.
Regardless...I'm nothing more than the coward in the corner.

# CHAPTER VI

It takes a lot of effort to convince my body to cooperate with my mind.

*Get up, Malin. Get up and get out!*

In a burst of energy, I roll from under the table and bolt out of the room. Fumbling through the now locked door, I think of Zain and Rune. *How could I let them take the blame? Why didn't I confess? Will I ever see them again?*

Through the second red door. *They're gone for good, doomed to suffer intense labor, all because I was hungry.*

Charging down the corridor, I frantically scan the patrolling guards, certain they must have passed Zain and Rune. They couldn't have gone too far, surely?

"Oi! Where are you running, Stretch?" One guard asks.

I want to ignore him. But it'll only cause more trouble in the long run. Coming to an abrupt stop, I look down at the fierce little man and search for an excuse. "Umm. I heard there was spaghetti in the chow hall."

"Ha. Well you missed out. It's all gone. Pudding was good, too." His amusement is suddenly replaced with irrefutable rage. "NO RUNNIN'!" He jams his baton into my sides, flooring me. Snickering at my wheezes, he marches off as I cradle my ribs.

I don't *think* anything is broken, but that doesn't matter now. I need to get up. Winded, I crawl towards a wall so that I can drag myself into a standing position. When I regain my breath, I hobble forwards, tears flooding my eyes when I can't locate Rune or Zain.

Careful not to walk too quickly or urgently, I slink past the other guards who only raise an eyebrow at my slumped posture.

I arrive at my cell, whimpering at the empty state. It was stupid to think Rune might be here. Didn't the female guard mention something about branding? As if we're not already branded enough with tattoos and drained blood. What else could they *possibly* do to them?

I linger by my cell door, too distraught to go in alone. It's all my fault... I could've yelled or distracted the guards in some way. It would've given Zain and Rune ample time to find an escape...

"Yooooou...l'wight?"

My stomach churns at the icy finger repetitively stroking my arm. Unsettled, I look down at the malnourished woman, her head shaved and her tattered, faded dress hanging off her bones.

But there's something in her eyes I haven't noticed in the majority of prisoners.

A flicker of life.

"I'm...just upset," I say, my heart sinking at her kind smile which only reveals her lack of teeth. "What's your name?"

"Droooogaaaa." It's almost as if she's forgotten how to speak, but the happiness in her gaunt, pale face is uplifting.

"Droga?" I confirm. "I'm Malin. They fed you well today."

She nods eagerly. "So m-much. I f-feel...l-life."

"That's lovely. I wish they'd feed you like this every day."

"M-me too. H-helps heal."

I take her bitterly cold hand and place it between mine, rubbing it gently. Her jaw drops, no doubt unaccustomed to body warmth. It must be an age since blood coursed through her veins.

"Angel," she mumbles, her eyes watering as she stares up at me.

"No," I say. "Far from it."

All I want is to escort Droga far away from this wretched prison. Give the immortals a warm shower, tasty food, a cuddle. But I'm helpless. Helpless and hopeless.

"There's...deeeaaaad...im-im-im..."

"Dead immortal, I know." I finish for her. "The rumor is spreading."

"I hope...I next!" The words are haunting, but her expression remains relatively pleased.

And there it is. The immortals don't fear this rumor. If anything, it's given them light at the end of the tunnel—that there is an end to this infinite torture.

In this small fraction of time, I make my decision. I *will* get these immortals out of here. They will eat, they will laugh, they will love again. They will heal and look back on their time here as nothing more than a fuzzy memory.

I *will* make it happen.

Or die trying.

I STRETCH out on the bed, twirling the strands of my greasy hair. The cell doors are wide open, but there's a tonal shift in the cell block.

There's chatter—chatter that's not coming from the heckling cannibals upstairs. Quiet murmurs, low hums and shuffling feet as immortals use their newfound energy to visit one another in their cells.

The guards don't appear concerned and continue about their mandatory patrol. Occasionally they stop to eavesdrop on what the immortals are saying, but it's difficult to translate. More often than not, the guard will get bored and continue down the corridor.

And all it took was one good meal. Imagine what a full week of eating could do. It'd be a gradual and *no doubt* painful process, but they could physically heal...and that would eventually lead to their mental state improving! These immortals aren't lost causes!

Whenever a guard passes my cell, I sit up and consider asking them about Rune and Zain. But I know better than that. Maybe I'm not supposed to even *know* about labor. There's only one guard I could even remotely risk conversing with and he's off duty.

I tried asking Droga about it, but I'd given her mental capacity too much credit. Halfway through trying to explain my situation, she blinked and walked away. Perhaps my conversation was too draining or maybe at her core, she's just rude. Guess I'll never know. But I spent the downtime replaying the earlier events over and over in my mind, figuring out my next move.

A whistle pierces the air, echoing down the hall. It doesn't stop and I have to grab the itchy, stained pillow to cover my sensitive ears.

*"Dead meat comin' fru! Lock up the cells!"*

The doors automatically slide shut, as guards round immortals back into their cells. I find relief in the clanging as it overpowers the shrieking whistle.

Footsteps march down the cell block, the cannibals above jeering at the new inmate.

*"Weird lookin' man!"*

*"Lots of you to eat!"*

*"We're coming for you, love!"*

It turns my stomach.

Out of sheer curiosity, I slink closer to the bars so I can sneak a peek at the new immortal.

And then my stomach does a full one-eighty.

Towering over the two guards, the cuffed immortal glares stoically ahead. Tattered three-quarter pants only elongate her already lean body. Her broad shoulders and strong jawline are a confusing paradox to people who aren't from the north. What probably makes it even more confusing for them is her auburn, short hair; her fringe covering the left side of her face. The look isn't androgynous to northerners, but folks down here will never understand.

I just can't believe it's her. What is she *doing* here?

As she nears my cell, I'm lost for words. Do I reach out to her? Or will the guards punish us? Can I say anything that might offer some form of comfort?

"Taylin," I whisper as I'm engulfed in her shadow.

She hears her name, her undeniable strength enough to halt the guards as she stops outside of my cell door.

"Malin," she says through gritted teeth.

"Come on, no socializing!" Both guards pull on her arms, but Taylin refuses to budge. Nostrils flared, she breathes heavily as she glowers at me.

"I will *murder* you," she spits, then succumbs to the guards bludgeoning her sides with their batons. Her expression remains emotionless, as they lead her down the corridor, far away from my cell.

Heart racing, I fall back onto the bed.

Murder me.

She'll *murder* me?

Her threat is on repeat in my mind, undeserved in its execution. What on earth did I do to warrant such an ominous greeting? We barely know each other. Now I have that menacing warning looming over me, meanwhile I still have to keep an eye on the cannibals and the imminent uniform assignment.

And nobody to confide in...

...time doesn't move forward in this place. We're perpetually stuck in a moment. It's impossible to tell time without natural light seeping in, and the guards don't stick to a schedule. They shout *sleep* or *breakfast* at any given time, seemingly based on their own mood.

I spend the rest of the day ripping the fabric off the end of the mattress to fashion a belt around my frail waist. I've always been slender, but the lack of food coupled with dehydration is already showing.

I'm naked beneath my robe; a regrettable decision. It was all I had in the moment. When the guards came knocking, it was either grab what you have and flee, or get arrested. At least this crummy belt will add a tiny layer of warmth and keep the material from getting in my way.

Tying the fabric tightly, I take this very small moment to feel like a pretty woman again. It's been a long time since I've had that opportunity—survival has always been the priority. But here, in a place where I have nothing, the tiniest bit of flare suddenly means the world.

With the realization that part of a mattress can invoke such a powerful emotion, I pause. I swallow when I notice my hands smoothing out the wrinkles in my robes. It's like I remember where I am. I'm not blinded by false hope. The cold stone reveals itself again in all its glory, along with the stained pillow, the rusted bars. Delirious, I collapse to my knees and sob.

I'm tired. I'm hungry. I'm confused. I'm lonely. I'm freezing. And I'm *scared*.

"Stop it," I admonish. "Stop it! You can't cry. It'll only make it worse!"

I barely recognize my voice. It's weak, deep, hoarse.

I used to sing. They said my voice was like a bell. But those days are long gone.

A faded memory...just like everything else...

...and in the silent prison, Taylin screams at the top of her lungs pleading to be released...

...I hardly know whether it's a dream or a memory...

"WAKE UP!"

My eyes fling open, the abrupt arousal jarring. I don't know where I disappeared to; the faint images from the dream-world slipping from my mental grip. A town...a town...

The doors roll open.

Fire...no, it wasn't a fire. There was a town, though. And a shop... did I know the woman in the dream? I remember feeling associated with her...but I can't piece it together.

Mind hazy, I listen to the slurred murmurs of immortals who pile out of their cells. Most of them seem to be returning to their daily routine, lining up to meet in the chow hall. They must be convinced they'll be served edible food again. I can't fathom what the odds are of that happening two days in a row. Either way, I'm considering risking a gassing for the possibility of a good meal. That and the idea of sitting vulnerable and alone in a cell where Taylin or the cannibals can find me is extremely daunting...

Reluctantly, I slip out of my cell and into the line, sticking out like a sore thumb. Nobody understands how awkward it is being considerably taller than the majority of the population.

I weigh up the options of running to the showers before the chow hall. I'm remarkably thirsty, but if I end up poisoned, I'm going to need whatever is dripping from the taps.

Shaking my head at the thought of Rune and Zain's face if they saw me lining up, I nearly chicken out. Gambling was never my strong suit, but I'd rather the devil I know.

Still bleary-eyed from sleep, we approach the chow hall. There's no turning back now. I'm mere meters away and the guards are waiting by the doors. They don't enforce mandatory attendance, but I'm sure if I turned back so close to the entrance, they'd react.

Inside, there's a different energy. Immortals still reside in their usual seats, but the vibe isn't as forlorn as before. Instead, there's an eagerness, an anticipation.

I find an empty seat and take my place next to a blind immortal who looks a lot older than the others. She must be extraordinarily ancient. Dressed in what looks like an old bed sheet, she stares at the stone table with a slight grin. Despite her milky eyes and multiple scars etched into her skin, she looks...happy?

The man across from me still has sauce stained on his lower lip and is smiling maniacally at the table.

I've never pitied anybody more than I do now.

"Will they really feed us two days in a row?" I ask quietly, but as expected, they don't respond.

It's as if I'm the only person still alive in this room. All except for the tall brunette who just walked through the doors. I stiffen at the arrival of Taylin, wondering if it'd be appropriate to hide beneath the table. After all, it's what I'm good at.

But she's already seen me. The advantage of being so tall is you can generally scope the perimeter a little easier than the average man. Her shoulders rise and she makes a beeline towards me.

I forget to breathe. I actually forget how to breathe as she nears the table.

She sits across from me, grinding her teeth. Without a word, she raises her hand and slaps me across the cheek, the force burning my skin. She clenches her fists, pauses, then stands and leaves as quickly as she arrived.

I nurse my cheek, waiting for the follow-up confrontation but she's secured a seat elsewhere.

Nobody at the table reacts. Not a slight eyebrow raise or a comforting pat on the back. I'm just a ghost. A ghost who is feeling the sting of a woman who detests every fiber of my being.

The selfish side of me hopes for a gassing, just so she can experience the discomfort. But I know better than to wish negativity on others. Hatred is self-punishment. Who needs that when the prison punishes us already?

Tense, I anxiously await the poison, wondering if I can hold my breath for that long...again. My skin is still peeling from the last gassing and my throat is perpetually raw.

But something unexpected happens. Several mortals dressed in a pale gray uniform appear from the back doors with trays in their hands. One by one, they serve the meal and famished immortals tear into it.

I don't know what to do when the tray is delivered in front of me. Steam sizzles off the steak, the smell mouth-watering. Some beans are scooped onto the side, along with mashed potato.

It's not a huge meal, but it's more than I've had in years.

Remembering Zain's words, I wonder about the poison. Carefully, I dig into the mash and beans with my finger, unsure what I'm looking for.

The other immortals finish their meal in a couple of gulps, eager for a second helping. If I'm going to eat, I better do it quickly before somebody steals it. Taking a gamble, I lick the mash off my finger, the warmth instantly mollifying my taut state. I barely have control over my body as I shovel the food into my mouth, enjoying every energizing microsecond.

"I think I felt my heart beat," the man across from me says, his laugh carefree. "Oh goodness gracious. Is this what it feels to be alive?"

The question is rhetorical, but his eyes dance.

"Your heart restarts after eating a meal?" I ask, uncertain as to how his biology works.

"We can all regenerate to a degree if we take care of our bodies. Food is the energy our cells need to kick-start everything. Understandably, the speed and effectiveness of my regeneration is not an ability all immortals possess. I'm a lot luckier than most." He glances at the blind woman next to me. "I can be dead by all accounts, but if I eat, drink and sleep correctly, I will reset almost back to normal. Oh goodness, imagine a third consecutive day of eating! I might actually get some blood pumping through my veins again!"

The woman throws her head back and laughs, although the cracking sounds following the motion churn my stomach. Unless that's the poison talking.

"You don't think this is poison?"

"If it is, it's very well hidden," the man says, licking his fingers. "You can usually taste it."

"Why do you think they're suddenly feeding us so well? My first day was a gassing!"

"Yeah, it depends. Psychological warfare, no doubt. We're guinea pigs." He shrugs absentmindedly. "It's been years since we've received a good meal. Presumedly the prison has gained some funding. Perhaps a new law has been passed? I can't say I care. I just want more mash."

His theory doesn't add up, and I instantly regret eating my meal. We're in a prison hellbent on murdering us—why would they aid us?

Should I force myself to purge just in case? Surely there's an experimental potion in that steak...

"GET OUTTA HERE!"

The guards bellow at the energized immortals who obediently stand and make their way out of the chow hall. I stay close to the blind woman and man, frightened of running into Taylin again.

When we are released back into the cell block, I look over my shoulder, curious as to where she went. I swear my cheek still aches.

I stop at the door to my cell. At first, I muse if I'm at the wrong one. But no. The remains of my cell spill out into the corridor.

The mattress has been absolutely destroyed, the insides and springs scattered across the floor. The pillow has been defiled, and a message is smeared across the walls, but I can't fathom what it's been written in.

*You're next mortal.*

My heart is stuck in my throat. Woozy, I lean against the bars and tremble. Can I lock myself in here forever? I'm safe in here, right?

No, I need to calm down. I can sense the panic attack. The overwhelming dread hanging over me like a storm cloud as my vision tunnels and my breaths become somewhat audible.

This is why the immortals always go to the chow hall. Even with the promise of poison, it's a safer bet than staying in the open cells when the cannibals are free to roam. Without the protection of Rune and Zain, I have no other choice. I doubt the courtyard bargain will hold up without Zain around to uphold it.

Not one immortal stops to see the state of my cell. They may be feeling slightly better, but the majority of them are still brain dead.

Shaking, I attempt to maintain some sort of cool, but it's futile. I'm sick, I'm pale, I'm dizzy. I stumble through the cell block, accidentally bumping into every single inmate. Hurrying to the showers, I choose to purge in peace.

I push on the door, the leaky pipes oddly comforting. My legs are like jelly, so I drop to my knees and crawl towards one of the taps and relish in each slow drop that lands on my tongue.

I can't even survive a week here alone. How do the cannibals know I'm mortal? Is it a certain odor? Are they highly attuned to that sort of thing? Is it because I'm the only one in here without blue skin? Excluding Taylin and Rune, of course...

The drip runs dry. I fumble with the tap, desperate for more but it's as good as I'm going to get.

The serenity of lying in a stone-cold room only slightly larger than my cell has eased my panic attack, but I'm in the same position I was ten minutes ago.

Taylin has threatened my life. Then the cannibals violated my cell. And any day now the medic will return to unknowingly murder me. No doubt they will assume they've killed their second immortal and the mystery will continue.

Wait a minute.

Despite my cramping stomach, I pull myself into an upright sitting position. *The dead immortal.* What if *they're* mortals too? It's the only thing that makes sense. That means there's other people like me in here, and if that's the case, we need to rally together and speak up!

Speak up against what, I'm not entirely sure. Now doubt they'd have us silenced pretty damn quickly. If the public knew mortals were sentenced to an immortal prison, it would start a civil war.

"They said I'd find you in here."

My ears prick at the civil voice and I find instant comfort in Mitty's presence. He stands awkwardly by the door, glancing over his shoulder.

"Mitty?" I bite my lip. "Is it all right if I call you that?"

He hesitates, no doubt unsettled by the familiar way I've greeted him. "Did Zain call me that?"

"He did. Should I not?"

"No. No that's fine. He asked me to speak with you."

"They're okay?" I note the shrill urgency in my voice, but I can't suppress it. I stand, but keep a fair distance between us.

"In relative terms." He sighs. "I worked so hard to keep Zain from labor work. He hates it in here, I get it. The lack of company, the cannibals, the odors. But it's like royalty compared to out there. At least here you get a cell, a roof over your head, freedom from guards who barely pay you any attention."

"How bad is it working in labor?"

His eyes widen and I wonder how warped his perception is. Surely nothing is worse than this. "They've got the toughest guards out there. Those guys don't suffer fools. They happily punish and torture without hesitation. Immortals get fed a piece of bread every day to maintain some sort of energy, but you're expected to sleep outside chained to the ground. You're susceptible to the elements and coerced to toil nonstop. Only sound-of-mind immortals are sent out there. Considering the cannibals are a liability and the others are practically zombies, they'd be useless. I pulled a few strings over the years to keep Zain safe here. Convinced some of them that he's too unhinged to work."

"But you're so young. Surely you couldn't have kept him safe all this time. And, I mean, why *would* you?"

"Because that's what my father did."

The conversation comes to an abrupt halt. I can't bring myself to interrogate the poor man.

"Mitty. I'm going to die in here. The cannibals have a target on my head and the new inmate hates me. I should be in labor with Rune and Zain. *Please*, Mitty. See, I'm sound of mind. You have no choice, right? Let me be with them."

Pressing his lips tightly together, the conflicted guard shakes his head. "No. No. It already breaks me to see Zain out there. He told me to make sure you stay safe. So it's here you must stay."

"Mitty. I'm *begging* you!" I slowly lower myself back to the ground and pray. "Send me outside with them."

"No. I made a promise."

"Mitty, I'll *die* in here!"

"Immortals can't die."

"But I'm not immortal!" I screech, surprised by the high pitch resonating in the dank room.

Mitty's eyebrows raise ever so slightly, crinkling his forehead. "That's impossible."

"Evidently not."

"You're lying."

"Pretty stupid thing to lie about, isn't it?" My candor is probably perceived as a little rude, but Mitty doesn't appear too fazed by my tone. More so the words behind it.

"If it were true, you wouldn't be locked up. And the gas alone should've poisoned you. Perhaps not fatally, but definitely enough to make you sick."

"I was careful not to breathe much of the gas in." Closing my eyes, I brace for the truth. "I *was* immortal, but I gave it up, all right?"

Leaving his post at the door, he closes it behind him and shuffles towards me, speaking in a hushed whisper. "Immortals can do that?"

"Northerners can. How else do you think we all died out? It's like how some corners can regenerate efficiently. Zain seems to be able to make me blurt out anything, so I'm speculating that's an ability immortals from his corner possess."

"But why would you give up your immortality?"

"Because I thought they'd stop chasing me. Dumb idea, right?" I snort. "Sometimes you'd rather die on your own terms than be enslaved by somebody else's."

"So the dead immortal?"

"Maybe we share an ability. I'm assuming they've had enough of living here."

Mitty almost smiles, but masks it with a cough. "Unlikely. The dead immortal was recently transferred to better quarters. They were *very* well looked after. Four meals a day. Plush living. They were egotistical and wealthy, so despite the poor conditions of the prison, they always had substantial quarters. Most of you lot don't have a shilling to your name due to the years spent running and hiding. This immortal had slightly different luck. I can say with absolute confidence they couldn't have been suicidal. If anything, they had it better than us mortals, and we're not even prisoners. Something weird is going on, that's for sure."

"But you don't know what's going on inside someone's head."

"I suppose you have a point." Mitty pauses. "What if there's more of you with this ability? Why haven't others given up their immortality? Or what if they all start doing it?"

"I can't speak for everyone, but generally immortals can only use their abilities when the body is in decent condition. Which leads me to the next question. What's with feeding everyone so well?"

"I genuinely don't know. Sometimes the prison does this, but admittedly it's been an age. Maybe relatives of the dead immortal donated some of the wealth, but that's just speculation. We can only hope for your sake, this trend continues. Can you...can you get your immortality back?"

For the first time in my life, I don't view my immortality as a curse, a hindrance, or a plague. It was a gift that I carelessly gave away. "It's long gone."

"Oh." It's strange to see him so disappointed. "Shame. I am painfully aware of the stigma against your kind, but my father and I have never hated any of you. One malevolent immortal doesn't mean you're all bad. You're feared for puerile reasons. If I had it my way, you'd all walk free. Or at least be treated much better than you currently are."

I want nothing more than to hug this man, but it's far too inappropriate. "We're lucky to have you here, Mitty. Thank you."

He nods stiffly. "Don't get too cozy around me. I still need to do my job. But I'll do my best to keep Zain's promise. You must remain safe. He really took a liking to you. Maybe because you're the first sane immortal he's come across in decades."

"And Rune?"

"Like I said, you're the *first* sane immortal he's come across in decades."

I smile. It's not a great joke, but it's something. "Are you sure you can't get me working in labor?"

"I won't do it," he says firmly. "Especially if what you're saying is true, your death will not be on my hands."

We're interrupted by a whistle blowing outside. Flinching, Mitty readjusts his uniform and clears his throat. He needn't say a thing. Understandingly, we nod to one another as he exits the showers. I wait several moments and follow him into the cell block, using my best poker face. If anybody found out about such an intimate conversation, we'd both be in trouble.

Hurrying back to my dingy, ransacked cell, I await the official lock up. There's nowhere for me to sit, so I curl up in the corner and gather scattered feathers and fabric into a pile. It's not much, but it's the best pillow I can make.

The cannibal's haunting message drips off the wall, the liquid substance still an unknown entity. I'm content to remain ignorant to its origins.

And yet, I can't stop staring at the threatening words. It's difficult to ignore, so I actively turn my back to the wall and bury my face in my lap. *If I can't see it, it's not there. If I can't see it, it's not there...*

*You're next mortal.*

I've memorized it. It practically screams in my head, looming over my shoulder with each agonizing second.

I need to get out of here.

# CHAPTER VII

The message dries overnight on the wall, permanently inked into stones. I consider washing it off, but I haven't rationed enough water for that. Instead, it remains, serving as a constant reminder.

Days pass, and every morning we are fed warm, fresh food—bread, meat, and vegetables.

Every morning I find myself growing more and more suspicious.

As the immortals become energized with each meal, it seems to have the opposite effect on me, as I slowly succumb to a zombie-like state. I'm too on edge to converse with anybody. I'm constantly looking over my shoulder, wondering when I'll be attacked. I barely eat due to the incessant fretting that our food is poisoned.

I'm stuck in an unbreakable loop.

I spend the days either locked in my cell or safely grouped with other immortals. The majority still struggle to form sentences or comprehend simple requests, but some smile now. Some even make eye contact. It's a form of company. But it doesn't make up for Taylin's nightly screams—either night terrors or a form of seeking attention. She keeps me up, maybe deliberately. Maybe she's trying to make me delirious from sleep deprivation so she can make good on her promise. I'm not prepared to find out.

After a fulfilling breakfast, I return to my destroyed cell and hide in the corner, conceptualizing plans to break free and work in labor with Rune and Zain.

I hope they're okay. They're strong. Smart. Sneaky. *Of course* they're okay.

"Oi. You."

My heart skips a beat at the sight of Taylin standing outside my cell. Bloodshot eyes and lips pursed, she looks weary.

"Please," I whisper. "I don't want any trouble."

"I want to talk to you."

It's tricky to discern her tone over the low chatter of immortals socializing in the corridor. It only takes a few moments for the guards to remind them of their place, banging on the bars and shouting at them to shut up.

Taylin steps inside my cell to avoid confrontation with the guards, but maintains her poise. "Now."

"Do you promise you'll only talk?" I ask carefully.

She takes a little too long to reply. "I promise I won't murder you. I didn't leave that message."

"I didn't think you did," I confess, glancing at the threat on the wall. "It's the cannibals. They come in here every time I'm in the chow hall."

"I know. The immortal next to my cell was defiled by one of the cannibals when I returned. There's not much left of them. Why don't the guards do anything?"

"Because the less of us, the better. So long as we keep quiet and keep out of their way, they don't care what we do."

"Hmm." Taylin narrows her eyes, reading the message on the wall. "They think I'm male."

"They're not accustomed to tall females from the north. We're all but extinct."

"We *could've* been entirely extinct." Her response is vitriolic. "It's your fault I'm in here."

"I thought I was helping." I offer my hand to show I'm apologizing, but she refuses. "Taylin, if I had known, I never would've...I mean...I didn't...I'm sorry."

"Sorry will never rectify the consequences of your decision."

"Can't you...you know...give up your immortality?"

"I wouldn't give it up in here. Not when I plan to get out." She pauses. "However, I have chosen to be your temporary ally. You're going to help me escape this prison. I don't belong here."

I cringe at the thought of disappointing her, but she leaves me with no option. "Nobody has ever escaped."

"They've never imprisoned northerners before. You and I are stronger, faster, smarter than all of them. Tell me what you know so we can break out. If it means killing all these guards, then I'll do it."

She's conspiring with the wrong person. I barely know anything around here. Without Zain or Rune to guide me, I'm nothing more than a bumbling idiot.

"I've heard you can work in labor outside. Allegedly conditions are much worse."

"Outside?" Her eyes flicker with imagined freedom. "Great. How do we do it?"

"It's a punishment. Zain and Rune were sent because they stole food."

"So we need to misbehave? Piece of cake. We can do that."

I don't know how to explain that one of the guards is doing everything in his power to prevent me from working in labor. It's a conversation which won't be received particularly well by an already unhinged immortal. Cleaning the dirt from beneath my fingernails, I mumble incoherently under my breath.

"I don't want them to...uh, Taylin, the thing is, I'm well looked after in here. As you are aware, I'm mortal. I might not survive in labor."

"Well you definitely won't survive in *here*! As soon as the medic returns to drain your blood, you're dead. Your entire existence is a ticking time bomb! The very least you can do after getting me caught up in this nightmare is help me escape."

She unfortunately has valid points—all points my lucid state has internally screamed at me, but ultimately fear overrides my logic.

"I can't guarantee they'll send me to labor with you," I say cryptically, preempting Mitty's reaction. "But follow me."

Ducking my head as we leave the cell, I analyze the overall mood and tone in the cell block. The immortals are settling down and the guards seem to be in a bad mood. Some of them have damp hair and shoulders, so it must be raining outside.

Damn it. Had I known, I would've run to the courtyard for a shower and fresh drink.

Taylin and I stand in the corridor, her fists clenching when I don't move.

"What are we doing?"

"Taking advantage of an opportunity."

I turn around and head towards the direction of the courtyard. It's a selfish decision, but the thought of fresh water cleansing the sweat and grease from my body is overwhelmingly tempting. Surely Taylin will appreciate it too. It's just slight detour...maybe it's also a method of procrastination.

The icy breeze in the cell block is colder than usual and my feet have turned blue slapping against the chilled stone.

At least they're not as blue as the other immortals.

"Do you have a plan?" Taylin spits in my ear as I lead her into the courtyard.

I don't reply.

Despite the blustering wind sweeping my hair across my vision, I stand still. Various puddles of water are disturbed by enthusiastic cannibals rolling and kicking their heels.

There's about six of them. I've never seen them up close—only heard their heckles from above. But their appearance is so much worse than their gravelly voices. Their flesh is adorned in scars, frayed fabric clinging to their well-fed bodies.

"Cannibals," I utter.

I'm such an idiot. Zain warned me about the pact with the cannibals and I failed to notice the time of day. We can't even back away silently, as the crash of the door closing behind us startles them.

Their eyes are black, alert, soulless. While they don't possess all their teeth, the ones that remain are sharp and bloodstained.

"Well, well, well!" The one sitting on the same bench Rune, Zain and I had gathered on only last week, claps. "Innit a pleasure seeing you here! What a feast you towers ought to be!"

Taylin shoots me a fierce look. "You traitor!"

"No, I didn't think they'd be here!" I say. "Honestly, I didn't!"

Like a pack of hungry werewolves, the cannibals approach us with sinister smiles, circling their prey with delight.

"I'm friends with Z-Zain!" I stutter, my voice lost in the wind. "You had a pact."

"Zain's not here no more." The bald one cracks his knuckles, although he's missing about two of them. "And you're not Zain."

"Touch me and you die!" Taylin's stern voice booms over the rain. She puffs out her chest, her stature enough to dissuade the cannibals for a moment.

When they compose themselves, they laugh, excited to face such a challenge. They bounce on their feet as if preparing for competition.

One lunges straight for Taylin who swings a mighty punch, landing on his jaw. Stunned, he stumbles back and gapes.

And that one action triggers an onslaught.

I've always considered myself a hider, not a fighter. It's how I've avoided conflict for all these years. I have very little experience in self-defense and now seems like the worst time to learn.

But life isn't known for its perfect timing.

I crouch as a cannibal lunges towards me and throw my body weight into his abdomen so that he flips over my head and topples to the ground. I glance back and note his temple smacking into the corner of the building. A mighty gash soon appears, and he collapses to the ground, eyes rolling to the back of his head. Unless he's a regenerator, that could cause some unrepairable damage and I can't help but feel extremely guilty for such a severe repercussion. An eternity with brain damage is a cruel punishment, even for cannibals.

Taylin is a dirty fighter. She doesn't care where she needs to attack to bring the men to their knees. And in response, they tend to bite into the juicer parts of her body, clinging to the flesh like a wild animal.

Hoping that my scream is enough to startle them, I kick a cannibal in the face so that he releases Taylin, a disgusting chunk of skin now missing from her thigh.

I'm too slow to dodge the cannibal who sneaks up behind me. He's the petite one of the group and practically climbs my body, dangling from my throat. Gasping for air while he clasps around my windpipe, I scramble to knock him off. I attempt to shriek when he bites into neck, but can't find the air to do so.

Panicked, I run backwards into the wall and slam him into it. When he drops to the ground, I choke and splutter, using my bare foot to kick him in the face.

It takes me a moment to recover emotionally, wanting nothing more than to apologize to the bruised and bloody criminal. *Yes*, he's trying to eat us. But I hate hurting anybody.

Scoping the drenched courtyard, I shudder at Taylin who has pulled her opponent's eyes out of his sockets, rendering him blind and useless.

"Suck it up! And save the eyes for a meal later!" One of the cannibals shouts, seemingly annoyed by his pained wails. "I'm *STARVING*! Take these things down!"

Three cannibals stand tall; the others too injured to partake in the fight. Exhausted, Taylin and I inch closer to one another, as if uniting to form a threatening force.

The remaining cannibals are far more vicious than their fallen comrades. Madness glimmers in their hungry eyes, their blue skin camouflaged beneath dry blood that has stained their skin. Not even the rain can cleanse their souls.

"This is your last chance to back off," Taylin shouts. "You don't know what northerners are capable of."

The last sentence resonates with them for a moment, because they freeze and glance at one another. It's intriguing how others perceive the north. Clearly the rumors are enough to evoke some sort of fear.

"Although we're more than happy to demonstrate," I add, hoping my acting abilities are believable. "You saw how effortlessly we injured your friends."

Friend is probably the wrong word to use. Sociopaths don't have *true* friends, do they? And the truth is, nothing about that was effortless. Despite my attempt at a heroic exterior, I'm trembling from the cold and fighting the urge to vomit out of pure terror and trauma. Bruises are already popping up on my skin.

"We're better fighters than them," the cannibal with a hairy chest says. Without another warning, the three of them leap towards us, teeth bared. Their weight topples us to the ground as their long nails dig into our skin.

I cry—in pain, fear, and desperation.

I'm pinned beneath two of them, my mortal blood no doubt tantalizing them. I could very well be their first warm meal in years. Between the pressure, the rain, and the shouts, I can't discern what is actually happening, but I know I can't move. Pockets of warmth appear and trickle down my body, a pool of blood gathering beneath my chin.

Vision cloudy from the rain, I try to make sense of the feeling. But life has turned hazy. My hearing fades and I gape at the cannibal on top of me...chewing. What...what is he eating?

"WHAT'S THIS DISTURBANCE ABOUT?"

I've never been happier to hear the grating voice of an irate guard. Within moments, the weight is lifted and I can breathe.

My vision tunnels, but I fight to maintain consciousness. Slowly piecing together my reality, I watch as the guards seize the cannibals who are covered in my blood.

A pale Mitty pulls me to my feet, his eyes solely focused on mine which are periodically rolling to the back of my head.

"Should've just let them rip into each other," one guard says as he hits a cannibal in the back of the head with his baton. The cannibal drops to the ground in a heap, likely a fatal blow had he been mortal. He's not going to be the same.

"No," another guard interjects. "We don't encourage the cannibals. It gives them energy which means they could come after us. You know the policy. *Subdued and sedated is highly rated.*"

"What about these two?" A guard waves his hand carelessly at Taylin and I. "The tall freaks. They look savvy. They require uniforms, but they look strong. Why has nobody sent them to labor yet? Is there something wrong with them?"

"Yeah, I always see the golden-haired one walkin' around relatively normal. Looks strong as ya say, so really should be out there. The other one has only been here a few days, so should be fitter than anyone 'ere. If it's engaging in fights with the cannibals, it should probably redirect that energy elsewhere."

Mitty tightens his grip around my arm, the quiver in his voice unnerving. "Ah, this one is mentally unstable. She is under the impression she's mortal, and behaves in a fragile fashion. Can't have that weak mindset slowing down progress in labor."

The overweight guard scoffs, then hits a restrained cannibal when he snaps at the air. "Is that all? That's a shite excuse! Send it to Torg and get it to work. Might as well send the other one too. Don't want them causing trouble in here."

Mitty is persistent. "But she's bleeding pretty severely. She might pass out before she can get to work. We should call the medic to clean her up."

"It's gotta get its blood drained, anyway! Jeez mate, you're not their protectors! They're disgusting criminals! Immortals *kill* and *control.* Don't you forget they're the enemy. Another protest out of you and we'll tell the superiors you're unable to handle the job."

Through my dazed state, I feel Mitty's shoulders slump forward as he clings to my arms. Taylin, meanwhile, is suppressing an excited smirk. She got exactly what she was searching for, and I got exactly what was coming to me.

The guards lead us out of the rain and back into the cell block.

The groggy cannibals are dragged upstairs, and I overhear some mention of throwing them into solitary confinement. I hope they're sentenced for a century or two.

Mitty and another guard guide Taylin and me through the cell block and several corridors, the rooms getting darker and darker. Or maybe that's just because I'm losing consciousness. I don't dare look back, frightened to see a trail of my blood.

"I'm bleeding...to death..." I murmur. Mitty squeezes my arm gently, but it's all he can offer.

Every room and corridor in this hideous prison is identical. The newer sections are built from concrete, which is ironic considering the stone holds up far better long term. Each room is windowless, bitterly cold and bland, leading me to believe it's some optical illusion. Maybe every room is the *same* room. Maybe this is some psychological trick to confuse us!

Or maybe I need to tend to these wounds.

I allow my heavy eyelids to close as we continue through the weaving prison. Seconds feel like hours and voices become distant. I barely feel the cold as my soaked hair and clothes stick to my skin. Everything is just...numb.

"Stay with us," Mitty's faraway whisper alerts me.

"Sleep..." I slur, only now aware of the slack Mitty has taken up. He holds me by my waist so that my feet scrape along the floor. From a distance, it would no doubt look like I'm walking but I'm far too weak for that. Keeping my arm around Mitty's shoulder, I fight to keep my head from flopping around.

"What you sayin' to that inmate?" The other guard who grasps onto Taylin is in no mood. "I swear mate, I'm *this* close to pushing for a transfer. First you mollycoddled that manipulative twonk, and now this one! You're a disgrace!"

Nothing more than a gentle giant in disguise, Mitty clears his throat. "I am not mollycoddling them."

"You bloody are! Look at you! Make that thing walk! You think we don't see you cringing whenever we hit an immortal with a foul odor or ugly face? Get over yourself. Go find a woman to knock up so you can mollycoddle them!"

There's no other justification; Mitty is bullied here. And as much as I hate to admit it; the rude guard might very well have a point. Mitty doesn't belong here. He's too kind and could fair better as an alchemist, medic, or caregiver.

For his own sake, I hope he quits. For my own, I hope he retires in fifty years.

Mitty doesn't verbally respond to the guard, but his muscles tense as we enter another room.

He props me up when we come to a halt and I force my eyes open. To the surprise of absolutely nobody, the room is gray, empty, and cold. Just like everything else in this hellhole.

We stand in silence, although I'm not entirely sure what we're waiting for. Taylin turns to look at me, her eyes widening when her gaze lands on my neck. She moves swiftly. Tearing off a piece of her damp pants, she applies pressure to my gaping wound. It stings, but the cold rag numbs my skin.

"Oi!" The guard is mortified. "What are you doing? Let it bleed out!"

"Just because immortals can't die doesn't ensure the quality of life," Taylin says through gritted teeth. "We can go blind, we can get arthritis, we can suffer from depression. Malin doesn't deserve to get an infection or pass out because you think immortals are evil!"

Stunned by her directness, the guard opens and shuts his mouth. He's a lot smaller than the three of us and has wisely chosen to ignore us. After all, we'll be gone in a matter of minutes and we're no longer his problem.

"How bad..." I am struggling to formulate the sentences.

"Bad," Taylin says. "You need stitches. They took a good chunk out of you."

A nauseated Mitty peers over to check the wound and quickly turns away. What are we waiting for, anyway? This Torg character? How long are we expected to stand?

"Anywhere else?" I ask, my extremities numb.

"A lot of bruises and cuts, but it's your throat I'm concerned about." Taylin applies more pressure to the wound. "Malin, I don't know what to do."

And there it is. Defeat. It's a tone I didn't think I'd hear from such a determined survivalist. She needn't say it, but I deduce the unspoken meaning.

I'm doomed.

Resigned to my fate, I crumble in a heap on the ground and find comfort in the fact that I can escape this nightmare once and for all... even if it's through death.

# CHAPTER VIII

They say that in death, your hearing is the last sense to go.

That makes sense. While I can't feel much or see anything, I hear a rather obnoxious ringing and...panicked voices.

"Are you sure?"

"Yes! All northerners have the same blood! Hurry up and take mine!"

"And why would you give a blood transfusion to an immortal?"

"I'm not doing it without a medic, obviously! Have you sterilized that needle?"

"No."

"Do it!"

"Why? She's a prisoner!"

"Oh, I'll do it. Pour the alcohol on the neck."

"Ow! Not so hard."

"Sorry."

The voices merge into one another, but it sounds like Mitty, Taylin, and the other guard. Something cold and acidic suddenly burns my neck and I want nothing more than to scream in agony...but I can't.

An unpleasant prick stabs my flesh. I'd writhe if I could feel my body. A cold line weaves in and out of my skin, tiny goosebumps popping up on my arms.

"Where did you learn to do this?"

"My grandmother. When I wasn't in the prison, I was with her. I've never sewed a human before, but it can't be much different from mending fabric."

"You *still* haven't sewn a *human*! It's an immortal! I'm reporting you!"

"Go on. Report him!" Taylin's voice. Hurried footsteps. "We dare you. Considering how grossly incompetent you are, you'd be fired long before him! Punished for misconduct! So shut up and stand over there!"

Silence. Until: "You have no idea what you're in for when you reach the fields. You'll be wishing for someone like me."

No reaction. Just heavy breathing. A prayer. Then silence once more…

MY EYES FLING OPEN, my vision crisp and rested.

Full of energy, I appreciate the surroundings as a powerful sensation overtakes my body. I could bounce off the walls.

I'm lying on a steel slab, Taylin's rag still wrapped around my throat. Mitty stands in the corner with his arms folded, but I can see dried blood stains on his wrists. Taylin stands with cuffs in the other corner, a golden metal band hugging her neck.

Her eyes are puffy, but the corner of her mouth curls when I stare at her. "You're alive."

I cautiously sit up, my throat dry and sore. "Surprisingly. Where are we?"

"Waiting for Torg. He said he needed the bathroom, and if you were still unconscious by the time he returned, he'd sound the alarm for the second dead immortal."

Mitty's bottom lip quivers oh-so subtly, but he doesn't hide his smile. "I thought I killed you. I stitched up your throat. I'm sorry it might leave a hideous scar. I panicked."

I go to touch the stitches, but stop when Mitty shakes his head. "Thank you both so much. I can't believe it. What happened to the other guard?"

"I told that imbecile to leave or else the three of us would hit him where the sun don't shine. He didn't feel so confident without the other goons to support him." Taylin puts her nose in the air rather petulantly. "What do I care? I'll never seen him again."

A door squeaks open and crashes behind me. I turn to see a broad man with scraggly red hair and a wide nose. The muscles in his arms are ridiculously well-defined, so much so I contemplate whether he's a descendant of the ogres.

"Oh good. She's up." The man who I assume is Torg is sucking on something, his lips smacking together as he speaks. "Thought so. One dead immortal is freakin' ludicrous, but *two*? Would never happen. Righto. Two more bodies for the fields. Let's check your sanity. Can't have deranged folk out there."

Could I deliberately fail such a test? Should I?

"I'm ready," I say when he doesn't continue. "What do you need to know?"

Torg cocks his head to the side, his inquisitive green eyes glistening. "I'd like to know why the pair of you don't have your uniforms yet."

"The medic has been busy," I say. "We're waiting."

"And she's mortal," Mitty blurts, which only leads to a skeptical Torg laughing boisterously.

"Good one, mate. All right, medic has been away. That checks out." He tugs on my wrist with his enormous hands. "Skinny little thing, but strong bones. Apart from the recent injury, you're physically in decent condition. How do you deal with starvation? Feel the urge to feast on inmates or mortals?"

"Honestly, except for the first couple of days, they've fed us pretty well," I admit. This answer stuns Torg, who looks at Mitty for validation. "Prior to that I...well...I stole from the guard's quarters."

Torg throws his head back and laughs again. "That's how most of you lot get sent to labor. Trust me, if you try to steal anything from a guard out there, you'll end up decapitated. They don't give a fig about your wellbeing. Interesting about the good food. Haven't seen that in a while. Must've finally got that funding."

It's only now I notice the leather pouch attached to his pants. He fumbles around and pulls out a gold band that matches Taylin's. Carefully, he adjusts it so it sits beneath my wound and clips it closed. I cough, uncomfortable. It's tight, itchy and cold. This might take some time to adapt to.

"What is this?"

"Branding," Torg says. "Doesn't come off once it's on, so think of it as a permanent fashion statement. There's also a tracking device, so if for some unspeakable reason you escape, we'll find you. Tell me what you think of immortals."

"Is this part of the examination?"

"All to measure your sanity levels, yes. What? You think I'm making conversation with you? Dream on."

I wonder what Taylin said in her assessment. Is there a right or wrong answer? Reluctantly, I tug at the golden band but it's fixated. "Umm. Immortals. I feel sorry for them. Sorry that they're unjustly paying for the crimes of their ancestors. Sorry that they can't die. Sorry that this is their legacy. Sorry for the unnecessary treatment and torture. Sorry...that I'm no longer one."

Torg leans in, his face mere inches from mine. He stares deep into my eyes as if trying to read my mind. "You don't think you're immortal? That's an insane thing to say."

"I gave it up," I reveal, hoping he might be able to report to the superiors. Maybe, just maybe, they will let me go.

"Oh. I see." Torg's fingers wriggle as if he's playing an imaginary piano. "You gave up your immortality—in the sense you gave up the glamor, the dignity that they once possessed. Of course you gave that up the instant you stepped inside these walls. Hopefully you also let go of their murderous intent, arrogance and compulsive controlling nature."

Answering is redundant. People—mortals and immortals alike—hear what they want to hear. The response is enough to satisfy Torg who chuckles and slaps my knee, signaling for me to get up.

My legs are like jelly at first, but once I take my first step towards Taylin, I feel more like my old self. Whatever that is.

"You two are qualified to work in labor. I cannot stress this enough—*behave* yourselves. The guards in here don't care what you do. It's a different world out there."

Mitty shifts in the corner, his duty to protect me coming to a crushing end.

I'm conflicted about the decision, but I'm relieved to get away from the cannibals and the lonely life inside my cell. I will be reunited with Zain and Rune, but everything else is a terrifying unknown.

Torg continues to suck on whatever lolly is hiding in his mouth, looking extremely smug. "Righto. You two are harmless enough. Mitty will escort you through the fifth corridor and Cell Block J. A few clearances, and you'll be transferred to the labor guards. Mitty, can you confirm you'll handle skinny and tallie? Do you need back-up?"

"I can manage." Mitty glares at Torg when he snorts. "Don't psychoanalyze me, Torg. I saved your ass when that immortal started pounding into you."

"I didn't say a word, mate."

"You don't have to. All functionalists overanalyze every tiny action. Stop."

A functionalist? It must be a term that came into use while I've been on the run. I assume it has something to do with understanding the mind, but I could be way off.

Mitty motions for Taylin and me to follow him. Taylin rattles her cuffs. "Hey. Why doesn't Malin need them?"

"Oh, right." Torg reaches into his pouch and pulls out a rusty pair that have seen better days. "I was supposed to do this earlier. Here you go."

He slaps them on, no longer wary of my injuries. Shooing us out of his diagnosis room, Taylin and I follow a disgruntled Mitty into the corridor.

"Absurd," Mitty says under his breath. "Mark my words, no mortal should be trapped here. No *immortal* should be trapped here. I'm taking this to the top."

"Will they even care?" Taylin asks, struggling to scratch her nose in the cuffs. "If word got out to the public that a mortal was trapped in here, it'd be pandemonium. Or maybe they won't care. Especially considering she gave up her immortality. She still has a direct lineage. Plus the whole northerner thing. I'm from the north and I hate what they did. Face it, Mitty. You're chasing a dead end."

Mitty shakes his head, refusing to make eye contact. "No. My father died speaking up for the immortals. I intend to do the same."

"Maybe without the death part?" I suggest, but he doesn't reply.

We continue down the corridor until we're in Cell Block J, multiple cells lined up for what seems like miles. The doors are all open, several guards leaning against the bars and chatting to one another. Immortals in this block aren't quite as chipper as the ones in mine since their big feed. They're quiet, malnourished, walking zombies.

What is going on?

"Walk faster," Mitty directs. "They'll see your golden branding and swarm you. Grass is always greener on the other side."

But I've already slowed my pace significantly. I can't help myself. In an open cell to my left, a gaunt immortal sits by the bed where a sleeping inmate remains motionless. Unable to control the urge, I enter the cell.

Frantic to regain his power, Mitty appears behind me and uses his authoritative voice. "Oi, immortal! Back in line!"

"Mitty," I whisper. "There's something wrong with this one."

"There's something wrong with all of them!"

"No. No. Look."

I point at the sitting immortal who is gazing forlornly at the filthy bed. She barely notices our presence. In the bed lies a very stiff inmate who stares vacantly at the ceiling. They don't breathe. They don't blink. They don't move.

Mitty hesitantly enters the cell, squinting in the dull light. Born mortals have never had great eyesight in comparison to immortals who take care of their body. He gently nudges the frozen inmate and when nothing happens, he snaps his fingers. The inmate doesn't react. Mitty shakes the immortal harder this time, but again...nothing happens. Directing his attention at the grieving immortal, he lowers his voice.

"How long has he been like this?"

The immortal has long lost the capacity to speak. Exhausted, she raises two fingers. It's hard to translate. Two hours? Two days? Weeks? Months? *Years?*

Disheartened, I turn away from the corpse. "He's dead."

"No he's not!" Mitty says firmly. "He's just...he's just...immortals can't die!"

"This is the second one this week," I say timidly, gazing at a concerned Taylin.

"He's just paralyzed," Mitty is only trying to convince himself. "It's hard to tell with immortals. I mean, you lot can walk around with chronic disease, hold your breath for days and walk into a blazing fire. Sure, it's unpleasant to say the least, but my point is this guy could still be...still be...*but*...immortals can't die..."

Unable to spend another second in the small room of death, I exit the cell and wait outside with Taylin who is staring at the corpse.

"Perhaps he gave up his immortality?" Taylin suggests, but her tone is far from reassuring.

Now is the only chance to confirm the theory that immortals who aren't northerners possess this ability. I duck back into the cell where Mitty is pacing, wondering what the protocol is. I get the strong sense he's never really seen a body before.

"Excuse me?" I ask, smiling kindly when the grieving immortal lifts her chin and stares at me. "Did this man give up his immortality voluntarily?"

At first, she appears confused, probably due to her lack of brain power. After some hard processing, she eventually shakes her head.

It's not concrete evidence, I understand that, but it still turns my stomach.

As far as I was concerned, only northerners could give up their immortality, but stranger things have happened. What's to say others didn't evolve and gain such a gift...or a curse?

But why would something evolve just to die?

The disturbance is attracting other inmates who shuffle closer to the cell, curious as to what the commotion is about. A few of them stare at our gold necklaces, just as Mitty suspected, so I pull up my robe in an attempt to cover it. Taylin takes a more direct approach and snarls at anyone who gets too close.

"Mitty," I say gently. "What are you doing?"

"Fretting." He regains composure after his admission and embraces his role. "We must alert the superiors. The body will need to be disposed of."

Masking his terror, his shoulders lightly brush against mine as he exits the cell and blows on the whistle dangling from his neck. The sound alerts the inattentive guards who equip their batons and head down the corridor, barging into me despite the significant distance between us. Keeping out of their way is impossible, apparently.

"What's up? Need help escorting these freaks to the fields?"

"No." Mitty keeps his head slightly bowed. "There's a dead immortal in here."

The guards exchange skeptical glances. "No such thing. They play dead so they can escape. Doesn't work, obviously. We outsmart them every time. Call their bluff when we go to cremate them." They laugh and fist bump one another as if reliving a favorite memory.

"This is different," Mitty insists. "His eyes aren't dilating. There is no brain activity or movement whatsoever. Something is going on."

"Conspiracy theorist, much?"

They chortle again which is the trigger Mitty needs to take command. "Listen to me, you lazy ingrates! A second immortal has defied everything we understand and ceased to be! Fetch a medic or somebody equipped to transport the body out of here and deliver the news to the superiors. If you don't, I'll report you and your jobs will be on the line! Understand?"

His directness is clearly something the pair are unaccustomed to. Awkwardly, they mumble to one another and leave the cell block.

"I'm not...I'm not the guy for this," Mitty says, covering his discomfort with a cough. "I mean, death was just never in the job description."

"It's all right." Hesitantly, I reach out and pat him tenderly on the shoulder. Reassuring a guard is the last thing I ever thought would happen in this place. "This isn't your responsibility."

"He needs respect. A prayer. A proper send-off. The guards aren't going to do that for him." Mitty locks eyes with the glum immortal sitting next to the bed. "We need to wait by his side."

Taylin pushes an immortal breathing heavily beside her, their eyes fixated on the glowing gold around her neck. "Mitty, I don't want you to think I'm rushing to get to my next punishment, but if we stay here much longer, I will need to knock these guys out. Why do they like gold so much?"

Mitty raises an eyebrow at the passive swarm and shrugs. "Legend has it immortals and gold went hand in hand. Didn't you lot used to eat it for power or something? That's the thousand-year rumor. Maybe it's just pretty. The guards only use it because it helps you stand out so they can keep a better eye on you, especially in the dark. And something to do with the tracking device is more accurate. But you're right. I need to get you out of here first."

"Will you come back for him?" I smack away the hand of a brain-dead immortal who reaches out to touch my gold band. "Perhaps you could have him buried in the fields? We're laborers, aren't we? Can't we help?"

"I'll ask." Mitty promises, clearing the way. "All right! Everyone out! *Out!* Don't make me put you in solitary confinement!"

The immortals obey, gazing longingly at Taylin and me. Returning to their cells, they keep to themselves, forever nursing their starving stomachs. Even with the decent breakfast, it's not enough to counter the consistently low calories inflicted over decades.

Mitty rolls the cell door shut behind him so the immortal can rest in peace until the guards return. *If* they return.

"Was there a burial for the other immortal?" I query as we continue on route. When Mitty doesn't respond, I consider pulling a Rune and repeating the question until I get an answer.

But I can't do that. Not when Mitty very swiftly wipes away a rogue tear.

"Not much further now," he announces when we walk across a grated bridge that presses into the balls of my feet. A steel door awaits us on the other end.

"It's beyond the door?" I ask.

"Yes." His shoulders rise as he inhales. We stop as he gingerly reaches for the handle. "I'm not exaggerating about the rough conditions. There's nobody to help you out there."

"So what?" Taylin says. "Beats the boredom inside. Besides, outdoors means better chances to escape."

Mitty's eyes nearly pop out of their sockets. "Is *this* what you're intending to do? Didn't you hear a word Torg said? There are trackers in your bands! Not to mention the constant supervision and chains. You can't escape!"

"No?" Taylin is rudely sarcastic, and it's difficult to figure out whether it's a bold performance or her genuine attitude. "*Watch* me."

"Lost cause," Mitty says under his breath, redirecting his attention to me. "Malin, stay with Zain. He'll watch over you. Preserve your energy when you can and listen to orders. *All* orders. If I can bring the dead immortal to the field for burial, I will."

Wild emotion bubbles inside of me. What have I done? Leaving the safety of the cells was the most absurd notion I've ever had. Constantly conflicted by the impulse to be a hero, I have accepted that at my core, I am a coward. I *want* to do so many things. I *want* to help others. I *want* justice. I *want* to flee. I *want* to fix everything.

But I *need* to look after myself. I *need* to play it safe. I *need* to be grateful.

"You've survived so much already," Mitty continues, his pep talks uninspiring. "A gassing, wounds, poor conditions."

"That was just dumb luck," I say timidly. "I've never had to rely on a skillset in this place—only the help of others. How am I supposed to make it out there?"

Taylin, visibly bored with the conversation rolls her shoulders back and groans. "We all make choices, Malin. You made yours the moment you gave up your immortality and landed me in this nightmare. It's time you faced the consequences. Suck it up."

Mitty tilts his head to the side. "Landed her in this nightmare? You knew each other outside of here?"

"Not many northerners left. Chances are we were bound to know one another," Taylin says before I have an opportunity to explain my side of the story. "I mean you lot all look alike. If our height weren't enough of a clue, then the 'lin' in our names certainly seals the deal. We're not very creative up there." She pauses. "Ugh. Can we go already?"

No. *No.* I want to procrastinate for as long as possible. Even the pungent smells have been tolerable recently. Could I volunteer to be a cleaner? The prison could certainly do with a good scrub. I could learn to be the new medic. Something. *Anything.*

But wishful thinking gets you nowhere. Exhausted and defeated, I do the one thing that would probably get me killed if it weren't Mitty. *I embrace him.* Trembling, I relish in his soapy scent and find sanctuary in his arms. In this moment, I'm protected.

A moment that vanishes the instant he releases me.

"Come on." He can't bring himself to look at me and pushes on the steel door.

And then...we step outside.

# CHAPTER IX

I t must be the middle of a moonless night. Clouds from the afternoon rain still drift in the sky, blocking out stars and neighboring planets.

The grass squishes between my toes, the lush sensation a treat compared to the hard stone and concrete inside the prison. It's hard to believe sleeping in damp grass used to be so degrading; and now it's the favorable option of two nightmares.

"It's quiet," I say. "Where is everyone?"

"Most likely down by the bridge they're building. It's a bit of a hike from here."

"Why do they need a new bridge?"

"The prison is overcrowded and underfunded, but medics and new guards still need transport to and from it. The last one has seen better days. Besides, the prison is anticipating guests. If they go the long way 'round, it will add days to their trip. We need a back entrance." Our golden bands glow dimly in the darkness, providing light as we navigate downhill. Mitty occasionally slips in his boots, but Taylin and I have better grip as we curl our toes into the dirt. "They don't care about immortals but nobody wants to see mortals die in an accident."

His words ring true as he leads us farther into the field, the terrain getting rockier as we progress. Taylin, finding it difficult to do anything wearing cuffs, moans.

"When do we get these off?" She jangles them.

"Certainly not in my custody. If you're lucky, they unlock them while you're working. Otherwise, you may as well think of them as ugly bracelets."

"Well, that makes escape a little trickier. But not impossible," she adds defiantly, already scanning the inky fields. It's a wonder how big this place truly is. It appears they've even grown their own crops at some point, but they appear to be long dead. Or maybe it's just the darkness.

"Ah. See down there?" Mitty places his hand on my shoulder and steers me towards the right. "That's where the camp is."

I follow his gaze, my heart leaping into my throat. He wasn't wrong about the poor conditions. It's not easy to see, but the immortals are sleeping betwixt rocks and dirt, curled into small balls. It looks like there are chains attached to their golden neckbands, keeping them tied to the ground. The rain has stopped but I imagine they'd be shivering in the bitter breeze. Even though I've been inside for a few hours, my clothes and hair are still a little damp.

"There aren't many prisoners," I say.

"About twenty, yeah." Mitty swallows his words, his somberness a grim reminder of my new reality.

Twenty. *Twenty.* There's twelve thousand immortals existing in this nightmare. How could less than two dozen be working in the fields? "Why so few? Have there been more?"

"Not all the prisoners can maintain the grueling lifestyle. Some of them get trapped under falling objects. They're still there, crushed beneath the weight. Others have been mauled by the hybrids, scattered along the fields. When they go mad or zombie-like, they're sent back to their cells, nothing more than a shell."

"Cute poetry," Taylin snorts. "You mentioned hybrids. What are those?"

"Deformed pack of beasts descended from wolves. I'm sure the immortals can tell you more about them. No doubt they've given them a proper name. They hang around the prison, patrolling. They know there's an endless supply of meat here. Not sure if the guards have managed to train them or not. That's not my business."

We creep closer to the camp, lowering our voices to not disrupt their sleep. I gently shoulder bump Taylin to grab her attention. "We're still allies, right?"

"Depends on whether you'll help me escape. If not, you're dead to me. And you'd better watch your back."

I'm stunned by her bluntness, having downplayed her intense hatred for me. How long can she resent me? Eternity? That's one of the downsides to being immortal; memories never fade.

"If you even *think* about escaping, you'll suffer a fate worse than death," Mitty admonishes, his flustered words running into one another. "Nobody can help you!"

"I don't need help," Taylin says defiantly, her obnoxious attitude beginning to grate on me. "I'm already outside of those walls. I'm still strong because I haven't been drained and I intend to stay that way! I'm tall and athletic. I have everything I need to make it out of here alive. So you can kindly keep your nose out of it."

I can't believe how openly she talks about breaking out in front of a guard. Yes, he's helped us so far, but to disrespect him like that? Part of me hopes he turns us around and locks her back in her cell.

"Yep. Lost cause," Mitty mumbles the sentiment again.

And that's when I realize he genuinely doesn't care about her fate. His warnings are for me and me alone. It's a surprise considering he barely knows me, even if he made a promise to Zain...who also doesn't know me particularly well. What do they think they owe me?

We're not far from the sleeping immortals. I turn to the right and cringe at the wide silhouettes. I've never seen a mortal so huge. There's not an ounce a fat; completely shredded and muscular. Their arms are easily the size of my entire abdomen. I count the silhouettes.

Six. Six guards currently. Each one upsettingly enormous, almost matching my height. I glance at Taylin who suddenly doesn't appear as confident.

Keeping quiet, Mitty waves to the shadows and points at Taylin and me. Five of the guards remain in place, quiet in the shadows while the biggest makes his way towards us. He isn't as concerned about disrupting the immortal's sleep. With his massive boots, he marches towards us, stepping on hands, ankles, heads...whatever is in his way. The immortals are either too sleepy or too conditioned to utter a sound. They rouse, but that's the extent. Not a single word escapes their lips.

The menacing guard halts just in front of us, his amber eyes flickering with intrigue.

"New recruits?" His voice is a smooth bass, fitting for his appearance. Indistinguishable scars line his hard face, trailing all the way up his shaved head.

"Yes," Mitty nudges us forward. "Sorry for the late notice, Garu."

"They're not blue."

"Yes, the medic has been too busy to assign their uniforms. Means they should have more energy than the others, so they'll be an asset."

The guard known as Garu makes a throaty sort of sound, like a skeptical grunt. "Troublesome?"

"No. They were caught fighting with the cannibals. Self-defense no doubt, but the others suggested they come here due to their healthy physique." Mitty pauses and looks at the immortals on the ground. "You're letting them sleep now?"

"Only three hours a night. They proved useless when they were sleep deprived." Garu's movements are slow and deliberate. "Names?"

Oh no. Aren't we supposed to go by numbers? I can't remember what mine was. Six thousand...no, it was twelve thousand and something...

"Malin and Taylin," Mitty speaks for us and I'm mortified. How can he use our real names so casually?

"Northerners?" Garu doesn't use inflection, so it's impossible to analyze his reaction to Mitty's solemn nod. "Must be the last ones."

"Perhaps," Mitty replies, his eyes darting down to his boots.

My stomach churns at the thought, aching for the lost promise of my loved one's safety. It's a slim chance, but they could very well still be in hiding. They're so much stronger, smarter and faster than me. If

I made it out, they definitely did too. They just weren't stupid enough to get caught and sent to this nightmare.

I shake the images clear, frantic to not lose myself within memories and possibilities. The present is the focus. Survival is key.

"Malin and Taylin." Garu's acknowledgement of my name pricks my ears. Instead of feeling gratitude for hearing somebody refer to me as a person, it instantly fills me with dread. I am now targeted. Recognized. In trouble. "Join the others. There is an hour left of sleep. We will wake you for breakfast. Labor will commence shortly afterwards."

Theoretically, his description sounds a lot better than hearing disturbed guards shouting at us to wake up, followed by begrudgingly shuffling towards a chow hall that usually dishes out poison. But the tone behind his voice is chilling...menacing...threatening.

Mitty reluctantly turns to face me, anguished. His arms lift as if he wants to touch me, but instead he inhales deeply. "Right then. You two, uh, better behave. I mean it. Night, Garu."

"Hold it." Garu demands, his blinks slow. "Is it true about the dead immortal?"

"Which one?" Mitty winces when he realizes his error. "Apologies for miscommunication. There was a second death tonight."

Garu raises one eyebrow, a hint of surprise in his stoic face. He then looks at me, his gaze boring into my soul. "Interesting."

"Yes. I'm unsure what the superiors want to do about it and whether there will be an investigation. I assume it will be swept under the rug considering the immortals don't have any family or friends to inform."

"It will certainly be investigated." Again, Garu's eyes pierce mine, nausea rippling through my stomach. He makes me want to be physically sick. "Bring the corpse to us for burial. We do not have the resources for cremation."

Mitty seems anxious to leave, perhaps experiencing the same sensations I'm enduring. He bows his head only slightly, glances at me once more and then leaves us to our new master. I gaze after Mitty as he disappears into the darkness, ascending up the slippery slope. Chances are this is the last time I'll ever see him.

"What did I tell you?" Garu address Taylin and me. "Join the others on the ground."

Even Taylin looks a little bewildered by his intimidating presence. As if dealing with a wild animal, we carefully avoid Garu's vicinity and crouch down in between some immortals.

"Heads down. You'll arise in an hour."

Garu stomps back to his post with the other guards, who spend every second staring at the immortals. It's an ominous energy, having hateful eyes watch my every movement.

I curl into a ball next to Taylin, squished between two other women who have a sun-kissed tan and muscular bodies. They're certainly not as famished as the others in the prison, but it's obvious they're still underfed and overworked. Dark rings hang beneath their eyes, their cheekbones prominent.

I get the impression it's best not to talk to them or ask questions. We were instructed to rest, so rest we shall. Anything to keep Garu from speaking to me again.

Shivering, I find myself instinctively reaching out to strangers to keep warm, but they don't seem to mind. If anything, it seems well received.

Just when I manage to control the anxiety and drift into a light slumber, the howl of hybrid creatures echoes through the fields...and I lament every stupid decision that led me here.

# CHAPTER X

I'm awake long before the guards clap their hands. It seems everyone is. And most disturbing of all, the guards look far more alert than any of us and they don't appear to have slept. Where's the bloodshot and puffy eyes? Is there a special pill they're consuming to ward off tiredness?

Taylin and I patiently sit in the dirt, but the other immortals are chained to small posts hammered into the ground. The guards systematically unlock the chains attached to the prisoner's neckbands, releasing them so they can stretch out and bathe in the warmth of the sun. When they've detached the prisoners, the guards return to their post, unmoving.

The fields look different in the morning light. It's so much more expansive than I initially thought. We're at the bottom of the slope, the prison looming over us as a constant reminder. The tower above the prison seems both majestic and out of place, leaving me to wonder who resides inside. Perhaps the warden? The so-called *superiors* the guards often speak about? Even at this early hour, a purple haze drifts out of the open window, a phenomenon the others seem accustomed to.

I turn away from the prison and scan the fields. Not far from here is a half-built bridge over a dried gully. To the right of that is a crop of wheat, and I immediately think of Rune. Are they utilizing the farmer to grow food? Is that why the food has suddenly been better? I really hope I can reconnect with him soon.

To my left are various woodwork projects—carts, trays, tables. They don't appear to be a priority and haven't been touched in a while. Beyond that are valleys and forests; or as Taylin would deem, the perfect hiding place.

There are no walls to keep us in, no cage to contain us. It feels like freedom until I swallow against the golden band around my neck.

I watch as the motionless guards finally bend over in perfect unison and untie the bags beside them. Pulling out loaves of bread, they break them in half and then in quarters and throw them at the prisoners.

Catching mine, I cringe at the staleness.

*Beggars can't be choosers, Malin. Be grateful for what you have.*

"Malin. Taylin." My heart thrums at Garu's voice, who is holding a loaf of bread. Perhaps he refuses to eat in front of company. Or maybe he's just as disgusted by the texture as I am. "There is a man-made well by the bridge. You may access water there."

"Th-thank you," I say, unsure whether speaking is allowed.

"May I escort them, sir?" a familiar voice asks.

"You may."

The owner of the voice stands amidst the resting immortals, having already demolished his breakfast. At first, I don't recognize him, a scruffy beard concealing half of his face. But there's no denying that boy-like spark in his eyes.

"Rune?" I ask, rushing to my feet.

"Please follow me," he says automatically. He motions for us to follow him, and we don't waste the opportunity. Our long legs don't take long to catch up as we approach the well, which is really more of a deep hole in the ground with murky water at the bottom.

"Classy," Taylin mutters. She crouches and scoops up the water in her hands, washing down the stale breakfast we endured.

"Rune," I repeat, wanting nothing more than to hug him. "I've been so worried about you. I'm sorry I didn't reveal myself."

"Don't worry about it," he whispers, his energetic nature somewhat suppressed. "What would've been the point? Anyway. How did you get here?"

"The cannibals attacked us," I mimic his quiet tone, then tested the dark water. "The guards thought we were strong and of sound mind so they sent us here. It doesn't seem so bad."

His eyebrows raise skeptically, leaning in to splash some water on his face. "It's grueling, Malin. We lost some immortals two nights ago when the hybrids attacked. Occasionally I hear them crying out in the middle of the night...but I can't find their heads. It's a different kind of torture to the one in there."

"Not many immortals are blue here," I say hopefully, wondering if it means they'll reconsider assigning my uniform.

"It's because we're getting food and water. It gives regeneration a fighting chance. I've been told they still drain us monthly, to keep us from rising up. Low energy slows down progress out here, but at least they can continue to control us."

I understand I'm short on time, so I try to get as much information out of Rune as possible. "Who is that Garu guy?"

"The head guard. He...he makes me sick. I can't explain it, but yeah, he's frightening."

"And Zain? Is Zain still here?"

My knees almost give out when Rune hesitates. If Zain's suffering *all because I wanted something nice to eat*, I may as well throw myself into this well. Rune notices my chagrin and is quick to mollify me. "No, no, he's okay. Yes, I'm concerned, *but* he *will* be back. When we have another free moment, I'll show you something." He glances over his shoulder. "Time's up. Come on."

I begrudgingly swallow the tainted water and hope for the best. The three of us return to the campsite and sit, awaiting instruction.

Garu and his large minions don't speak much. They breathe in unison, they blink in unison. It's a haunting scene.

"Immortals," Garu finally announces. "Good morning. There will be a slight amendment to our agenda today. Before construction continues on the new bridge, we will be burying the second deceased immortal."

How frequent would these burials become? Hopefully, this is the second and last of an unfortunate run. Checking the area, I look for the graveyard. Sheepishly, I raise my hand.

"Excuse me?" I regret it immediately. Everybody turns to look at me, Garu sending that energetic nausea once more.

"Yes, Malin."

"Where...where will we bury him?"

"Next to the last immortal."

"Where is that located?"

"Beneath your feet."

I feel Taylin freeze next to me, the sickly sensation worsening. I look down at my filthy feet and wriggle my toes in the hard dirt. They forced the immortals to sleep on top of a corpse they buried? What would possess them to be so cruel and disrespectful?

Garu smiles; the expression unnatural on his hard face. "Before we begin preparation, be sure to relieve yourselves. I do not care for the scent of soiled clothes."

I expect the prisoners to disperse, but they keep in place. Satisfied by this, Garu flicks his wrist and the immortals collectively begin scratching at the dirt.

"Rune? Aren't there any tools?"

He's already on his knees, scratching away at the earth. "Nope. Your hands are the tools. Hurry up before they send the hybrids over."

Taylin exchanges a concerned glance, but soon complies. Shoulder to shoulder, we dig. Tiny rocks etch beneath my fingernails which are bending backwards with each motion. This is an impossible task. Why would they do this? Are tools allowed to construct the bridge? Or is this some sort of sick experiment?

Hours pass and sweat stings my eyes, the rising sun blistering my pale skin. The warm weather is certainly making up for yesterday. Taylin curses periodically beside me, but the rest, admirably so, bite their tongues. A few grunts and groans escape, but that's the extent of their complaints.

We've barely made a dent in the ground. I'm assuming that with such a short deadline, we won't be required to dig six feet, which only makes the burial position all the more disturbing.

A shadow from behind blocks the sun, relieving me from the incessant burn. When I recognize it as Garu's shadow however, I swiftly realign myself with the fiery ball in the sky. I'd rather sizzle than be in his presence.

"Faster," his thunderous voice commands. "We have one hour."

"How deep must we go?" I ask when nobody else responds. I can't bring myself to look at him; only the shadow which subtly shrugs.

"Up to you lot. If the corpse pokes through the earth, then you're the ones sleeping with it. Best dig faster if you want peace of mind."

A few immortals instinctively dig faster, their hands bruised and bloodied.

But I don't. I'm too distracted by his mention of sleep. When I arrived, Garu and his goons stood overlooking the immortals. There was no chair, no bed, no shelter onsite. They, for all intents and purposes, didn't rest. That's difficult for an immortal, let alone a mortal. What is with these guards?

Tears involuntarily prick my eyes as my fingers throb with each grind. The faster we try, the slower we become. I try to separate myself from the job, but it's hard to accept that this uneven, rocky hole is reserved as the final resting place for an immortal who deserved better.

I ignore the blood on my fingers, considering the likelihood of an afterlife for an immortal. What's the point of an afterlife if you live forever? It just seems unlikely.

Time loses all meaning. The repetitive and draining nature serves as an infinite loop, but I'm so mentally exhausted that the hours pass relatively quickly. It's a strange combination.

Eventually, Garu tells us to stop digging. The sun is still shining, just not as high in the sky. Maybe it's only afternoon. I've never been great at understanding time. It's never meant anything to me before.

"The guards are delivering the corpse," Garu announces.

We step away from the hole, which is only two and a half feet deep, at best. Barely enough to cover the inevitable stench.

Walking downhill from the prison are Mitty and two other guards, their noses scrunched as they carry the immortal on a steel slab.

There's silence as the guards approach, dropping the slab on the ground in disgust. Mitty stays beside them, wincing as the body clumsily rolls off. If they didn't respect us while we're alive, it figures they wouldn't when we're dead.

"Get rid of it!" The guard says, sticking out his tongue. "I was told we didn't have to worry about death here!" He kicks at the body, then dry heaves.

Garu keeps his arms folded and his brow furrowed. "Don't kick the body."

The guard is initially affronted, but doesn't protest beyond a petulant grunt. "Can we go?"

"Your services are no longer required."

"Right." The guard sniffs and motions at Mitty and the other to follow. Mitty reluctantly turns back to nod at me, but the action is over in a flash.

Without another word, several immortals mumble a prayer over the body and delicately drag him into the shallow hole. It's a tight fit; they have to curl up his legs and twist his neck into an awkward position.

"Should we say a few words?" Rune asks, his expression vacant.

"No," Garu says. "There's work to be done."

There's no arguing. Like a choreographed dance, the immortals maneuver around one another as they throw dirt onto the body, uttering quiet farewells as they do so.

I bend over and take a handful of the dirt, watching as it spills through the gaps in my fingers. It feels wrong to throw this onto a body. He needs to be respected, buried properly in the safety of a coffin.

But as always, I'm helpless. Destined to comply with orders I don't believe in or agree with, despite how unfair they may be.

Closing my eyes, I throw the dirt, wincing at the thought. What if this foreshadows my future in this prison? My days are numbered, and nobody believes I'm mortal. Maybe attempting escape with Taylin isn't such a foolish idea after all...

The last of the dirt is thrown onto the mound, having only just covered the departed immortal. We're not given a minute to rest or process the scene. Instead, Garu's guards move us towards the well, encouraging us to drink.

They never speak. They barely blink. They're...*soulless*...

"You have two minutes to hydrate," Garu calls. "Construction on the bridge must continue."

"I don't know how to build a bridge," I say on the verge of hysteria. Rune only smirks as we line up at the well. I wipe away sweat that has merged with stray tears, glancing back at the campsite substituting as a graveyard. "What am I supposed to do?"

"Relax, you're tall and strong. You'll mostly be carrying stones to and fro. Taylin, too."

"I can't believe they make you do this. You're a farmer. Couldn't those skills be put to better use?"

"They most likely would've assigned me to the crops, but apparently the prison's received a donation. Gourmet meals allegedly; at least in comparison to poison. Not sure if that's true or not."

"It is true. I was scared to eat just in case it was a trick, but the immortals were speaking coherently from the energy gained."

Rune's eyes widen, a hint of resentment flickering. "The day after we are exiled for stealing food...they give you..." He can't bring himself to finish the sentence. Instead, he focuses on his breath, determined to compose himself. "Nope. Nope. Not worth the aggravation."

I know his rage isn't directed at me, but I feel like I'm the one to blame. In reality, life is definitely easier on the inside so long as meals are provided. There will probably be fewer cannibals with the introduction of proper food, too. Luck just hasn't been on Rune's side in this instance.

"How is your investigation going?" I ask.

"With the dead immortal?" Rune clarifies. "Terrible. They buried the first one before I got here. I'd love to dig deep and see who it is. Check for signs of struggle or suffering. Just get a better understanding, but the guards are always watching. Plus I'd hate to disrespect the dead. This guy looked unwell, but no different from the others here. Looked like he was from the south."

We approach the well as the other immortals disperse, heading towards construction, Taylin in the mix.

I graciously drink, no longer concerned about the color of the water. Anything to stay hydrated in this heat. Rune doesn't drink much. Instead, he pulls out a crumpled bowl from his pants, made from a material I don't recognize.

"What are you doing?" I ask.

He scoops the water into the oddly shaped cup and folds it over to keep from spilling. Carefully, he tucks it back into his pants. "Zain needs water."

Perplexed, I look around. "Where *is* Zain?"

"Not now. Come on." He tugs on my elbow. We join the others by the bridge, who are waiting for Garu's instruction.

Taylin isolates herself from the group as much as possible, her attention on the surrounds. I can practically hear the cogs in her mind turning as she calculates an escape route.

"No need to micromanage," Garu instructs. "Strongest carry the stones to the bridge. Wooden foundation is almost complete; finish that today. Tall ones. Gather the stone."

I flinch at the way he addresses me, glancing at Rune for reassurance once the immortals commence work. "Rune. Where am I meant to go to find stone?"

"Follow me. I'm not supposed to carry, so hurry."

I follow Rune down the slight decline, Taylin trailing behind.

Two other scrawny immortals are making their way down with us, their bodies frail. The whole thought of them picking up something heavy makes me cringe. I could snap them in half with a hug.

Rune stops and points at the bottom of the decline where massive rock deposits have formed. It's a beautiful showcase of Mother Nature, but my heart sinks.

"We carry those up?"

"That's it. Sorry Mal. I can't stay. They'll punish me. My job is stacking and cutting into the bridge. Plus I need to get the water to... you know who. See you tonight."

He runs back up the slope, leaving me to stare at the quarry below. The rocks are *massive*. Even Taylin looks a little intimidated.

"We're going to look so buff," she says, but I don't think she's joking. "And uphill too."

"Both ways," I joke, but at this stage, something so absurd wouldn't be surprising.

The two immortals beat us to the bottom, purely focused on their job at hand. They don't rest or hesitate for even a second. Working together, they lift at their knees and communicate through expression, lugging a rectangular shaped rock. They move at an impressive pace back up the slope, returning almost as quickly.

"We better move it," I suggest. We can't still be standing here when they've already brought back one massive block of stone.

"You mean escape?" Taylin whispers. "I haven't figured out the best course yet."

"No. These. Pick one."

"It's impossible. They're huge."

The two immortals return, frowning at our immobility. The one with wild, red hair points at a giant rock in front of us. "You two better hurry. The hybrids hang about here and sniff out sweat pretty easily. The longer you stand around, the sooner you'll be found."

The warning is enough motivation for Taylin and me to squat and fumble around the edges of the rock. Not only is it going to be heavy, but the shape is awkward, too.

"We can do this," I encourage. "One."

Taylin breathes out rapidly, mentally and physically preparing. "Two."

"Three!"

We lift, my knees almost buckling. Taylin isn't faring well either, her entire body quivering as we carry the block. I grunt something incoherent and we manage a small step forward.

We're both trembling violently and without warning, we simultaneously drop and jump out of the way of the stone.

Taylin bends over, resting her hands on her knees. "How are we supposed to do that?"

"We can try a smaller one," I say, determined not to be next on the hybrid menu. "Come on, Taylin."

"This place sure knows how to break your spirit. And your back." Wincing, she checks the area. "Okay, let's try this."

It's certainly a smaller block of stone, so I happily oblige. We go through the same process to prepare ourselves, lifting a little easier this time.

Shuffling forward, we grunt and groan as each agonizing step rips at our calves. My arms scream for relief, but I can't let go. Not this time.

"I need...ugh...rest," Taylin says.

"No," I push. "We're only halfway."

I sneer at the two immortals who overtake us once again; practically seasoned veterans in such an appalling task. And to think I had the arrogance to consider them weaker than me. I'm better than that. At least so I thought.

Taylin isn't trembling like she was with the first stone. I know she can make it to the top. We have a long day ahead of us and we have to learn how to put mind over matter. Mind over stone. Mind over these big...awful...stones.

"The summit!" Taylin gasps as we reach the top of the slope.

"It's not a mountain."

"It may as well be!"

Picking up the pace, we clumsily sidestep towards construction and drop the stone next to the small pile the other immortals have started. Taylin thrashes her arms out like a sea creature, stretching out the muscles that must be as upset as mine.

I want to rest, but the silent guards lock eyes with mine, unyielding.

"Come on, Taylin," I say. "Hybrids down there. Guards up here. I don't want to find out what's worse."

She doesn't argue, although she is a little distracted by the workers. I look at the immortals who drag stones to the side, chipping into edges that need rounding off. At least they were given tools. I half expected them to use their teeth. The stones that are completed are then carried a short distance to the bridge and systematically placed. Their task looks much better than ours.

We replicate the arduous procedure eleven times before we find ourselves sprawled across large rocks that won't be budging any time soon.

"I don't think...we should stay like this," I warn breathlessly, my body too exhausted to move.

"I don't care anymore. Let them eat me," Taylin says, staring vacantly at the sky. "I can't lift another damn rock. I just can't. You've had more practice than I have."

My head shoots up, only for a second, before falling back onto the rock. "What do you mean?"

"You were immortal. No doubt in your centuries of living you've encountered heavy objects. Your muscles would be semi-used to this. I'm in my twenties. My body doesn't know what's going on. It has no muscle memory."

I forget how young Taylin is. It's so commonplace for immortals to look the same age over hundreds of years.

The two immortals jog downhill, scrutinizing our position. When they're in earshot, they scorn us. "We're serious. The hybrids will get you. We're not helping you if they attack."

"Same to you," Taylin snaps, lifting her hand to reveal a rude gesture northerners use. I doubt they even know what it means. They certainly don't pretend to care, finding the next best stone to lug. When they leave, I force myself into a sitting position.

"They're right. We can do this."

"I can't. I want to die right now. How many stones are we expected to take? Look, it's getting late! The sun is close to setting. Aren't we supposed to sleep?"

"This isn't a retreat. We were warned about this place," I remind, massaging my biceps. It's going to hurt so much more tomorrow. "The sooner we do it, the sooner we're finished."

"How insightful." Despite the sarcasm, she rolls onto her stomach and carefully pushes herself into a position that is close to standing. "What's that?"

I don't pay her any attention, focusing only on rocks we can physically move. What if we brought a pile of considerably smaller stones to the construction site? Would they be usable? Do they *have* to be *so* big?

"Oi! Malin!" I jolt at the powerful force on my shoulder—far more powerful than it should be considering her exhaustion. "Look!"

I follow Taylin's gaze beyond the quarry, landing on a strange colored rock. A...*bloody* sort of rock. A...*hairy* sort of rock. Fighting the urge to purge, I look away and shake my head fiercely. "Nope. Nope. Taylin, I'm not. I can't."

"Is it a head?"

"Yes. No. I don't know. It'd still be alive. Oh, it's so inhumane."

"I'm going to talk to it. Try, anyway. Maybe it can tell us something useful."

I grab onto her arm, lowering my voice. "The only thing it will relay to you is to do as you're told! What is *wrong* with you?"

"What is wrong with *me?*" she shrieks, insulted by the accusation. "What is wrong with this *place?* I don't belong here, Malin! I'm only here because of you! I deserve better than this and you know it!"

Her words sink in as I release my grip around her arm. She

frowns before slinking off towards the decapitated head wedged between the rocks. Navigating barefoot, careful to avoid the sharp edges she springs closer and closer.

I stay back, rubbing my sunburnt shoulders, dreading the sting of tomorrow. Taylin reaches the head, crouching down and nudging it with her pinky finger. It rolls ever so slightly to the side, groaning.

"Hello. Can you hear me?" Taylin asks.

The neck is severed just below the voice box, so theoretically the immortal should be able to speak. But for all I know, the tongue could've been cut out, but it's most likely suffering from brain damage.

"Who...?"

"I'm Taylin, a prisoner. How did you end up this way?"

Uncomfortable, I chew on the insides of my cheeks, wishing to either reunite the head with a body, or put it out of misery. What are the dead immortal's secrets? You can't burn an immortal; they wind up charred and miserable, but still very much alive. Decapitation is a variant of hell. Short of giving up their immortality like me, there's nothing they could've done. The corpse we buried was not a northerner, so he certainly couldn't have given it up.

"Hybridsss..." The voice is barely above a whisper, hardly audible from where I'm standing. "Don't try escape...don't try escape...my body...I can still feel...my body...they're...they're...they're still chewing on it..."

"What are the hybrids?" Taylin asks with little regard for the immortal's suffering.

I don't listen for a response. It seems pointless when I can already see them.

They're unlike any creature or humanoid I've ever come across. Perched on rocks across the way, their jet-black fur seems glossy in the sunlight. My heart thrums at the sight of the terrifying beasts. I've never met an animal bigger than me, but these things tower over me. Their hind legs cause their upper body to stoop over, where two ferociously bulky arms drag by their side. Blood and dirt cover their snouts, their black eyes sunken in.

I clear my throat. "Taylin. Run back to me."

She raises a finger to hush me, listening to the head's monologue.

"Taylin," I repeat firmly. "The hybrids are watching."

Time hits a standstill as I consider my options. Save myself or save Taylin? No matter the choice, I'll be wrong. I thought I was saving Taylin the night I met her, but instead she blames me for her imprisonment. What if that happens again? I might rush towards her and she could scream because I interrupted the important talking head information.

"TAYLIN!" I shout when the hybrids take a calculated step forward. There must be a dozen of them.

She turns to chastise me, but instead stares at the direction I'm focused on. Suddenly very spirited, she picks up the talking head and cradles it in her arm. Springing from rock to rock she sprints uphill, leaving me behind. Panicked, I chase after her.

"Were those...? They were...! That was close!"

The other immortals are above, running down the hill to collect more stone.

"Hybrids are watching," I say as we continue upwards. I don't stop to see their reaction. It's not my problem.

Before we reach the 'summit' as Taylin calls it, I grab her hand and slow her down. "Stop. What will the guards say? We can't return to the construction site with no stones."

"I'll hedge my bets!" Taylin says through gritted teeth. Tense, she checks over her shoulder. "All right, they're not coming after us."

"They don't like crowdsssss..." The muffled voice in the crook of her arm says. "They won't harm groupsss..."

"Oh, good, thanks. That's good to know. Oh. This is Marn. He said he was attacked and shredded to pieces last month by the hybrids when he tried to escape. He believes the guards have something to do with it. A treaty, or exchange. Otherwise the hybrids wouldn't hang around this place," Taylin speedily recounts.

"Hi Marn. I'm Malin." I introduce myself somewhat glumly.

"*MALIN?*" His gray eyes widen. "Malin from the north?"

Taylin readjusts the head, lifting him so they're face to face. "Do you know her?"

I recoil, praying he doesn't overshare. Taylin is far too young to know about any of the events in the north. Avoiding his gaze, I become interested in my feet.

"I know *of* her," the head responds gravely. "Malin...it isss an...honor."

My head shoots up. Is he *joking?* Has he mistaken me for somebody else? Judging by his sincere expression, the head is deathly serious.

Taylin's disgust, merged with confusion, is equally sincere. "Why would anybody say that? Malin is...is...the worst."

The *worst?*

"Thisssss cannot be," the head objects. "She isss the savior of her people, isss she not? That isss her role."

"HA!" Taylin throws her head back and laughs. "She's a selfish coward, Marn. She landed me in this place and tried to get off scot-free."

I can't bring myself to confront either of them. The past is in the past for a reason, nothing more than a faded memory. Shielding my flushed face, I turn away and run. Where to, I don't know. I just can't bear to delve into unnecessary history. Shame and mortification don't even begin to cover it.

I'm careful not to run towards the construction site, because returning without stone seems like a remarkably stupid idea. Instead I remain on the slope, running on an angle like a petulant toddler. There's a chance I'll charge straight into a hybrid's mouth. Or face-plant into the guards. But it doesn't matter. I *run*. Because running away from my problems is what I do best.

Red spots scatter my vision, slowing me to a halt. Dizzy, I kneel between the shrubbery, cursing myself for running in such blistering heat when I'm already beyond exhausted. I bat away the coarse, but verdant thicket.

Taylin isn't far away, but she doesn't chase me. It's difficult to make out her face from here, but no doubt she's glaring after me with an obnoxious scowl. As well she should. She cradles the head once more and continues back down the hill, interrupting the two immortals to offer to carry a particularly large stone. They're too immersed in their task to notice the head, most likely confusing it for a strange rock. Or maybe they're smart enough not to ask questions. Either way, she uses one arm to lift the stone from behind, barely contributing her strength.

Settling into a comfortable position, semi hidden behind the brier, I allow my patchy vision to restore. My mind is hazy from the labor, to the extent of fearing I've imagined the talking head. I mean, *really*. What's the odds of him even knowing who I am?

"Deep breaths, Malin," I instruct myself. "Day by day. Hour by hour. Minute by...lousy minute. This is your life now. It's temporary. It's only temporary..."

Too stunned to scream, I seem to suck in the air as an icy hand emerges from the ground and grasps onto my ankle. Writhing in its clasp, I frantically attempt to shake it off, but it only squeezes tighter.

Do I yell for help? What will Garu say when he sees me resting on the job? Should I admit defeat now?

"Hey, hey!" A voice from below mollifies. "Ease up, ease up. You're safe."

Instinctively, I trust the familiar voice, relaxing my aching muscles. When I stop fighting, the hand releases me and disappears back into the ground.

"Move the shrub," he says.

Complying, I effortlessly sweep the bush to the side and audibly gasp. Beneath the foliage is a tight, man-made hole. It tunnels deep into the ground like the burrow of an animal. Only instead of an animal, stands a filthy, smiley immortal by the name of Zain.

"It's so good to see you!" I say, reaching down to take his hand.

He squeezes tightly, his face thinner than the last time I saw him. "What is all of this?"

"My way out!" Zain motions at the tiny tunnel. "Rune has been feeding and watering me. You didn't bring anything?"

"I...I didn't know you were h-here," I stammer, instantly guilty. "I could go back and find something?"

"No, no. It's fine. You're planning on joining us when I complete this glorious trail, aren't you?"

Keeping on my knees, I peer into the dark hole. "Hold on. You've been *living* in here? The guards haven't noticed your absence?"

"Yeah, yeah. Hey, I've lived in worse conditions. Feeling mighty proud of myself. The guards think I died with another when transporting those ridiculous stones. Hybrid attacked, so I faked my death."

"Marn?" I ask forlornly, thinking of the talking head.

"Pfft, I don't know what his name was. Tell Rune I'm aiming for two more months. I think I'm getting close to an exit. It's difficult to map out, and it's probably not the best route if you're claustrophobic, but you can be free with us."

My fingers brush over the golden band tied around my throat. "And what about this? Can't they track us?"

"Or is it an empty threat?" Zain taps his own band. "They haven't found me yet, have they? Unless they think a hybrid is recklessly tossing my body around underground."

My attention shifts to Taylin and the two immortals heading back downhill. I press my body hard into the earth, hoping it's enough to conceal me. They don't look in this direction, so hopefully it did the trick.

Spitting out bits of dirt, I crawl closer to the hole. "What do you plan to do when you escape?"

"Isn't it obvious?" Zain says, his energy contagious. "Start a revolution."

I blink, having trouble comprehending the statement. "Excuse me, a what?"

"A revolution."

"Against who?"

"The mortals."

"The mortals? All of them?"

"Yes."

"Why?"

"Because they hate us, they control us, and they deserve to die."

I lean back, mind blown by the revelation. Zain's lost his sanity in this tunnel. "Zain, not all mortals are bad. They don't all hate us."

"Sure they do. I haven't seen mortal protesters fighting for our rights. Not in all these years. We're more powerful than them and it scares them. It's time to take back what's rightfully ours, ruling the land as the gods that we are!" His passion only amplifies his voice, so I immediately hush him.

"No, Zain. We *aren't* gods. Living forever and possessing a few abilities does not give us the right to control anyone. That's how we ended up in this position. The humans began a revolution all their own, far outnumbering our kind. Now we're weak and mindless. It will be a short and pointless battle. Why contribute to a never-ending cycle?"

"Because we can *break* the cycle!"

It's useless arguing with someone who has no intention of hearing another viewpoint. He is decidedly stubborn and there is no negotiating with somebody like that. The best thing I can do is remove myself from the conversation.

"I need to return to work. Not sure what they'll do to us if they catch us talking." At least I'm not lying. "It was genuinely a relief to see you, Zain. If Rune doesn't get to you soon, I'll bring some water. Stay safe."

"Of course. They'll get suspicious if they find you. Hurry out of here! Don't forget to cover up the hole before you go."

Nodding, I wait for him to sink back into the depths of the man-made burrow, and cover the entrance with the shrubs.

I catch up with Taylin and the other immortals who are lugging a stone up the hill, their life on a constant loop. Only this time, Taylin doesn't have the talking head in her arms.

"Do you need help with that?" I ask.

"No," the immortal huffs. "We certainly do not need four of us to carry one item."

"I can't go back down there alone," I whisper. "The hybrids."

"Ugh. Wait here. The four of us moving quickly will be enough to keep them at bay."

Obeying, I wait on the slant as the three immortals carry the stone to the bridge and lightly jog back.

Taylin rams into my shoulder as we stride downhill. "I can't believe you ran off like that. Who does that?"

"Where's the head?" I ask dismissively.

"He wanted peace. Didn't enjoy my body odor either, apparently. I returned him to where I found him, but promised I'll keep him company when I can. And maybe keep an eye out for his body. It's not fair for him to live like that." She clears her throat. "Is what he said about you true?"

"I can't remember what he said," I reply truthfully, having only memorized verbatim Taylin's colorful description. Selfish coward. Selfish coward. *Selfish coward.*

"About you being the savior of our people. He didn't go into much detail after that. Each syllable causes him excruciating pain. You could probably hear the rasp in his voice."

Her tone is softer than before, if not inquisitive. Her mood swings are exhausting. When we reach the bottom of the slope, the other immortals have already scooped up their stone. I scan for the hybrids, still perched and watching. My heart races, desperate to pick any rock close enough.

Taylin and I settle on the same one, heavy, but manageable. Wasting no time, we trek back towards the construction.

"Well?" Taylin grunts. "Is it true?"

Me being a savior? Definitely not. I'm a *selfish coward.* Maybe if northerners weren't on the verge of extinction, I could be considered worthy of a heroic title if given the chance. But those days are long gone and I no longer know the person who I was.

"I've only ever wanted peace and zero division," I decide. "But there's nothing left. You know that."

"I'm left. You're left. There might be others."

"Taylin, seeing you that night was a miracle for me. For decades, I thought I was the only northerner left. You gave me hope."

"I dashed that hope, I'm guessing? Considering I'm an orphan from a line of northerners who hid away from the world?"

I don't respond. Mainly to conserve my breath, but also because I have nothing to contribute. Sweat trickles down my forehead to my lips, and I resent the stone for using up both of my hands.

Taylin reciprocates by keeping her mouth shut for the duration of our task. It's not long before nightfall makes it near impossible to see a thing, and if not for the glow of our golden neckbands, I would've tripped several times by now.

"Dinner time," Garu's voice booms.

Gracious, Taylin and I return to the campsite, flinching when we see the fresh mound. I'm presented with instant guilt for forgetting about the dead immortal already.

And this is only day one.

Every muscle in my body screams as I sit cross-legged, my lower back suddenly the victim of gravity. Is this how it feels to be old? Because I certainly feel my age.

Rune takes a seat next to me, my heart singing at the very sight of him. Taylin reluctantly sits next to me, our relationship constantly in turmoil. She doesn't engage with me, though. Instead she turns her back to me, focusing on the dark surrounds.

The silent guards make the rounds and hand the immortals a slightly larger slice of stale loaf from this morning. Only there's a surprising treat. This bread has a smear of butter on it. I study the prisoner's expressions, their eyes hungry for the delightful surprise. The first thing most of them do is lick the butter, before shoving the bread into their mouths.

I'm less inclined to eat it that way, but enjoy the taste and filling sensation, nonetheless.

"Are we allowed to speak?" I whisper to Rune as we eat in the void.

"Yes, we have ten minutes of quiet talk before they chain us up. Sorry, it's been a big day for everyone. We tend to zone out after dinner!" He tries to laugh, but he looks as tired as I feel. He looks around and lowers his voice, something I know he struggles with. "I wanted to talk to you about something."

"I think I know what," I say. "Is it regarding our friend?"

Rune lets out a stunned gasp. "How?"

"I...stumbled across him. Do you know what his plans are?"

Terrified of the guards, Rune only mouths the next words. "Escape?"

"And then?"

He shrugs. "Live free?"

"No." I can barely hear myself as I talk. "He wants to start a revolution against the mortals. He's hoping we can take them all down."

Rune looks at me as if I'm the crazy one. Eventually, he licks the remaining butter from his glossy lips and shakes his head. "He has a weird sense of humor. That's east coast immortals for you."

I return his skeptical expression. "Rune. Listen to me. Either he's gone crazy down there or he hasn't filled you in on his master plan. Maybe it's because he knows you happily lived amongst the mortals. Believe me."

"But it's so much better if I don't believe you," he exasperates. "I'm too tired to think about this. The thought of starting a war against innocent people is, is...I can't. A demonstration, sure. But violence is never the answer. An eye for an eye and the world goes blind."

"I'm relieved you feel that way." I reach out and place a tender hand on his shoulder. "I've missed you, Rune."

"Aww, Malin." A wide smiles spreads across his face. "I've missed you too."

"And I miss your bare face," I tease, motioning at his patchy beard.

"Yeah, me too." He rubs his scruffy chin. "You know what else? Weirdly, I miss that uncomfortable bed. Funny what you get used to."

"You're looking healthy otherwise," I compliment, noting his golden tan.

"Gotta love regenerating."

"I don't think I had a chance to ask you. If somebody chopped off your thumb, could you grow another one?"

Rune pauses, considering the scenario. "It's not something I'd be willing to do for an experiment, but I'm sure some might be able to do that. I've developed a theory after working with these lot. You know how I didn't really know any other immortals before I came here? And how I thought we could all regenerate? Turns out the ability is predominately reserved for those in the central land."

I feel my forehead crinkle. "What do you mean?"

"Well, you know how northerners all have that similar look? You and Taylin are super tall, broad shoulders; it's just how the north evolved—for lack of a better word. Zain's from the east and their hair, skin, and eyes are always a little darker. My crew rock the pale face and golden locks. In the same way we have specific physical attributes, the immortals from those places have a tendency to possess the same special abilities. Regeneration comes from the central land. I know what you're thinking. There are some immortals who can regenerate who are from the east or the west. But it's only if they're further inland. Those on the coast don't have the ability at all. The theory is that living in a central area meant you're more prone to attack from all sides, so regeneration would've been a handy ability. I learned a lot of this from Rara. Oh! I haven't introduced you."

"That's okay," I say, not in the mood to meet new people. "What do they say northerners possess?"

I can't figure out Rune's expression. It's an odd combination of pity and reservation. "Considering the northerners have all but died out...the belief is they're the only immortals who can give up their immortality. The theory is being so wealthy and having it all, they could actively choose when they were ready to move on to the next life, if there is one. The tall friends of the gods." He pauses. "Malin. Is there something you need to tell me?"

Sighing, I nod and shuffle closer to Rune. The cold night breeze is making me wish for the boiling sun again. "Immortality doesn't always need to be wasted. It can be transferred. I'm technically mortal now. It's why I was so hysterical about getting drained. I knew I'd die."

"Mal, I...I don't even know what to say. It was always important that I look out for you, but so long as I'm around, I'm going to do everything in my power to keep you alive. We will get you out of here, one way or another. You shouldn't be here!" Frustrated, he grinds his teeth together. "What actually happened to your people, anyway? There are conflicting stories."

I slump forward, glancing at Taylin who is sitting with her back to me. I know she's eavesdropping on our conversation, taking it all in.

"Civil war killed a lot of the mortal northerners," I explain to Rune who is listening intently. "All of them, we thought. When the corrupt immortals turned on each other for power, they performed heinous acts equivalent to the vile things they do here. We can't regenerate. If your head was separated from your body, it can't reattach. You're destined to live in physical discomfort. Most northern immortals chose suicide over the infinite torture."

"You chose a mortal life?" Rune's eyes appear amber against the glow of his neck band. He's so engrossed in the narrative that he seems to have forgotten how to blink.

"No. Not at all." I have an overwhelming desire to snatch my heart out of my chest, just to find some relief from the pang of guilt. Deep breaths suppress the feeling enough to continue my story. "I ran and hid for decades. It was only recently I transferred my immortality to another. I couldn't bear to see an innocent killed. Not when they were the first northerner I'd seen in years. It was an instinctive process to protect my people. Their life mattered more than mine."

Taylin shifts behind me, but doesn't utter a word. Neither does Rune. He stares, then places his hand to his chest. "Malin, that is a noble, courageous act."

"Doesn't feel like it..."

"It is. I'm just...sorry. Sorry for everything. Even back in our cells I was obsessed with finding out about the dead immortal. I should've been more empathetic. I mean, I'm still a little obsessed. I keep wanting to dig up the mound just to find out who they are but I know that's disrespectful."

"Don't be sorry," I say. "It's an unpleasant thought exhuming a grave, but I'd be lying if I said I wasn't curious too. If the body is a northerner who gave up their immortality, it would give me hope that there are more of my people still out there. And if it's not...then I suppose it just raises more questions."

"Time for sleep," Garu commands, his voice harsh in the silence. "Get into position."

Automatically, the immortals curl themselves into position next to the various posts sticking out of the ground.

"Oi. Newbies." Just as I curl up next to Rune, an angry immortal storms up to Taylin and me. "Nope. Not here. Pay your dues. Newbies sleep on the corpse."

It's as if my stomach falls out of my body. "Sleep...on the mound?"

"Look how cramped we are. Somebody's gotta take up that space. That somebody is you."

"Can't we spread out a little more?"

"Get up!" The immortal kicks dust into my face, and I splutter awkwardly.

Taylin stands, towering over the tiny immortal. Nostrils flared, she pushes the immortal so that he stumbles backwards. "Don't. Do. That."

Garu and his guards approach, their presence enough to stifle the situation. Not wanting to stir up any trouble, I make my way towards the mound, Taylin on my heels.

"You're going to listen to that thing?" she whispers.

"I'm not going to make enemies on my first day in labor," I reply. "You don't have to follow me."

Taylin hesitates as I kneel on the mound, cringing at the thought of sleeping on a departed immortal. She follows my lead and purses her lips. "I don't have to, but I want to."

The guards are already chaining the immortals to the posts in the ground. Struggling to get comfortable, Taylin and I readjust our positions, our limbs dangling off the mound. It's physically impossible to settle in, but mentally it's even worse. I feel like I'm disrespecting the dead.

Garu appears, clipping a chain to my neck band and then to the post. He does the same for Taylin then exhales quietly. Leaving in a flash, I test out the chain only to discover its primary purpose is to choke anyone who tries to roll over in their slumber. Combine that with sore muscles and sunburn and you're left with a sleepless night.

"Malin," Taylin murmurs. "I miss my cell."

To protect me from the brink of insanity, I laugh.

Despite the discomfort, I quickly fall into a dark, vivid world where the hands of the dead reach out to me from the earth and pull me into their eternal resting place...

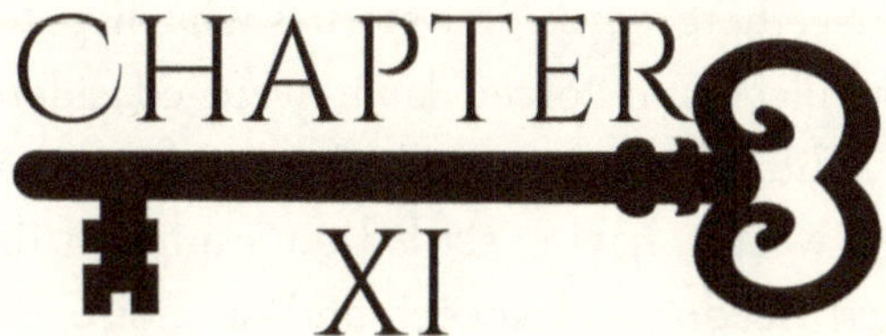

# CHAPTER XI

The north was once a revered land of wealth, power, and prestige. For centuries, its people lived in exquisite homes built entirely from marble. Beautiful infrastructure designed by only the best architects.

Each majestic building had glorious domes, columns, and grand entrances. Its people enjoyed pastel robes made of satin, the flowing fabric dreamlike against the skin.

They enjoyed perfect weather set at the perfect temperature, the men and women living in harmony. Hobbies were thoroughly explored, as wealth allowed the northern inhabitants a life of leisure.

At its peak, mortals worshipped immortals as gods—the eternal protectors and dictators of the land. They understood the importance of mortal sacrifices and an annual event was accepted. One life in exchange for the continuation of a luxurious existence, as proposed by the immortals.

Immortals secretly knew there was no real benefit to sacrifices—merely a means of control. Fear is a powerful weapon. It did, however, become a tradition, and to not have an annual sacrifice felt like a bad omen.

When exports from other corners of the land became scarce due to bad crop and disease, the immortals decided it was fair to request northern mortals to toil in the fields and perform other lowly duties. After all, there was no point in buying from other corners if it could be produced locally. Mortals understood how crucial it was to keep the immortals happy, as they were the rich, educated ones who only did what was best.

Life was fair, life made sense.

Of course, there were a few mortals who disputed this way of life. Annual sacrifices and forced labor were considered cruel in their eyes. They didn't care how rich the north was, after centuries of bequeathed wealth, having settled on a mine of diamonds. Instead, they wanted freedom—of speech and of choice. Their opinion was unpopular, but it eventually gained steam. Mortals came to the conclusion their gods were obnoxious, pathological liars. Immortals were no different from them—only older and out of touch with the common man.

And thus, a civil war commenced.

Word of corrupt immortals spread across the land, mortals becoming highly suspicious of anyone who lived a lengthy life. It didn't take much to segregate the two entities, mortals soon calling for any immortal to be safely locked away, to keep from using their godly powers.

After a while, the northern mortals died out, specifically when their uprising didn't go according to plan. A sword is only fatal to the person wielding it.

Soon, all that was left were immortals fighting for supremacy, disfiguring bodies and destroying prized possessions. After all, with no mortals to rule over, somebody had to be the slave.

They were all strong.

They were all fast.

They were all smart.

They were all greedy.

They all died.

And I fled like a coward...after starting the war in the first place.

I DREAM of the north all week, the memories hazy and muddled. It feels like a character I imagined into existence and not a life I once lived.

I've managed to convince myself that the north was evil; that the lifestyle was something I resented, but I fear it's nothing more than a coping mechanism. I've told myself for years that I hated the pretentious nature of the marble architecture, the golden facilities, the satin robes.

But the truth is, it wasn't all bad. I had a close connection with my unihorn, and enjoyed riding with her through the flowery fields. I loved painting with the elderly in the evenings. The immortal children were particularly obnoxious to the mortals, but there was one young boy who always gave me a flicker of hope. He listened whenever I explained how fragile mortals were—emotionally and physically. Fragility like that should be respected, not degraded. I don't know what became of him, but I like to think I had some sort of impact.

My family was distant because I was different, but I didn't hate my home. I just hated how corrupt it'd become.

Meanwhile, I'd happily trade my disdain for my northern lifestyle with the tough conditions I'm currently enduring.

The days working in labor all roll into one.

Each morning we eat, drink, and work.

Each morning, Rune gives me his share of food because as a mortal, I need it more.

Each afternoon, Rune sneaks what's left of the bread to Zain.

Each afternoon, Taylin and I complain about our aches and pains to one another.

Each night, Taylin and I begrudgingly sleep on the mound.

Each night we're chained.

And then we do it all again.

But one day, Taylin breaks the routine.

"I'm leaving. I've had it up to here!" She is looking even skinnier than before, her cheekbones more prominent than ever. Kicking at a rock she grabs at her hair and screams. "I'm going *insane*. The monotony, the exhaustion. I'd rather be a talking head alongside Marn!"

"Don't say that," I warn. "He's not living."

"He somehow learned to whistle recently. Between bouts of nonsensical rambling, he seems much happier than me."

"Ready?" I ask, bending over to lift a large stone. Call me crazy, but it's getting a little easier to carry these mini boulders. Maybe I'm getting stronger after all.

She doesn't budge, her gaze settled on the valley beyond. "I've been studying the perimeters. The hybrids prefer this area, but they don't seem to nest towards the south. I've decided those guards are freakin' zombies or something. Mal, they don't sleep. *Ever.* Or blink. I stayed up all night just watching them. *And they watched me back!* Have you noticed Garu is the only one who speaks? Or even has a name? Anyway, they're mostly focused on those building the bridge. We need to escape before they finish up. See if we keep to the bottom of this hill, we can sneak between the rocks to the south. Should be about fifteen minutes if we jog. Keep to the shrubbery. Then we bolt. We need to do it before nightfall because these stupid necklaces glow in the dark. Easy plan, right? Oh, and we either take Marn with us or we leave him here as a witness so he can say we were killed by the hybrids so they don't come after us."

No. No, that's not a good plan at all. Besides, what are we expected to do beyond the perimeters? I'm the mortal here. I will die out in the wilderness.

It's what I want to say. But I can't. All I can focus on is the fact I have one immortal asking me to escape with her and another quietly digging underground in the hopes of starting a revolution. I respect their ambition, but it's not the way to do it.

No more war. No more fleeing. I've done enough of both.

"Mal? Answer me. Come on, you of all people can't survive on stale bread and work in these conditions! I'm struggling. I puff walking uphill, I'm dizzy every day, and my arms feel like they're about to fall off. Seriously, you won't survive here much longer. Are you going to leave with me?"

"I'm dizzy too," I confess. "Constantly. Anguished. Fed up. But we could die in the wilderness. Or worse, be captured and brought straight back here."

"Isn't it worth the gamble? You know the second the medic returns to drain us, you're dead."

I hate that she's right. What's worse is I hate that if we don't leave now, we might never leave. But can I really leave Rune behind, who has been nothing but supportive and generous? Or maybe now is the time to tell her about Zain's tunneling? Only he's nowhere near finished, and I doubt Taylin would share a space with someone who wants to kill mortals.

"All right," I say through gritted teeth, stunned that the words are falling out of my mouth. "Now."

I'll come back for Rune, I tell myself. Once we're free, I'll come back for them all. I don't know in what capacity, but I'm not an abandoner. I'm *not*.

Taylin's eyes light up, as she leans forward to stretch out her calf muscles. "All right. You know the plan, right?"

"Run, don't get caught, hide."

"Yes."

We navigate through the maze of rocks, keeping low to the ground. Stopping at Marn, Taylin lowers her voice. "Hey, Marn. We're leaving this place. Do you want to come with us?"

The talking head gives the closest thing resembling a laugh. "Essscape isss futile. My home isss here."

"Fine." Taylin rolls her eyes. "Suit yourself. If the guards come looking, tell them we've been compromised by the hybrids."

"Tell them the truth? Will...do..."

In this moment, I swear Taylin wants to kick the talking head like a ball. Instead, she exhales sharply and leads me in the other direction.

This doesn't feel real. Am I actually doing this? It was so sudden, so soon, so *wrong*. I should be with Rune. And yet I've left him *twice*. How could I do that to someone I care about?

I feel ridiculous running so stooped over, but I follow Taylin's posture, trusting her alleged plan. It's true, the guards would have difficulty spotting us from this angle. That fact doesn't make our plan any smarter, though.

"I can't go through with this," I blurt after several quiet moments creeping through the thistle. "Taylin, I have a really bad feeling."

"Is that a special ability you have or something?"

"No, just centuries worth of instinct." I come to a decisive halt. "I can't go another step. And I don't want you to go either."

"It's now or never."

"But why?"

"Because looking at you is making me ill, all right? You look sickly, we all do, but the difference is you *can* get sick and die."

This poor girl flips and flops more than a reaperfish out of water. "You're risking all of this because you're worried about me?"

"Well, I also really hate these conditions. Our sleeping arrangements, the labor, the food. I'm done, I'm out. I'm selfishly selfless. If you want to stay here, then so be it."

"I don't want to leave Rune behind," I say quietly, wondering if he's the only reason why I'm choosing to stay.

Betrayal is written across her face. Rising above it, she forces a strained smile. "All right. It was nice knowing you. I wish you the best." Her tone is dripping with disdain as she crawls through the brush.

She can't be told or convinced in any way. Stubbornness can be a curse. As her dirt-stained body vanishes into the camouflage of the bushes, I genuinely hope it's the last time I see her. That means theoretically she's free and safe. The worst scenario would be finding her body scattered across the fields.

Wincing as thistle scrapes across my sunburn, I pull myself to my feet and watch the horizon. I don't know why. Processing hasn't been my forte lately. Hunger, dehydration, and sleep deprivation can do that to a person.

I remain hidden until the sky transitions to a beautiful blueish pink as the sun prepares to set. Watching the outskirts, I mourn

Taylin. For all her complexity, she was an important aspect in my life. The very fact she was the only northerner I'd met in decades meant we had an instant connection. It was like she was a metaphorical daughter; hope for all that was lost.

Just as I'm ready to depart from my hiding spot and face the punishment for not doing my assigned work, I notice a lean, vulnerable speck running from the wooded area and back towards my direction.

My heart leaps to my throat. Standing tall, I freeze as Taylin pumps her arms. I don't need to guess what's chasing her. Within moments the ferocious hybrids spring out of the wooded area, gaining on her faster than she can run.

There's nothing I can do from here except watch her gruesome demise. Struck with sudden courage, I pick up a rock the size of my head and leap forward. Bolting, I charge downhill and across the quarry. Ahead are large animal traps, something that was placed either to dissuade hybrids or to trap escaping prisoners. My tall physique has its advantages, especially when it comes to jumping over objects that others find challenging. Various other traps are scattered throughout the area, making it somewhat difficult to avoid when my only focus is Taylin.

Three hybrids are on her tail, her shrieks echoing across the valley.

"I'm coming!" I scream, clutching onto the rock. "Taylin, I'm coming!"

Realistically, I know I'm only serving as a distraction so they won't shred her to pieces. But I'll go down fighting to protect my people.

We're almost face to face. Stretching her hands towards me, Taylin squeals as one of the hybrids lashes out, its claws slicing into her back. It's with enough force to send her flying forward, landing into my arms. I push her to her feet, rock at the ready.

The hybrids are even more terrifying up close, but I don't have time to focus on their tenacity.

"Run, Taylin!" I demand.

"No way." She appears by my side, wielding a fallen tree branch.

I don't have an opportunity to respond. A hybrid lunges at me. I aim for its head, but it's pinned me to the ground before I even had a chance to swing. Dazed by the force, I release a bloodcurdling scream as I stare into its black, soulless eyes. Its breath is like death, its rogue tongue curled as it lets out a husky growl.

Taylin's flimsy branch hits the hybrid straight in the face, startling it enough to loosen its grip on me. Rolling out from beneath its heavy weight, I get to my feet and bash its skull with my rock.

It does very little to hurt the magnificent beast.

The two others join in on the action, effortlessly knocking us to our sides. This is it, then. At least I'll have the fortune to bask in the relief that is death. Taylin has a far more grueling process to endure.

Closing my eyes, I embrace the end.

Before the hybrids can sink their teeth and claws into our delicate skin, a loud whistle cuts through the air, stunning the beasts.

Opening my eyes, I glance behind us, shocked to find Garu standing tensely, whistle in his mouth.

"Leave them," he instructs.

I watch in fascination as the hybrids grunt and begrudgingly retreat to the wooded area. All except the one who had me pinned. It remains in place, glaring at Garu.

"Leave," he repeats. "Do you wish for pain?"

The hybrid growls aggressively as if taunting Garu. It isn't willing to listen to the guard, unintimidated by the threat. It stands on its hind legs, preparing to strike.

Nonchalant, Garu solemnly shakes his head. "Be it on your own shoulders."

Taylin and I shield ourselves as the beast leaps over us toward Garu. Only it doesn't get very far. It drops just in front of us, twitching and spasming violently.

I scramble into a better position so I can see what's going on. Garu remains in place, blue energy sparking from his left hand. No, not blue energy. Current. Tiny little jolts electrify his hand. But it doesn't impact Garu. Only the unconscious beast.

Amazed, Taylin sits back and gapes at Garu. "Thank you, sir. We were told nobody would help us if the hybrids attacked."

Garu doesn't budge, his blinks slow and precise. "We need as many workers alive as possible."

Taylin and I help one another to our feet, standing in place, waiting for instruction.

"What are you doing so far away from the designated quarry?" Garu asks, a hint of suspicion in his voice. We're easily a ten-minute stroll from where we should be.

Lost. Toilet break. Temporary insanity. Prison break. Wanted to find better stones.

There's no good answer.

"So I thought," he replies smoothly. "No dinner for either of you."

We exchange confused glances. That's *it*? No decapitation? No solitary confinement? No lashing? Simply bed without supper?

Not wanting to provoke him, we nod in unison and follow Garu silently back towards the unfinished bridge.

"Only I control the hybrids," Garu says rather spontaneously. I jump at his voice, having not anticipated a conversation. "They are good creatures. Loyal. Faithful. Not as sporadic as a werewolf but not as stupid as doggan. My family has always had a way with the animals."

Neither of us are sure how to respond to his origin story. The man evokes fear and nausea in those he so much as gazes at. How am I supposed to carry on a conversation with him?

"What about the current shooting out of your hand?" I cringe, unsure why the words tumbled out of my mouth. Taylin thwacks me on the back of the head.

A small smirk appears on the side of Garu's mouth. "My personal talent."

This man has no intention of elaborating. For some reason, I get the impression he is full of *many* secretive talents.

The sun wastes no time setting, as if it's anxious to end the day. We reach the campsite as it gets dark, the immortals all gathered by the well to cleanse and drink.

They notice us with Garu, puzzled expressions on their faces, but nobody dares to question it. Rune in particular is concerned, somewhat flustered by the scene.

Garu leads us to the campsite and instructs us to sit. "No water either."

"We're sorry," I say sincerely. "It was stupid."

"Stupid is a matter of opinion," he says dismissively. "Rest while you can. The time for fresh uniforms is here."

My stomach lurches, and not just because he's looking straight at me. "Uniforms? You mean the medic is back?"

"Yes. A guard will collect the group in pairs throughout the night. Newbies first, of course. This is your first time, yes? Do not fear. Within a few days, the laborers regenerate the blood. It's a faster healing time considering we feed and water you. You'll get used to it."

I'm not listening. I just can't wrap my head around it. Was today always the day I was destined to die? If not by a hybrid, then by severe blood loss? Or is this our punishment for running away?

Finished with the conversation, Garu redirects his attention to the other immortals, yelling out instructions I block out. They're not important. Nothing is. I'm going to die tonight.

Taylin grips onto my arm, determined. "Let's try again. Let's steal that whistle and run. You're not dying tonight, Malin!"

"It's over Taylin," I mumble listlessly. "Give me the luxury of enjoying the stars."

I lay on my back and gaze at the cerulean atmosphere, the glistening specks comforting. Instead of letting anxiety and fear use up the precious time I have left, I welcome peace, acceptance, and relief.

It's out of my hands now.

"Please," Taylin whispers. "I'm not ready to let you go. I knew this was coming, I knew it was overdue. It's why I wanted to leave so badly. Call it a sixth sense or something. Please, please, we can find another way out."

White noise. Nothing more than white noise...

"Malin." Rune's voice is nearby, his face soon blocking my view of the sky. I look through him, unable to drag myself back into grim reality. "Malin, I just heard. I'll cause a distraction. You can hide with Zain in the hole! It's the only way."

A spark of hope. That's definitely not a terrible idea. Anxiety floods through my veins once more as my inner survivalist fights for the right to live.

"All right." I sit up. "Yes, we can do that. How do we distract them?"

Taylin and Rune beam at my sudden enthusiasm, having broken through my defeatist exterior. The other immortals are slowly gathering back to the campsite, the countdown on. In a moment, the guards will hand out stale loaves. Then they'll allow ten minutes of downtime, followed by chaining us to our posts. Who knows when the medic will arrive in that time.

"It's now or never," Rune says quickly, his words running into one other. "I'll scream that there's a hybrid nearby. It'll be enough for you to get out of sight."

"No, it won't be," I mumble as figures from the prison appear ahead. "It's never. It's never going to happen."

Lamenting at the sight of Mitty and another nameless guard sauntering towards us, I hug Rune as tightly as I can.

"*Now*, come on *now*. Get ready to run!" Rune clenches his jaw. "Ready?"

"Malin, Taylin?" Garu calls. "The guards have arrived. Please return as soon as possible. We do not appreciate time wasters. Time actually means something to mortals."

His sly remark is unnecessary and frantically, I plead my case one last time. "Garu. Mitty. Somebody, please listen to me. I'm mortal. I gave up my immortality. If you drain my blood, I will *die*."

Mitty looks like he hasn't slept in days, his eyes red and puffy. He clears his throat nervously, watching for Garu's reaction.

"But you were an immortal?" Garu confirms.

"Yes."

"Then you are successfully paying for your crimes. If you die tonight, as unfortunate as that may be, then you die. Find comfort in the fact that your friends will be the ones burying you tomorrow. No doubt, they will respect your body." He blinks, his grin unsettling. "And you don't know why the other immortals have died?"

"We don't think so," Rune interrupts, eager to share his newfound theories. "It's strictly a northerner ability. Just like how the central land immortals can regenerate."

"And the east have the gift of gab." Garu suddenly doesn't look so amused. "They have the ability to pull the truth out of anyone. Manipulate enemies. They are extremely dangerous. It's why I often send them on the risky tasks near the hybrids. They are better off dead, but alas, death is not their fate."

Stunned by Garu's chattiness, I turn to Rune for reassurance. Isn't Zain from the east? Is that who is he referring to?

And if that's true...Zain is looking to recruit others to begin a violent revolution...which means we're all in trouble. Mortals don't deserve death and immortals don't deserve war.

I utter a horrified squeal.

"*Run*," Rune whispers. "*You're fast.*"

"*But Zain is going to pull everyone into his cause!*" I say as Mitty gathers next to me, cuffing my wrists. It's only in this moment that I finally understand why Mitty has been so good to me. Zain has him brainwashed, under his charismatic spell.

My gratitude transmutes to pity.

Pity vanishes and is speedily replaced with terror as Mitty leads me away from the others. The other guard cuffs Taylin, who follows close behind.

"I'm sorry," Mitty says in a hushed tone. "I did everything I could to delay the medic. Asked her to treat others before coming to the laborers. I've even researched ways to get you pardoned, but there is no precedent. An immortal is a felon, period. It sickens me."

*Sickens you because Zain spent years twisting your thoughts...*

. Nothing comes out of my mouth. If I force words out, I'll burst into tears instead. I'm not ready to die. I must stop Zain and warn the others. I have to find out why Garu has such an interesting talent. I need to release the innocent immortals.

But most of all...I just want to live for the sake of living...

EVERYTHING IS dreamlike as we return to the dank infirmary.

Taylin is the first to be drained, making childish noises throughout the entire procedure.

"Goodness, you take a long time to drain. A lot more blood in these freakishly tall bodies," Angela, the medic, so kindly announces.

She has a point, though. In fact, seemingly bored with the process, she removes the syringe after only a short time. Taylin is certainly pale and her lips are a little blue, but she doesn't look nearly as corpse-like as the others.

Sluggishly, Taylin gets off the steel slab and meanders towards me, her eyes rolling to the back of her head.

"Maybe I need to spend more time on you two during the next drain," Angela mumbles. "Great. *Just* great. More time I don't have. Come on, second freak. Onto the slab."

Compliant, I sit down and stare at the stone floor. Here goes nothing. Hypnotized by surging memories, I barely notice the medic sticking the needle into my arm.

It is a weird sense of déjà vu being trapped between these walls again. Part of me wonders how disassociated I am, whether I'm already hallucinating from the trauma. The medic's voice is distorted, distant. Mitty's stoic expression is incomprehensible. Taylin's strange hand gestures in her cuffs are nonsensical.

If I still held spiritual beliefs, I'd convince myself that my soul was already disconnecting from my body, hence the twisted reality. But I know better than that. Immortals don't have souls. An eternal being can't have it all.

"Rotten prisoners!" The medic is speaking to the guards. "I'm run off my feet. Draining blood every hour on the hour. Who thought feeding them was a good idea? I'm exhausted from constantly draining them! Now they're energetic enough to complain about their arthritis or chronic illness. For years, we didn't need to stock up on medical supplies. Now we have to worry about a riot if we don't provide! What's this world coming to? They don't deserve rights! Who is in charge? Something fishy is going on."

I wince as Angela begins the process; already grieving the life force being sucked from my fragile body. I haven't checked if she cleaned the needle before jamming it into my vein. I suppose it's the least of my concerns.

My head throbs as blood is pulled from my body, and I can't resist the temptation to drift into a deep slumber. My chin drops to my chest, my eyelids fluttering.

"Sensitive one," the medic scoffs.

"Because she's mortal!" Taylin's fading voice shouts. "We told you that several times!"

Did she? I can't really remember much...

"Yeah, yeah. If I believed every prisoner who used that excuse, I'd be long fired. They all say they're mortal, then walk around as living corpses mere hours later. Immortals are the worst kind of liars. Especially those eastern ones. I gag them. Even cut out their tongues if the mood strikes."

Oh. That makes sense...a lot of inmates don't talk...perhaps that's why...

Nauseated, I succumb to the darkness, Taylin's imprint still in my mind's eye. Neither of us would be in this position if it wasn't for me. Neither...of...us...

∞

I crouch as I reach the bushes, my heart pounding in my ears. Pulling back the greenery, I check for animals. The burnaprays are particularly nasty critters, feasting in packs and digging through live prey's flesh until they reach their favorite part of the body—the bone.

Fortunately, I find no evidence of their nest or waste about. Twigs poke my eyes as I step into the bush and I brush aside the stinging nettle. Here I can hide. Here I can rest.

I can't remember the last time I slept. Being on the run will do that to you.

As my eyelids droop, I shiver in the harsh breeze. Just a few minutes. A few minutes of shut-eye will be fine...

...a scream sounds in the distance.

Now wide awake and alert, I peer through the bushes, trying to locate the scream. It's a woman. She sounds desperate.

Unable to help myself, I pull back the shrubbery and investigate the shrill cry. It's impossible to see much in the dark, and the intense wind only adds to the eerie vibe.

Several lanterns are just down the path, hung by a carriage. Two horses whinny as six guards surround their captured criminal.

I chastise myself for being so curious. If the guards are busy with this immortal, it gives me another day or two of peace. Why would I sabotage that?

Listening to my better judgment, I turn to flee back to my hiding place until I'm stopped by a hysterical sob.

"Please, sirs. Please, I'm mortal. I swear that I'm mortal. You don't need to shoot me!" I've never heard anybody plead like this before.

A guard snorts. "Yeah, sure you are, mate. You're that bloody northerner we've been trying to track down! Last one they say!"

My heart flutters. A northerner? That can't be! I thought I was the last one. Creeping closer to get a better look, I nearly let out an audible gasp. On her knees with her hands behind her head is a tall, strong woman. Practically a giant compared to others around these parts. Her long neck, her shoulders, her hair...everything about her points to a northern heritage. The guards aim their rifles at her, unsympathetic to her plights.

"I'm not! I'm only twenty! My parents died when I was young. We lived in a quiet village. Please, I'm a humble seamstress. I can offer free services for your wives? Or mend your jackets? Please, sirs, I beg of you. I'm not who you think I am. Immortals are evil. I'm not one of them!"

Her words fall on deaf ears, the wind howling in response.

"I don't know where you get the audacity to lie to us, but mortal northerners died out when my great-great-grandmother was a kid."

"No, some went into hiding! My family did that for generations!"

A guard groans. "Just shoot it. If it's telling the truth, then it'll die a saint. If it doesn't bleed to death, we'll take it in."

I can't stand to look at this. I should be protecting my people and now the only one I've come across in decades is about to be killed or imprisoned. This girl is a metaphorical daughter, regardless of her mortality, and she needs my assistance.

Without a game plan, I dash forward. I'm long. I'm quick. I'm tall. I have little experience, but I can fight these smaller guards.

In the darkness, I lunge forward and kick the rifles out of two of the guard's hands. Stunned by the assault, their sluggishness gives me a chance to headbutt one between the eyes, who stumbles back into the mud. One of the guards who lost his gun attempts to strangle me from behind, but with the height discrepancy, I manage to kick him in the face, watching as two loose teeth fly out as his head hits the ground.

With two incapacitated, I only have four more to fight.

"Get out of here!" I scream at the girl. "Run!"

A loud shot is fired and I jolt as a bullet skims my waist. Bullets are unpleasant, but nothing I've not managed in the past. They take forever to heal, especially if I don't get an opportunity to remove the bullet.

"There's two of 'em! We're under attack! Two of the freaks!"

Scrambling for the dropped gun, I pick it up and shoot two

guards in the leg. Perhaps they'll choose to believe it's because I'm a lousy shot, but the truth is I can't bring myself to murder anybody, even a guard. They drop, crying out in pain, and despite the circumstances, I still feel guilty for my actions. I *almost* apologize.

Dodging another bullet, I spring towards the remaining guards and use the rifle to smack them in their jaws. It's enough to drop them, but not for long. Holding onto the gun, I run to the northern girl and kneel beside her.

"I'm Malin, daughter of Theralin. Come with me!"

"T-Taylin," the girl stammers. I'm puzzled by her trembling until I glance down at her abdomen and notice the blood pouring out. Hands shaking, she reaches to me as she drops to her side, mud covering her face. "I'm d-dying..."

Oh, no. She truly is mortal.

The guards are already regaining stamina and composure. I fire a warning shot toward those who reach for their own gun. "Stay back!"

"Help..." Taylin utters. "I'm...I'm..."

Could lack of sleep truly be the reason why such a ludicrous thought flits through my mind? Or am I so desperately lonely that I'd do *anything* for my people?

Sucking in my lips, I decisively place my hand around my chest and mumble a quick incantation. A misty, blue light shoots out of my body and I suddenly regret my choice. Instantly, I feel less powerful. Less alert. Less flexible. It's like everything my body has learned over the years has been wiped. Instead, it feels feeble and fragile.

The blue light shoots into Taylin's wound, my immortality rushing into her cells and speedily aiding her body to recover. She stares up at me, awestruck by the transition.

"Go. Run!" I demand.

"But...did you...give me immortality?"

"Yes!"

She responds in a fashion I never would've predicted. "How could you? I hate you! Why would I want to live forever? Why?"

Too distracted by her emotional outburst, I don't hear the guard approach me from behind and hit me in the head with the back of the rifle.

Dazed, I drop to all fours, not accustomed to such a beating. Mortality already has a lot of downfalls. For starters, a hit to the head certainly hurts a lot more than it used to.

As the guards surround me, I watch in relief as Taylin scurries away, her trail of blood vanishing in the slippery mud.

"Another northerner! Wha' a treat!"

"We'll make sure you suffer in prison! How dare you accost us!"

"Wait! Where'd the other one go?"

Having resigned myself to my fate, I don't resist the guards as they cuff me. Why bother? My story is over. It's up to Taylin to live... to hide...to fight...and find the rest of our people...

"MALIN? MALIN? CAN YOU HEAR ME?"

I can. I *can* hear things. Is this the great beyond? I can't seem to feel anything. Or really see. But I have a sense of existence. Oddly, I feel a lot of love. A lot of emotional warmth. People I care about are nearby. Only, I can't seem to reach them.

"Are you sure she's alive?"

"She's breathing, see? Her heartbeat is faint, but that's normal after a draining, right?"

Someone holds onto my hand and I now feel how ice cold the touch is. "Hold in there, Malin. You're so strong. You can recover, all right? If only I could pass on my regenerative abilities!"

"You can't?"

"No. It's a stupidly selfish ability. You northerners can gift your immortality. How sweet is that? I can't even heal someone."

*Rune.* Rune! And Taylin?

"She's stirring! Malin! Malin, can you hear us?"

It's difficult to string a sentence together. My mind is eager to shout out that yes, everything is fine, but my body won't cooperate.

Eventually, and after a lot of willpower, my eyes open and I take in my surroundings.

We're back at the labor camp. A pale Rune and Taylin are sitting by my sides, with Garu curiously overlooking us. Once I seem alive and well, he nods and returns to his post with the silent guards.

"You're not...blue..." I rasp.

"Regenerator." Rune winks. "Crazy fast healing, eh? And Taylin here wasn't drained much, having been the first northerner. You copped the brunt of it once the medic learned you had more blood. She made sure another bag was prepared."

"Yeah, she said I'll be going back again soon. She didn't want to waste time on me this round." Taylin rolls her eyes. "You scared us, Malin. Passed out on the slab. If it weren't for Mitty to help carry you back here, they probably would've left you to rot in the cells. I tried but...yeah, I feel weak. Like a mortal again."

Rune shoots Taylin a confused look. "All right, so just to confirm. Malin gave up her immortality for you, right?"

"Yes," we reply in unison, but I'm too exhausted to explain.

"We only met for a second," Taylin recounts. "The guards had mistaken me for her. The land was on the lookout for an immortal northerner, little to my knowledge. When they broke into my home, I fled. Ended up in the middle of nowhere, but they pursued. Not one guard believed I was mortal. When they shot me, Malin exchanged life forces and took my place. I escaped, but not for long. I was only a seamstress. Had no idea what I was supposed to be doing. It wasn't long before they caught up to me. I hated Malin for turning me into the thing I despised. Immortals were evil beings who thought they were godlike. But now I see Malin is far from evil. You're a true light in the darkness, sacrificing yourself for a stranger. That's nothing short of heroic."

I hold back tears, too dizzy to formulate words. I catch a glimpse of my arms, a blue tinge reflecting off my golden neckband.

And there it is. Officially branded. It finally happened. I now looked exactly like the other imprisoned immortals, our bruised skin a uniform, which only proves our infinite sentence.

I trace the surface with my finger, already nostalgic for the olive tan.

"Strange, isn't it?" Taylin says. "If only you could see your face. You look bruised."

"Hopefully, Garu will let you rest," Rune says quietly. "I mean, you're pretty useless right now. Maybe they'll let you work on the bridge for a few days."

"Mmm..." It's all I manage to squeeze out.

Sympathetic to my condition, Rune squeezes my leg fondly then turns to Taylin. "Hey, you said you were a seamstress. So what, you lived amongst mortals?"

"I was a mortal myself," Taylin says, somewhat vitriolic.

"No, I get that. But you were a northerner. Your parents would've been in hiding for years after such a bad reputation. Most of the land assumed any northerner was immortal because they killed all the mortals. How did you work as a seamstress?"

Taylin possesses a stereotypical northerner trait, and that's a reluctance to discuss the past. Regardless, she stretches out her leg and pokes at her corpse-like skin. "When I was orphaned, an older woman was kind enough to house me. She taught me how to sew, but knew my appearance would trouble her customers. Bad reputation, as you said, and my height was frightening. After explaining the need to remain concealed, she allowed me to work in the back of her shop. There, I would mend clothes and sew wedding dresses. I hated the wedding dresses. So much unnecessary work for a pointless ceremony. I digress. She confided in her friends and they didn't have a problem with me being from the north. It's amazing how hated our people are. Nobody likes the wealthy, whether it's earned or not. But everyone assumes our kind are rich killers, regardless of our mortality or not. It's a gross assumption."

"I'm sorry," Rune apologizes. "If it helps, the mortals in my village thought the northern stories were nothing more than tales of mythology. Part of me always hoped they were true. Giants who lived in beautiful homes seemed so majestic to me. They say there's nothing left of it now. But I'm a hopeless dreamer. I like to think it's still there. And despite where we've ended up, the little boy in me is excited that I now have two legendary friends. It's everything I could've asked for."

Taylin snorts. "What? Two freakishly tall women with masculine features?"

"No," Rune says. "Two strong people with big hearts who have my back and I have theirs. I know we're prisoners, but I'm the luckiest guy in the world."

I listen carefully to the way Rune worded his sentence. I'm touched by his heartwarming admission, but I suspect the second person he's referring to is Zain instead of Taylin.

Through my haze of pain and confusion, I think of Zain and how despised immortals from the eastern corner are. Patchy memories of the medic declaring she cuts out their tongues to prevent them from manipulating others flash in my mind's eye. I don't know much about the east, but there's clearly some bad blood I'm not privy to.

But I can't deal with that tonight. I just want to sleep. As if reading my thoughts, Garu and his guards gather around us, chaining our necks to our posts. It's only now I realize Rune has bravely taken the unpleasant sleeping position on the mound, allowing me to stretch out next to him.

Beyond that observation is a sea of black, as deep sleep carries me far away from reality.

# CHAPTER XII

It takes a few days for the wooziness to subside. Despite having been drained less than me, Taylin is in rough shape, languid and nauseous. She complains of headaches, but beyond that, she mostly curls into a ball and shivers, sweat glistening all over her body.

"Do northerners not respond well to draining?" Garu asks on the second day, allowing us to remain in the camp. I'm stunned by his generosity, but the faster we can heal, the better we can work.

"I don't know," I mumble. "Have northerners ever been imprisoned here before?"

"Not to my knowledge," he says. "Do you require more bread?"

I glance at Taylin who is laying on her side, clutching her stomach. After a moment, she nods slightly.

"Yes please," I reply, closing my eyes to ward off the dizziness.

Garu returns swiftly, throwing the bread at our feet. "Tomorrow, you must work. We need the bridge completed by the end of the week."

"Why?" I ask, careful not to look directly at Garu. His presence only enhances my nausea.

Taylin reaches for the bread, bringing it to her pale blue lips. She nibbles it delicately, staring vacantly ahead. She looks exactly how I feel.

"We have visitors arriving," Garu says.

"Can't they take the prisoner entrance?"

"These are important visitors. It is not good etiquette for them to traverse the treacherous terrain. It will add days to their journey." Finished with the conversation, Garu turns away from us and strolls toward the construction of the bridge. I don't know how he expects us to finish by the end of the week.

"How are you coping?" I ask Taylin once he's out of earshot.

"Like death!" Her voice rattles. "It's like when I caught the plague as a child. Only the hag's potion gave me relief. I don't think I'm getting better."

"You're definitely not as pale," I reassure. "Only your lips. You're fairing much better than me. My fingernails are disgusting." I glimpse at the dark blue coating, repulsed by my body.

"Fantastic," she responds sarcastically. She can't be too sick, then.

Garu is facing us again, his neutral expression twisting into a scowl. "What is this lunatic doing here?"

Bewildered, I mistake him for talking to us. Glimpsing over my shoulder, I spot Mitty on his own, walking down from the prison, his uniform wrinkled and untucked.

Garu meets Mitty before he gets too close to our campsite, but they're near enough to eavesdrop on.

"You do understand this isn't your territory?"

"Apologies, Garu. Sincerely."

"Well? Do you have news?"

"No. I...I would like to transfer to work here."

Garu tosses his head back, laughing boisterously. Only, it doesn't really sound like a laugh. It's throaty and belittling. "There's nothing to transfer to. We have it covered here. Is the inside getting too hard for you?"

Mitty looks like a little boy in comparison to Garu, nervously rubbing his hands together. "Admittedly, the inmates are more energetic since consistent feeding. They're asking questions, standing up to us more. I don't mind that. The prisoners *should* have more rights. But that's not the reason why I want to transfer."

"Then what? Why on earth would you leave the cushy job on the inside? We don't eat well. We don't sleep well. We're on constant alert. Do you think you could stand such conditions?"

Mitty stares longingly at Taylin and I, his eyebrows knitted together. "I've learned to sympathize with some of the prisoners. One in particular, but word is he was mauled by the hybrids."

"Marn?" Garu asks. "Brive? Or Zain?"

"Zain," Mitty says quickly, unable to lie convincingly. I wonder what he knows. "He was friends with my father."

"But they're both dead," Garu says bluntly. "Well, good as dead if he's been mauled. Your presence here makes little sense. We do not need your help unless you're considering becoming a laborer. Workers we *do* need."

"I could probably bring you more workers. The cannibals have behaved better since receiving regular meals. They're aggressively passionate so would serve you well here. They could redirect their rage towards physical labor. We were told to never bring them here due to unpredictable behavior, but that was before you took charge."

I want to scream at Mitty for even suggesting something so preposterous! He *does* realize the cannibals almost killed me and are the reason why I was sentenced to labor? What is this guy's motive?

Garu has a contemplative expression. "How many?"

"Dozens, but three in particular have been on their best behavior."

"As you can see, we're two down while the northerners recover. More workers would be good."

Mitty narrows his eyes at Taylin and I. "Why are you allowing them to rest?"

"We're on a deadline and any silly mistakes on their behalf will only slow down production. I'd rather they recuperate and make up for the delay."

The answer seems to alleviate any concern Mitty had, a relieved smile spreading across his face. "Oh, that's good. All right, I'll reconsider my transfer and bring the cannibals to you. If they cause any trouble—"

"Nothing causes me trouble," Garu interrupts, a sentiment I believe. "Is there anything else?"

Mitty's body language implies a firm yes, but he shakes his head instead. "No, sir. Thank you, Garu, for your time. I'll organize the workers."

"See that you do."

Garu dismisses Mitty, who stumbles back up the hill towards the prison. Locking eyes with me, Garu frowns and I try to focus on something, *anything* else.

"You seem displeased with the news," Garu says, unbudging from his position.

It seems pointless to deny anything to him. He's always in my head, anyway. "The cannibals almost killed me."

"Immortals can't be killed."

"I'm not an immortal anymore, remember? I gave it up." I exhale when his expression doesn't change. "I gave it to Taylin. For all intents and purposes, she's the true mortal gifted with my immortality."

Unsurprised, he folds his arms. "Interesting. This is why you are both sickly. One is mortal. The other is unaccustomed to their body preventing their permanent demise."

Growing frustrated, I take advantage of his chatty mood. "And there is no way to get pardoned? What if the public found out a mortal was trapped in this facility?"

"The general public would not care. An immortal is an immortal. Period. If you were born one or transitioned into one, you are the enemy." Garu focuses on the bridge. "Go drink. Hydrate. It will help the blood regenerate. Relieve yourselves if need be."

"I'm not moving from this spot," Taylin rasps. "Malin? Can you bring me some water if you're going?"

"Of course." Standing is tricky; in fact, I stumble back several times, narrowly avoiding landing on the post poking from the ground. Eventually, to the amusement of Garu, I make it to my feet. The world moves around me, like having sea legs. Taking my first step forward, I feel like a proud parent watching their toddler walk for the first time.

I did it. I *did* it.

Disinterested in the slow process, Garu overtakes me as I wobble towards the well. It's a huge accomplishment as I slump next to the side, scooping the filthy water between my hands.

When I've had my share, I pull out the grass on the sides, soaking them in the water. It's not ideal, but when I have nothing else to carry the liquid in, it'll do.

I want to conserve my energy, but the grassy water is not enough for Taylin. When she sucks the blades dry, I return to the well to try again. Resting on the ground, I watch Rune and the immortals hard at work, piling the stones and fitting them to the bridge. Everyone is testy, aggravated by one another, and shouting insults.

"Touch me again and I'll throw you off here!"

"I didn't touch you! Focus on your craftsmanship! You missed a spot!"

When they get too rowdy, a guard steps in and smacks them across the face. It's enough for one immortal to lose a tooth. Sheepishly, they quietly continue their work.

From an outsider's perspective, it's easy to see how rushed the construction is. The sides look well designed—sturdy, neat. The middle, however, the most important part, is askew. Stones have wide gaps between one another, seemingly loose when immortals walk across them.

Concerned about appearing judgmental as I hang by the well, I return to Taylin who sips on the water and dozes off. Poor girl is having a hard time.

I'm physically tired, but my mind is racing. With Taylin asleep, I don't know if I can sit here alone for hours on end. Restless, I consider telling myself a story through the shapes in the clouds, but the overcast prevents much creativity.

Listening to the immortals shout at each other once again, I think of Zain and how his own personal project is going. Still a little shaky when I stand, I pause before taking another step. Walking in this condition is akin to balancing on a tightrope. One misstep and I'm down for the count.

Under the guise of finding a private area to relieve myself, I casually make my way towards the shrubbery where Zain's invisible hideout is.

Carefully, I crouch and pull aside the bushes, somewhat surprised to find the hole has widened. Or maybe my memory is patchy.

"Zain?" I whisper, knowing it's pointless if he's managed to dig for miles. "Zain?"

No answer. I wait. I wait a little longer. Nothing.

Without thinking, I lower my feet into the hole. Slowly, I slip down, almost like a slide. It's considerably bigger than I expected. Crawling is the only way forward, but it's not as claustrophobic as I'd anticipated. A lot of work has gone into this. As I descend into darkness, I trip blindly over my hands. My golden neckband doesn't provide a lot of light.

"Zain?" I call. My voice doesn't echo. It's like it ricochets back towards me.

I don't know how long I crawl for. Too long. It's hard to discern time in the dark and part of me worries I've taken a wrong turn. Could this tiny tunnel cave-in at a moment's notice? Does it link up to some creature's burrow?

"Zain?" I ask again.

This time I'm met with a response. "Malin?"

Relieved, my heart hammers against my chest. It's only now I realize I'm panting and choking on the specks of dirt.

At the end of the tunnel, I spot a dull golden glow. The figure kneels, the tunnel ceiling significantly higher.

I pick up the pace, eager to get to the end. When I reach Zain, he helps me to my knees and pats me on the back.

"Good to see you!"

"Hard to see you," I counter. "Why are our neckbands so dull down here?"

Zain shrugs, his face blanketed in the dirt. "Maybe the tracker is what makes them glow. Perhaps the signal isn't so strong down here.

Or they're dirty. Who cares? I should welcome you to my humble abode. What do you think?" He smiles like a madman, and I suppose he is.

"I can't believe you've been living down here."

"How long has it been?"

I shrug, genuinely disoriented by time. "A month?"

"Oh. I'm ahead of schedule. I'm close to finishing. That's why I'm digging up. Once I get confirmation as to where I am on the map, I'll recruit the others to sneak out. Might be able to get this finished in a few days."

Zain speaks with such confidence that a weaker mind would follow him without question. But his plan doesn't make any sense, and no speech said with thorough conviction could defend the insanity of the concept.

"You haven't really thought this through, have you?"

"On the contrary," he says, his voice croaky. His ribs poke through his skin, his tattoos blending in with the dirt and mud on his skin. It's only now I notice he's at least had a tool to help him tunnel— the spade he either stole or manipulated his way into getting. Regardless, it's still been an impressive effort.

"Talk me through it," I encourage.

"What's the point? You're not going to follow me."

Taken aback, I falter over my words. Does he suddenly doubt his charismatic abilities? "Why do you say that?"

"Because of how you reacted the first time. Besides, your kind are difficult to persuade. Sure, I can get you to blurt out truths you wouldn't ordinarily. But I can't change a stubborn mindset. And northerners are all the same. It's how you lot died out."

"I'm not stubborn," I protest, somewhat stubbornly. "I mean, I'm wishy-washy at times. Indecisive."

"You're stubborn," he insists, picking up his spade and chipping at the ceiling. He barely blinks as the dirt falls into his vision, meanwhile I cough and splutter.

"Please answer my question, Zain. For the sake of transparency.

Just because I won't follow you doesn't mean I don't agree or won't help you." I hope he can't detect my attempt at manipulation.

"Uh-huh," he says passively. "I'm not a fool, Malin. Mad, perhaps. But I have faith that I'll regain my sanity once I'm free from this torturous prison. You know my intention is to escape and recruit other immortals. They may be from this prison, they may be still hiding across the land. They might not even be born yet, as their genes produce a throwback. One way or another, Malin, I can guarantee this prison will go down in flames. I will not see our people mistreated anymore. As a northerner, I thought *you* of *all* people would see the importance in that."

"I do," I agree. "I really do. But violence and segregation aren't the answer. War destroyed my entire corner of the land. All I ask is that you don't harm innocent mortals. Believe me when I say they're not all bad. Look at Mitty. Rune's village was kind to him, too."

Zain snorts, and this time splutters on the dirt himself. "You sure about that? You don't believe a bigoted, fearful mortal ratted him out? If you don't, then *you* are the fool, my friend."

Taken aback, I lose myself in a web of thoughts. It's only when I notice Zain rubbing his hand across the gold neckband and licking his fingers that I snap back into the present.

"What are you doing?" I ask, twisting my nose at the sight. What a peculiar thing to do.

"Licking the golden remnants," he says matter-of-factly, keeping his focus on the collapsing tunnel ceiling. "Why so surprised? How else do you think I've kept my sustenance down here? Certainly not with crummy leftovers and minimal water!"

His answer only raises more questions. "Zain, I haven't the foggiest what you're on about. Are you telling me gold helps your stamina?"

Zain stops what he's doing, looking at me as if I've insulted his entire existence. "Oh, Malin. How can you not know this?"

"You're irritating me now!" Once again, his ability coerces me into saying exactly what I feel. "Just explain it to me. I'm ignorant, I get it."

"It doesn't make sense how you can't know. You're northern! Didn't you lot live amongst wealth and such?"

"Yes. Not a huge amount of gold, but sure. Mostly diamonds and sapphires. It was the norm. Wealth was all we knew."

"Ever wondered why your kind are so tall? So strong? So *once upon a time* worshipped? Gold helps us. Increases stamina, smarts, strength. The more we ingest, the healthier we become. Growing up around it gives your kind a head-start in life."

Shaking my head, I dismiss the theory. "Taylin is mortal. Well, was. We had plenty of other mortals who were also tall. Gold wouldn't impact mortals the same way. That disproves your theory."

Jaw clenched, Zain leans in close. "Tell me, *princess*. Were the mortals *as* tall? *As* strong? *As* fast? And if your little friend is allegedly mortal, then the gold would be doing nothing to help her."

"Well, she's not mortal anymore. I gave her my immortality," I correct coyly. "And no. No, the northern mortals weren't as tall...or strong...perhaps only compared to other corners."

Compelled to smack me over the head with the spade, Zain inhales sharply, squeezing the handle. When a small smirk appears, he returns to digging. "There you go."

"But why would the guards give us something that makes us stronger? That doesn't make sense."

"Of course it does." He clears his throat, resting his arms for a moment. "Thought you were smarter than this, *princess*."

"Stop calling me that."

"There are a few reasons I can conceive as to why they'd give laborers gold. One: keep us strong so we work for longer. Two: Somebody is on the inside wanting to start a revolution. Three: They don't know its benefits. Four: They thought it looked pretty." He hesitates. "Unless you're planning on helping me dig, you better leave. You've been here for far too long. The guards will send their hybrids on you."

"Been there, done that," I brag jokingly, but it's wasted on Zain. "I'll leave you."

"Yep. Good luck and all that."

The farewell is unjustly callous, leaving me with a bitter taste in my mouth. He doesn't so much as wave, obsessively digging into the dirt. Shuffling around in the small space, I begin the incline up the tunnel, a little less apprehensive on the trip back.

I don't know how I'm going to explain the state of my skin and clothes when I surface. Sure, we're already pretty filthy, and sweat is an odor we've all become desensitized to. But the dirt caught in my hair and eyelashes is another matter entirely.

When I gasp in the fresh air, I splutter and choke. I didn't realize how oxygen-deprived I was in the tunnel.

Dusting myself off, I make do with my appearance and rejoin Taylin who is now wide awake and chewing on the blades of grass.

"Hey!" She certainly isn't happy. "Where have you been?"

I wish she wouldn't shout and draw attention. Maybe she's still affected by the blood loss. Her scowl only fades when I sit quietly next to her, stroking the golden neckband around my neck. In hindsight, I probably never could've lifted all those stones without a boost...maybe I'm only alive after the draining because of this ugly necklace. Or maybe Zain is nothing more than a liar.

"How long have I been gone?"

"How would I know?" Taylin spits. "I woke up, and you had vanished. I've been on my own for an hour at least."

She certainly has more fight in her spirit. She's beginning to heal.

"Can you keep a secret?" I purse my lips, hoping she understands the gravity of the question.

"From the guards? Yes. And I don't speak to anyone else."

She makes a valid point. "There's an immortal digging a tunnel out of here. The guards believe the hybrids destroyed him, like with Marn."

"Oh, Marn..." Taylin's face droops. "I haven't visited him in days. He needs company."

"Yes. Anyway, the immortal in the tunnel is nearly finished. He wants to recruit others to escape and start a revolution on the outside."

Taylin's jaw drops for a split second before she swiftly readjusts her clothes. Any emotion other than anger tends to be perceived as a weakness in her twisted reality. "That explains the dirt stains. So what does this mean? You're sneaking out of here to rebel and fight innocent mortals? As a former mortal, Malin, I can't support this. We don't deserve punishment because these monsters are torturing us."

"Oh trust me, I'm on your side!" I say, wary of Taylin's disdain. She scrutinizes my body language and relaxes. "But maybe we can pretend to agree with him. He has a way out. And if it means helping other innocent immortals escape…"

"What's to say he won't let you through if you don't side with him?"

"He won't know."

"Where is he from? The east? Because if so, his ability gives him a slight advantage."

"Not necessarily. He said northerners are stubborn, so he can't manipulate our perspectives as easily. I do tend to blurt out truths around him, but that's the extent of it."

Taylin nods, then scans the immediate area, a sadness in her intense eyes. "I couldn't find another way out of here. Not without tackling the hybrids. And after seeing Garu with that electrical hand…I'm extremely wary of him. If this tunnel is the way out, I'll fake it until I make it."

Hope flickers in my chest, amplifying my determination to protect those I care about. "It'll be dangerous."

"We'll have to find a way across the waters. Start anew in a different land."

"But mortal blood won't be shed because of us."

With mutual respect, we smile at one another, on the same page for the first time. After a comfortable pause in the conversation, Taylin draws in the dirt with her finger.

"Was the north really as breathtaking as they say it is?"

Given Taylin's youth, how sincerely should I answer? "We were all well-looked after. Delectable meals, beautiful buildings, stunning dresses. It was a life of luxury. But with the good comes the bad. I hated the mortal sacrifices. They were a stupid concept designed to control the masses. I never envisioned myself as godly or powerful and resented being presented as such."

"So you were there when the battle began?"

My gaze drops to my filthy feet, ashamed of what I'm about to confess. "No. I ran away before the uprising. The tension was palpable. Whispers of revenge circulated. I gave the family of mortals I'd befriended my wealth and disappeared without a trace. When I heard the immortals turned on one another after slaughtering all the mortals, I knew it was the beginning of the end. I was already in hiding, for people recognized my...*heritage*. But when the immortal cells were proposed, I knew nothing would be the same. And it was the northerners who brought this tragedy upon us all. Other corners never imagined worshipping immortals. They were respected and would offer sage advice. They were the politicians who prevented war through communication instead of emotion. But they were *never* idolized. Those corners did it right. They lived as one. The northerners messed everything up."

I didn't intend to work myself up, but releasing any bottled frustration over my history has always carried a risk. I never discuss my family, my age, my past. None of it matters now. It was a different lifetime, and it doesn't reflect who I am now.

Gulping back sobs, I blink up at the gray sky to dissuade the tears from rolling down my cheeks.

Taylin, all too familiar with repressing emotion, does nothing to console me. She simply waits until I compose myself, and we move on.

I like that.

After several moments of peace, we're disturbed by foul language.

"I don't want to work down here! You can't make me!"

"Shove it. You'll do as you're told."

Taylin and I glimpse at Mitty, another guard, and three cuffed cannibals who are looking almost plump. Their skin is a pale blue, only highlighting the various cuts and scars on their bare torsos. If Zain's theory is true, I cringe to think how strong cannibals will be with the assistance of a golden band.

"No! I won't do it! I won't do it!"

"One more word out of you and the medic will cut your tongue out!"

This threat works—probably because it holds a lot of merit.

I recognize the bald one who likes to run his mouth, his sharp nose twisted to the side as if recently broken. The other one has thick, black hair that sticks up like he's been electrocuted, but I can't remember if he was part of the group who attacked me. That whole incident is a hazy blur. The third cannibal is a woman with frizzy, brown hair and missing teeth. She's scrawny with an animalistic glint in her eyes.

"Recognize them?" Taylin asks.

"The bald one, yes. The other guy I'm not so sure. The woman is new to me."

We watch as Mitty brings them to the campsite, Garu quick to meet everyone. The bald cannibal scrunches up his face when he spots me.

"You two! It's your fault we're out here!"

"Shut up!" Mitty, displaying an act of violence I haven't seen from him before, punches the bald cannibal in the abdomen. The cannibal falls forward only slightly, then grins mischievously as if enjoying the pain.

"It's nobody's fault," Garu says calmly, his sickening presence enough to subdue the cannibals. "We needed workers, and we heard you were strong. Usually, we don't approve of your kind out here, but desperate times call for desperate measures. If you misbehave in any manner, you will be decapitated. Is that understood?"

A stunned silence befalls the new group.

"Is that even allowed?" The man with black hair glances at Mitty.

"I play by my own rules," Garu says, and they believe it. "Tell me your names."

"7-1-4-8," the bald man replies.

"No." Garu blinks twice, seemingly annoyed by the misunderstanding. "Your *name*."

The cannibals have been here a lot longer than I have—it's evident by their numbers. But in this moment, I sympathize with them. What was once their identity was stolen from them years ago, and to have someone with a shred of humanity request their birth name is quite a disorienting and confronting experience.

"Fello," the bald man says with great reluctance. How long has it been since he's uttered his own name?

"Thrillia," the woman follows.

So they're both from the south. I've not had much to do with southerners, having never visited, but the women all have names ending in 'a' and the men end in 'o'. They also tend to like the letter 'l'.

"Rosh," the last man announces proudly. Although it seems he presented a nickname, I assume he's from the west. They tend to be stouter in that region.

Garu clicks his tongue, committing the names to memory. It's an interesting approach he takes by humanizing us. Then again, everything about Garu is strange.

"Fello, Thrillia, and Rosh," Garu greets. "You will remain cuffed for the first day. Head towards the well to drink. You will begin work immediately."

"What about them?" Fello uses both his hands to point at us, the cuffs rattling with his movements.

"They are not your concern," Garu says. "They are mine. Now get to work. Keep your mouths to yourselves."

Cautious of the sudden freedom, the cannibals remain grouped together and shuffle towards the bridge where Garu's guards await.

Admittedly, coming from a cramped cell block, it is disconcerting when a superior tells you to walk without supervision. It almost feels like a test...or a trick.

"I don't feel comfortable with them around," I mumble, kicking myself for speaking out of place. It's a miracle we're allowed to even rest while the others are working harder than ever before.

"It makes me uneasy, too," Mitty admits. "I could still transfer here, Garu. Specifically, I could keep watch over the cannibals."

"I am more than capable, thank you." Garu folds his arms, scrutinizing Mitty's slumped posture. "However, given you've asked twice in one day, I'm succumbing to curiosity. You may stay for the night. I'll be watching you like a burnapray, though. I always find out ulterior motives."

Mitty's face lights, despite the warning. With a burst of energy, he salutes Garu. "Thank you, sir! Shall I join the other guards on the bridge?"

"No. Go to the top of the hill and ensure the immortals carrying the stones are not injured or toying around. They've slowed down significantly since yesterday."

"Right on it, sir!" Mitty jogs towards his new post, his body swaying side to side with each step.

Garu lets out a low, rhythmic grunt and I assume it's a low chuckle. Arms perpetually crossed, he continues his patrol around the immediate area, his focus predominately on the cannibals who are warily passing along the stones and putting them into place.

It's unsettling, seeing them so far out of their comfort zone. Their usual behavior is terrifying, but at least it's predictable. Watching their obedience is unprecedented. They'll reveal their true natures again. Soon, they'll learn the lay of the land. Soon, they'll starve from the lack of meat they're so accustomed to. Soon, they'll be accustomed to the new rules and happily break them.

They're a ticking time bomb.

∞

THE DAY DRAGS. Taylin and I have exhausted conversation so I've resorted to people watching.

Mitty is in his element, a perpetual grin on his face. It boggles me as to why. His whole demeanor has changed; there's a spring in his step and his forehead isn't crinkled. He appears younger, lighter...*relieved.*

But *why?*

Garu is yelling at the cannibals to work harder. Whenever they so much as look at another immortal, he slaps them across the face, scaring them into submission. They keep their eyes on their feet, knocking into one another as they place the stones.

Rune is having a break at the well. He wipes his mouth and glances over his shoulder. When he notices me watching, he makes a signal with his hand. Frowning, I watch as he repeats the signal, two fists smoothly digging into the ground.

"Dig?" I mouth to him, but I'm not sure he can make it out from the distance.

He points at me, so I look down.

*Oh.*

He nods then returns to the bridge as I contemplate the action. He wants me to uncover the first dead immortal to find out who it is. Is curiosity really worth disrespecting the dead? Or facing the repercussions of getting caught?

So *what* if it *is* a northerner? Doesn't mean I can do anything about it. So *what* if it's someone else? That doesn't help the mystery as to why immortals are dying.

While Taylin dozes, I pull myself up and head towards Mitty.

"Hi," I say.

"Malin!" Shoulders rolled back, he inhales deeply like he's breathing fresh air for the first time. "Tremendous day, is it not?"

"Why did you want to work out here?"

"Many reasons! So many reasons..." Mitty trails off, focusing on the horizon. "How are you feeling?"

"Alive," I say after a pause. "I have a question about the first dead immortal. You mentioned they were well-looked after. Were they northern?"

Reverting to his usual uneasy state, he clears his throat and averts my gaze. "I'm not sure. My department don't manage those in the tower. It's prohibited. Even the delivery guards don't enter the top headquarters. They drop off food and leave."

I furrow my brow, then look up at the menacing tower, the purple haze drifting out of the open window. "So nobody knows who lives up there?"

"It's the superiors. Those who control the prison. But no, I have never met them. Word is, they changed hands recently. Something's coming. The prisoners inside are getting stronger and more coherent. I know I'm not safe in those walls anymore. If there's an uprising, they will kill all the mortals in the prison. We've turned them into monsters. Centuries of mistreatment will certainly change their mindsets." Mitty glances down the hill towards the shrubbery where Zain's hidden tunnel is concealed. "Why don't you ask the other prisoners who the dead body is? They buried them."

"I don't get a chance to speak to them. And when I do, they're quite flippant," I confess. "Do you really think there will be an uprising inside the prison?"

"Yes. Call it instinct. Call it paranoia. But something is coming. The thing is, I agree with the immortals. They *should* fight back. I just don't want to be there when it happens because I won't survive it." He swivels his short neck, checking the area. "Garu is busy. The guards are distracted. If it's that important you find out who the first dead immortal is, dig now. I won't look."

My stomach lurches at the thought. "Does it really matter who it is?"

"Any information is power. I'll leave it at that." He turns his back to me, finishing the conversation.

I'm quick to slink away and return to Taylin, my mind swarming with various outcomes. Skidding to my knees, I shake her shoulder.

"Tay, wake up. Wake up."

She groans and opens one eye. "What?"

"Help me exhume the first dead immortal."

The statement is enough for her to open both eyes. "Have you lost your mind? Are you dehydrated? Go drink!"

"I'm serious," I whisper. "We're on a severe time limit. The others are working and Garu is distracted with the cannibals. It's now or never."

"Why is it important?"

"Because Mitty said information is power, and he thinks something is coming. Please. We need to know what's killing immortals. You or Rune could be next. Either cover me or help me."

Begrudgingly, Taylin pulls herself into a sitting position and waits for me to lead the way. I scurry towards the first mound, which has been significantly flattened in comparison to the second grave.

"My fingers are still destroyed," Taylin mumbles as she reluctantly scratches at the dirt. "Great. It's worse than I remember."

"I know, it's awful," I agree, wincing as I join in. "At least it's not as deep. We just need to see the face. That's all."

We work as covertly as possible, taking turns to keep a lookout and rest our hands. It doesn't take long to dig at least. I anticipate a rotting corpse, but we must still be at surface level. We dig deeper. Deeper. Sweat rolls down our noses and into the grave.

And there's still no corpse. No bones. Nothing.

"This is impossible," I say breathlessly. "Seriously. They buried the first dead immortal here. There's a grave. The body can't decompose in a month. There'd be remnants."

Frustrated, Taylin reaches in the hole and rummages. "Hmm. There's definitely nothing in here."

"I can't believe it." Listless, I lean back. "Maybe this was the wrong spot?"

"There are two mounds in this campsite. One where we buried the last guy, and this one. Maybe Garu lied. Maybe they never buried the immortal here."

"Why would he lie?" I ask. "That doesn't make sense. Maybe the immortal faked their death and escaped?"

Taylin shrugs, not that invested in the scandal. "All possibilities. Either way, there is a non-existent dead immortal in this grave. Nobody seems to know who they are. They were supposedly buried instead of cremated. And yet there's no body. Definitely a conspiracy. Just goes to show you can't trust anyone or anything here."

Truer words have never been spoken. We quickly throw the dirt back into the hole. Before I have a chance to speak to Mitty again, Rune pretends to drink at the well again, then sneaks towards us, checking over his shoulder.

"Well? Anything? I can't stay long."

"There's no corpse," I say breathlessly, sitting on the pile of dirt to try to flatten it. "There's nothing there."

Rune blinks. "What? Like a fake grave? You sure you dug in the right place?"

"Where else would it be?" I wave at the flat surfaces. "You're on good terms with the other prisoners. Can you check with them? I mean, did they even bury a body?"

"Yes, yes. They say they did! It was a few days before I came here! That's why I thought now would be a good time to investigate. After I signaled to you, I had a chance to ask Halla while Garu kicked the cannibal for trying to lick a guard. The first dead immortal was a short, pale woman in a blue dress." Rune runs his sweaty fingers through his hair. "Then I shut up because Garu turned and gave us a threatening look. Halla wouldn't lie. What could no corpse mean?"

"And Halla knows nothing else about this woman?" I press, conscious of the time limit.

"No. The guards dropped off the body. They buried her. That was it. Halla didn't mention injuries or anything. Just that she dressed well and seemed well-fed." Rune gulps. "I better get back. Speak soon."

He bolts to the bridge, leaving Taylin and me alone once again.

"Well?" She drops to her side and returns to a curled-up position. "What do you think this all means?"

I hate questions that don't have direct answers. I glance at Garu on the bridge. I watch the prisoners hard at work. I turn to face the tower. Then my focus lands on the smiling Mitty, the man with the sudden shift in personality.

"It means somebody is lying."

# CHAPTER XIII

Lying wedged between Rune and Taylin during the night is surprisingly comfortable, as I nuzzle into their bodies for warmth. The chains around our necks are endlessly annoying, but I've come to terms with it. It's vital to pick your battles.

I stir from my slumber when something close by smacks its lips together, humming quietly. Lifting my head to get a better look, I gape at Rosh who has one hand over a squirming immortal's mouth while gnawing on her arm.

Before I even cry out for Garu, he whips through the camp like a tornado, kicking Rosh in the face with his boot. Rolling backward and landing on his side, Garu bends over and wraps his electric hand around Rosh's throat. Tiny sparks flash and Rosh spasms in his grasp, froth bubbling at his lips.

Garu releases Rosh who instantly collapses, twitching and spasming. A fatal blow for any mortal; absolute torture for an immortal.

Locking eyes with Garu, he glares at me as he returns to his post. "Go back to sleep."

I dare not disobey. I try to find the victim in the crowd of sleeping bodies and notice her curled over on her side, nursing her bleeding arm. Through sobs, she snuggles into the closest immortal. If I could physically move from my position, I'd comfort her. The poor thing needs a medic.

"Garu," I whisper. "We're all tied up. Rosh can still reach her. He'll attack again."

"Go back o sleep!" he grunts. "That thing won't be moving anytime soon."

It's wise to trust Garu on matters such as this, especially if I wish to avoid his electrical jolts. He doesn't appear to be in the mood for backchat. Maybe it's because he doesn't sleep. Anyone would be grumpy.

"What happened?" Rune mumbles, his eyes fluttering open.

"Shh," I say. "Rosh was trying to eat an immortal."

"What?" Rune almost shouts. Desperate to keep him quiet, I kick him in the shin.

"It's all right. Garu stopped him." I hesitate, trying to avoid eye contact with Garu, flitting over his post and back to Rune. "You know, I don't think mortals can physically stay awake for as long as Garu has. It's tricky even as an immortal."

Yawning, Rune scratches at his head. "What are you saying? Do you think he's an immortal? That's impossible. He's a guard."

I motion towards Mitty who is standing by the other guards, but has fallen asleep standing up. "He controls the hybrids. He has electricity coming out of his hand. He seems to puppeteer the other guards. He makes me physically ill if he stares at me. Whatever he is, he's not one of us. Mortal or immortal."

My heart hammers as I utter the words, terrified of what Garu might do if he overheard me. Rune processes the observation, picking at his dry lips. "I guess the real question we should be asking is whether he's on our side or not."

"He's a guard," I say automatically. "He's our enemy."

"Mitty's a guard. He's been our helper," Rune counters. "Life isn't so black and white, Mal. Just check out the shades of blue in the night sky. There are a lot of layers. A lot of depth. A lot of variety. If there's all that in a color, imagine how complex a personality is."

His answer silences me, which is probably for the best. Wearily, he flashes me a weak smile and returns to his deep slumber, leaving me alone with my thoughts.

I don't know who or what to trust anymore. I don't know who I identify as; an immortal or mortal. I feel like I don't know anything.

As I spiral into an existential crisis, lost in the otherworldly constellations above, I'm dragged back into reality by the sound of hybrids howling nearby. I bolt upright, choking myself on the chains.

"Garu!" I'm not quiet this time. I don't want to come face to face with those beasts again.

The majority of immortals stir, half their faces smeared in the dirt with tiny, rocky bumps imprinted on their cheeks.

Garu doesn't respond, but he motions at the other guards to follow.

"Stay here." He hits Mitty between his pecks, jolting him awake. Mitty's eyes almost pop out of their sockets, but he is quick to stand his ground and watch the rest of us.

The immortals murmur to one another, suddenly feeling extremely exposed out here, tied to our posts with our watchers gone. I don't have much faith in Mitty's ability to ensure our safety from something as vicious as the hybrids.

I've never wanted Garu by my side more than I do now.

"Calm down," Mitty spits, approaching us carefully. "We only get one shot at this."

"One shot?" I repeat, gawking at Mitty who crouches down to unchain the immortal closest to him. "Mitty? What's going on?"

He places a finger to his lips, unchaining the second immortal. What is he *doing*? The guards might behead him for such a betrayal! Is he seriously aiding an escape?

"Mitty, mate! We have sixty seconds!" A flustered voice calls in the darkness.

I twist my body to locate the owner, and covered head to toe in the dirt is Zain; his filthy beard thicker than ever before. He jogs towards the camp holding a saw. I have no idea where he got it from, but no doubt he found various tools left scattered around the bridge.

He begins hacking at the chains, releasing confused immortals one by one.

"Zain?" Rune waves from our position.

"Hi, buddy. Thanks for all the food. Everyone listen to me. The second you're released," he grunts with each saw, "run downhill where you'll find shrubbery. Beneath it is a tunnel. Begin the descent and we'll make our way to freedom. We will be back for the others and find those still hiding across the land. Then we shall start our revolution."

"What about our neckbands? They'll track us!" A panicked immortal cries as her chain snaps in half.

"Yeah, we'll see," Zain says as he approaches Rune, sawing into the rusty shackles. "Mitty reckons they don't have the technology for that; that it was fearmongering to dissuade escape. It was Mitty's idea to give us the golden bands to keep us strong."

"It was your idea, Zain. And a great one," Mitty adds.

"Yeah, but you executed it! You got the guards to listen! Whatever lies you told them worked!"

"Thirty seconds," Mitty says, unlocking one last immortal, turning on his heel. "It's now or never, Zain!"

The chain splits, freeing Rune. Zain stands up and motions at Rune, leaving Taylin and me still tied to our posts.

Mitty herds the ten freed immortals towards the hill, following them into the darkness. He doesn't glance back. He doesn't hesitate.

He leaves us...

...*that's* why he wanted a transfer...

...he's nothing more than Zain's puppet...

Zain offers Rune his hand, glancing over his shoulder at the sound of Garu's footsteps returning. "Quick, buddy."

Conflicted, Rune looks back and forth at the hand and me. Clenching his jaw, he shakes his head furiously. "No. No, I can't leave them behind."

Zain drops his hand, his tone callous. "Foolish choice. You better find a way to escape before the visitors arrive across the bridge. Mitty says they're mortals who know how to kill immortals permanently. This prison is a death camp. Good luck."

His final words are flippant, his face scrunched up into a disgusted expression. He speeds away, running faster than anybody I've ever seen.

Rune sits up, rubbing his throat in disbelief. There are only half of us left—Taylin, Rune, the three cannibals, and about five others I never learned the names of.

A perplexed Garu and his fellow guards run uphill back to their posts, their eyebrows raised in unison at the abandoned camp. Mortified, Garu approaches me, sparks flying out of his hand. Grabbing me around the throat, I squeal at the thought of him strangling me the way he did the cannibal.

"*WHERE ARE THEY?!*" His spit flies into my face as veins pulsate in his temples.

"I...I..." I can't get the words out.

Distraught by the fact one shock could kill me, Rune stands and boldly taps Garu on his shoulder. "Sir! Please, let her go!"

Turning on Rune, Garu releases me and clasps his huge hand around Rune's tiny neck. Choking on air, I feel Taylin place a tender hand on my back.

"*WHY AREN'T YOU TIED? WHO DID THIS?*" Garu screams at Rune, his voice giving us shell shock. Rune can't formulate words either, his breath caught in his throat.

"A prisoner released us," I speak on Rune's behalf, terrified for his safety. Garu could quite easily behead him here and now. "I'm not sure who he was. He sawed the chains, and they fled with him. Except for Rune. Rune decided to stay."

Garu listens intently, snarling at Rune. "Foolish boy."

Rune is dropped to the dirt, tight gasps escaping his windpipe. When he recovers from the assault, he scurries back toward me and holds my hand.

Garu paces back and forth, his anxiety boiling. I get the impression he's never experienced such a disaster.

"It was that easterner, wasn't it? He took that pliable guard!" Garu halts in place and screams at the stars, his goons standing motionless in a line behind him. "You. Malin. You know where his hideout is. Take me."

Oh, no please. *Please*, no more targets on my head. My throat still burns, his imprint still sizzled into my skin. "Excuse me?"

"Don't act coy. You were covered in dirt when you returned to camp. Where is his tunnel?"

"I...I..."

"Don't let his eastern ability manipulate you into hiding the truth! That man is a danger to all of us! If he starts a revolution, he will be the cause of a mass war, segregating all corners! Needless deaths, including mortal children, will be on *your* hands if you don't tell me where the tunnel is!"

And with that, all attention is officially on me. Confused faces urge me to speak up, their peer pressure overwhelming.

How can Garu possibly know Zain's plan, or the alleged outcome? More importantly, what happens if I show him where the tunnel is? Will he punish those who escaped? Will he close up the entrance making future escape for Taylin, Rune and me impossible?

"It's on the slope," I say, wincing as I speak. No matter my choice, it's a mistake. "Beneath the bushes."

"Don't lie to me."

"She's not!" Rune jumps in. "Look, I'll take you to it. I, I don't think you guys will fit. It's pretty narrow. Mitty will be struggling. But I can show you where it is."

"Mitty?" An agitated Garu runs his hands through his short hair. "The guard?"

"That's what we call him."

Rolling his eyes, Garu begins walking, his goons close behind. "Absurdity. He's beyond brainwashed. The idiot will die first. Lead the way."

Without another word, Rune nervously hops forward with the guards close on his heels.

I feel sick to my stomach, and not because of Garu's overbearing presence in the vicinity, but because I ratted somebody out. Because I destroyed our only chance at escape. Because I was left behind. Because now we're left alone with three cannibals.

We lay tied to our posts, listening for any clue as to what's going on. But they're too far away to hear anything. Not a voice carried in the light breeze. Not the sounds of struggle or confrontation.

Turning to face Taylin, I gape at her white lips. The girl looks so different drained of blood—her spark, her zest, her *fire* drained with it.

"Are you all right?" I ask.

"I don't know," she says. "Not the best way to wake up. What did Zain say about the visitors?"

"That they're coming across the bridge we're building. He warned us of their arrival, something about them permanently killing us."

Her eyes water with hopelessness, her bottom lip quivering. She's never looked so small in this moment. "We're dead no matter what. If we ran with them tonight...if we stay and complete the bridge...we're dead, regardless."

Nothing I can say will console her—because she's right.

A revolution will end in war.

Submission will end in death.

There's only one thing that could give us a glimmer of hope, but I don't think I'm capable of such a sacrifice.

I couldn't do it hundreds of years ago and I don't think I can do it now.

But I could be left with no choice. There might be only one way to set things right.

I'll have to reclaim my birthright and claim my throne to do it.

And the thought terrifies me.

# CHAPTER XIV

Garu throws obscenities about as they return to the camp, kicking at the dust like a petulant child.

"We'll never reach them!"

I don't want to give Garu ideas, but I wonder if he has bombs or ammunition that could prevent the group from tunneling any further.

"I will not obliterate them, Malin!" Garu snaps at me and I stare at the furious guard, wondering if I said something out loud.

"I...sorry?"

"You heard me!" Garu snaps, his thick boots hammering against the earth as he walks. "Hybrids won't fit in the hole, either. Pursuit is useless. That prisoner really thought of everything as he constructed the escape. And right under my nose. I was certain the hybrids got to him so I stopped listening. Rotten easterners! We must complete the bridge. The guests will fix everything. Everyone up! We must continue construction! Northerners, no more rest. We need you."

My stomach churns at the thought of hastening the process, especially if these guests truly are on route to permanently killing the immortals. Rune looks physically ill, his forehead crinkled as he stands next to the guards, dwarfed by their gigantic builds.

Within seconds, we are released from our chains, unused to such a procedure in the middle of the night.

"No time will be wasted," Garu continues. "We will finish the bridge!"

Taylin nudges me as if to say she has no intention of completing it. As we stand, the guards hurriedly throw down stale loaves of bread —a bigger share than usual. Despite the ungodly hour, we shovel it down and are physically pushed towards the bridge.

Rune gathers next to me, his voice tight. "The guards closed the tunnel entrance."

"Why didn't Garu stop the prisoners?" I ask, coughing up crumbs.

"They tried. No guard could fit. Garu sent down electrical shocks, but it didn't seem to do much. He said...he said he *read Zain's mind*. He saw the future Zain envisioned. Can mortals do that? Can *immortals* do that? Isn't that impossible?"

Gobsmacked, I stare at the bridge as we stride closer. "I...I mean, nothing is impossible. But...that...I mean, no. No, Garu shouldn't have the ability. Certainly not. But he also shouldn't be able to send electricity from his hand."

Rune doesn't react, keeping his face neutral as we approach the bridge. I have no idea what I'm supposed to do. My experience thus far has involved transporting heavy rocks. Beyond that basic ability, my bridge-building knowledge is zero. I hope I can utilize the same skill by fitting the blocks together, especially considering today is the first time I've woken up feeling semi-normal. The dizziness has mostly subsided, replaced by ravenous hunger instead.

I can't speak for Taylin. She looks like a walking corpse, her eyes dark and vacant. I'm surprised by how lengthy her recovery is. Even I, a mortal, am coping better.

"We're sabotaging this bridge, right?" Rune says out the corner of his mouth. "Slow it down. Make mistakes. Whatever it takes. We can't let the visitors cross."

"We destroy it," Taylin corrects, her fiery spirit suddenly alight. "Watch it crumble."

"How?" I ask, careful of my volume. Garu's outburst and alleged mind-reading abilities have me on edge.

Rune scopes the bridge. "I'll climb down and knock out the columns. Don't stand in the middle of the bridge. Keep to the edge and delay as much as you can."

"I'll help," Taylin says, her voice raspy.

"Me too," I say.

"No," Rune dismisses. "You're the mortal. If anything falls on us, we'll find a way out. Keep watch for us."

Nodding, I find the pile of stone and lift a smaller one as Taylin and Rune slink into the darkness and scale down the bridge until they're in the gully, finding ways to knock down the hastily constructed columns.

Riddled with anxiety, I constantly bump into other tired immortals who are speedily carrying stones and stacking them into place. They dare not speak, avoiding eye contact with Garu and the guards, but their disheartened expressions say it all. I can practically hear their silent screams as they curse the universe for not being included in the great escape, wondering what they'd done to deserve such awful misfortune.

The bridge shifts ever so slightly. Too immersed in their task, the other immortals don't seem to notice the tremor. I can't see Taylin and Rune from this angle, but the bridge at this stage is only held up by those columns. Break those, and everything falls.

"Malin! Hop to it!" Garu shouts when he notices I've come to a standstill. Eager to avoid conflict, I nod and rush to the center of the bridge and place a stone. I still can't see Taylin or Rune, but I run back to safety to collect another. If I can time it so I'm not on the bridge when it collapses, then everything will be fine. An immortal barges into me and steals a stone I was considering selecting. I barely recognize her face against the dull glow of the neckband, but Thrillia's harsh glare cuts me deep. It's hurtful to be so hated for no reason.

As I carry a stone along the half-completed bridge, a violent tremor shakes all of those on it.

The immortals instantly stop what they're doing, frozen in fear, midway through their task.

Garu curses and bolts towards us, leaping onto the bridge. He tugs on the prisoners closest to him and shoves them to safety. "Get off! Get off!"

Panicked, I leap off the bridge and roll onto the dead grass, my long limbs a blessing in scenarios like this. On my side, I watch as Garu manages to aid four immortals just as the bridge gives out. As the stones crumble and the shape of the bridge reduces to rubble, Garu catapults towards me, half of his body dangling off the side. He attempts to protect his head as small debris flies upwards, and I do the same, peeking through the gaps in my fingers. I scream as a rock flies towards the back of his head, knocking him out cold for several seconds.

In the silence, I crawl to Garu, who is now conscious, but struggling to come to. His large body begins to slide off the edge, but I'm quick to latch onto his arms, moaning as I drag him away from the cliff.

Ears ringing against the deafening destruction, I check for the others. All the guards are gone. Vanished into thin air. Three immortals lay on what's left of the grass, staring at the chaos. The fourth is the cannibal Fello, a devilish gleam in his eyes as he grins at the destroyed bridge.

A small shriek escapes my throat as I think of Rune and Taylin. Did they find safety in the gully? Please tell me they're not trapped beneath the rubble with the other immortals who didn't get off the bridge in time. I couldn't live with myself.

"Are you all right, Garu?" I ask, but he doesn't have the energy to respond. No doubt he needs medical attention, but I can only think of my friends. "I'll be right back. Promise."

I climb down the gully, fumbling and slipping on damp walls. Sliding to the bottom, I cringe at the moans and sobs of the immortals caught in the debris. A couple of feet hang out, sandwiched between rock and earth.

"Taylin? Rune?" I cough as I dig through the rubble. "Say something!"

"*Something!*" a deliberately high-pitched voice mocks. Glancing over my shoulder, I find a stern Thrillia clenching her fists. "Just you and me, freak. Guards are dead. Immortals are buried. Me? Well li'l ol' me is *starving*. Famished. Bread? *Stale* bread? Are they *kidding?* I desire flesh. Meat. Warmth. *Fresh.* And I'm hungry for the fight."

"Please don't, Thrillia," I warn, emotion bubbling in my chest. "This is a tragedy. We need to help them!"

"Why?" She shrugs, her aloofness unsettling. "My fellow cannibals are weak. Trapped meals will be easier on their stomachs."

"One of the cannibals is *in* there!" I scream. "You're prepared to eat your own? You're not going to help? Don't they mean anything to you?"

"You're joking, right?" Thrillia is suddenly perplexed, taking an unsteady step towards me, unbalanced for some reason. Perhaps she's just as weak as the others. "Do they mean anything to me? Hmm, let's allow that to sink in. Do. *They?* Mean *anything.* To *me?*" She places a theatrical finger to her chin. "That would be a huge, resounding no. See, kid, it's a hybrid-eat-hybrid world out there. When you're immortal, you can't get attached to anything. People and materials rot around you in what feels like months. And when you become like me, eating your own kind out of desperation and boredom, there's no turning back. You see the fragility in our existence. The hopelessness. The absurdity. Nothing matters. Don't you understand that? *Nothing* matters! Not me. Not you. Not any of those poor bastards trapped under the bridge. The only thing that matters at this moment is my unrelenting hunger. My animalistic ambition to survive overpowers the analytical mindset. I *want* to give up. But what's the point? The alternative is even worse than this. It's death upon death upon death with no release. So it's every immortal for themselves, no matter how pointless their existence may be. And I'm starving."

She's finished with the conversation. Leaning to the side, she flicks up dirt with her hands and throws it directly into my face, temporarily blinding me.

Flailing as I stumble backward, I yell out in pain as I land on the debris, the arch in my back crunching from the impact.

Within moments, Thrillia is on top of me, her teeth bared and her face savage. For somebody so little, she's remarkably strong. I free one hand from her sweaty grip and swing an awkward punch, but it doesn't even leave a mark. She grabs my arm and bites into it, ripping into the skin.

I scream at the blood, a little surprised to see so much of it has regenerated. Not that it matters now. This abhorrent being will eat me alive unless I wriggle out of her strong grip.

*Mind over matter, Malin. Mind over matter…*

Drawing on the little energy I can muster, I use my leg and lift, propelling her into the air. The folks from her corner are small—usually no taller than five feet, three inches, but they make up for it with power and speed. She lands on her feet and springs towards me just as I manage to stand up.

*She's tiny, Malin. She's tiny. I can do this.*

Ignoring the throbbing sensation in my arm, I pick up a small stone as a weapon, anticipating the moment I get to slam it into her temple.

Thrillia weaves towards me, bounding over the debris. I utilize my long limbs and kick the air where she would've jumped, stopping her in midair. She lands flat on her back, but rolls out of the way before I can stomp my foot.

In that slight second of hesitation, she's already climbed up the collapsed bridge and leaped onto my back, gnawing into my neck.

Too surprised to vocalize, I run backward, crushing her into the debris behind us. She slides off my back and remains in a heap on the ground.

"It's pointless," she says, looking up at me with tired eyes. "We could literally fight forever."

"For you maybe," I say, tightening my grip around my makeshift weapon. "I gave up my immortality."

There's a hint of surprise in Thrillia's tense face, but she relaxes when she smiles. "No, you didn't. You're not mortal."

"Yes, I am."

"Being a cannibal has given me a sixth sense for these sorts of things. Mortals smell better. At least, in here they do. The guards have blood constantly pumping through their veins. The few mistakes that have been made when they imprisoned a mortal were some of the best meals we've ever had. We licked the bones clean because they were fresh. The immortals in here are old. Stale. Dry. They smell that way, too. And they're impossible to digest fully because even in their weakness, their bodies regenerate before we can get to their bones. It's exhausting. Their eyeballs are delicious, though. Those don't grow back. But you, Malin? You don't smell *or* taste like a mortal."

If she's trying to distract me with bamboozlement, it's working. "Maybe it has something to do with the fact I *was* an immortal because I can wholly confirm that my infinite youth has come to an end."

Why? Why do I bother to engage? Thrillia only smirks and pulls the same trick; throwing dirt into my face. I don't react as poorly, but it's still enough time for the cannibal to wrap her arms around my waist and charge me into the ground. She scrambles onto my abdomen, a sense of déjà vu as she pins my arms and sinks her teeth into my throat.

"Cut it out," a gruff voice orders.

Thrillia's face is smeared with my blood, and I dread the inevitable grisly end. She pulls herself off of me and stands tall for a microsecond before she convulses and drops to the ground, foam frothing at her mouth.

Placing pressure around my neck, I sit up and find Garu limping forward, electrical sparks flying out of his hand.

"Garu!" I say. "You're concussed! You must rest!"

"Show me your neck," he instructs, towering over me. When I gently release pressure, he nods. "That's not so bad. Keep your hand on the wound. It will heal."

"Great." I fumble as I stand, concerned about the immortals trapped in the remains of the bridge. Their cries are getting weaker. "Taylin! Rune!"

"Shh!" Garu demands, his glassy eyes focused on the debris. "You can't stay here."

"I know. I'm sorry for climbing down here. I truly am, but we need to get you to the medic. And we need others to come so we can rescue the immortals!"

"They're good as dead," Garu says, deadpan as always. "The bridge is destroyed. Immortals are trapped. You can't stay here."

Blinking at his brevity, I dismiss his answer. "Taylin and Rune should be around here somewhere. Please, sir, if you'll let me search for them, we can collectively carry you to the infirmary. You shouldn't be walking with a concussion!"

"Malin!" It's the first time I've heard true inflection in his voice—frustration, intensity, and hopelessness combined. I recoil at the tone. "Listen to me! *You. Can't. Stay. Here.*"

I glance at Thrillia, hoping she stays incapacitated for as long as I live. "Why?"

He wraps a firm hand around my arm, squeezing it gently. "It isn't safe."

I don't know what to say. His sense of urgency implies something drastic, but *nothing* has been safe since I arrived. Why is my protection only now vital? And what about the others? These are all questions I don't have the opportunity to ask as he drags me towards the debris and orders me to climb up, which proves difficult when one hand is practically glued to my neck wound.

When we reach the top, the four prisoners are still in their place. Something is off about them. It's like they're sedated...

"Are they coming with us?" I ask.

"No." Garu speaks out of the corner of his mouth, his gaze on the tower which overlooks the prison.

"Don't they need to be safe too?"

"They'll aid in retrieving what's left of the crushed prisoners."

"I can help."

"No!" Garu snaps, tightening his gaze around my arm as I unsuccessfully dig my heels into the dirt. "You saved me when you didn't need to. I could've fallen and severely injured myself. For that, I must protect you to show my gratitude."

I'm not buying his excuse. Twisting in his grip, I peer over my shoulder at the mess. Surely Rune and Taylin are fine...surely...

"Where are the other guards?" I ask, having not seen them since the collapse.

"They'll return," Garu utters under his breath, ending the conversation.

I pick up the pace to keep up with his gait, wincing whenever a pained cry echoes through the gully.

"Why were the uninjured immortals languid?" I ask, thinking of their overly relaxed state. "Did you do something to them?"

"Yes," Garu replies. "I haven't got the other guards to help me and I need to escort you. They're in a meditative trance."

My mouth hangs open, as I feel both fearful and fascinated. "What *are* you?"

The questions unnerve him, as he sniffs and pulls me closer. "Somebody who doesn't care for your friends who destroyed the one chance we had at saving your people."

I try to calm my pulse, worried that it'll intensify the blood already trickling out of my neck. But I can't help it. Breaths heavy, I attempt to analyze his words but I'm unable to form a coherent sentence.

"What?"

"Rune. Taylin. I overheard their thoughts when it was too late. That bridge was a one-way ticket to freedom. Now be quiet."

We approach the all-too-familiar cage which houses thousands of innocent immortals. Instead of carrying on through the double doors and down the steps to the infirmary, we enter through a side door. We continue up a narrow, spiral staircase, where the cracked cement turns to uneven stone, step by step.

There's no natural light as we proceed upwards, but Garu doesn't slow down. Seeing in the dark must be on his growing list of talents.

We halt at the top where a velvet curtain is drawn. Soothing panpipes are playing, as a hazelnut scent wafts through the air.

Compared to the blood, sweat and vomit I've been inhaling every day for the last month, this aroma leaves me practically floating.

"Permission to enter?" Garu projects over the panpipes, which stop at the sound of his voice. In the silence, I hear a soft bubbling, but a three-note melody answers Garu. The notes must grant us access, because Garu pulls back the curtain and we step inside.

I'm amazed by the luxurious interior. The room is circular, so I assume we're at the top of the tower which overlooks the prison. Plush, white rugs are laid over the stone where a pretty woman lays with the panpipes pressed against her lips.

She smiles, shifting into a more comfortable position. She is neatly spread out next to a roaring fire; the flames a striking violet against a cauldron. Her golden hair is wrapped in a beaded snood, which matches her crimson dress. I have flashes of my past, as I recall resenting the abysmal accessory. Eventually, I ended up cutting my hair off, much to the dismay of my family, just so I didn't need to wear the expected dress code.

"Hello Garu. Excuse my informal manner," she says, motioning at her position. Gracefully, she pulls herself up to sit and gently taps the rug. "Please, take a seat."

"Unfortunately I can't stay," Garu says, his voice tender; an unsettling contrast to his usual demeanor. "My guards have evaporated due to the shock of the collapse and the prisoner's trance won't maintain without me around."

"I saw," the girl's eyes dart at the circular window where the violet haze drifts out. "By all means, hurry back. We might still have a chance."

Garu bows deeply and releases his grip. "Listen to them, Malin. These are the superiors who run the prison. Respect them."

Turning on his heel, he hurries from the tower without another word. I awkwardly remain in place, taking in the divine I.

My stomach growls at the sight of fruit and meat laid out on the table in the corner. My muscles ache as I long for the four-poster bed. My heart swells at the woman's clean, glowing skin and fresh clothes. Here I am, still clinging to a tattered robe that barely keeps me protected against the elements.

"Malin?" The woman asks. "I am Sharnique, one of the superiors. Please, take a seat so I may inform you of your duties here."

Cautiously, I inch closer and fight the urge to react when my calloused feet land on the gloriously delicate rug. I can't remember the last time I felt anything so pillowy. When I cross my legs, I run my fingers through the fur, wondering if it's real or not.

"We don't kill animals, no matter how much of an annoyance some are," Sharnique says, amused by my puerile actions.

Embarrassed, I shove my hands in my lap and stare into her amber eyes. What corner of the land is she from? Her name isn't like any I've ever heard before.

"It's a pleasure to meet you, Sharnique," I say. "If you don't mind me asking; why have I been brought here?"

With a feminine shrug, she sweeps an imaginary stray hair behind her ear. "Garu's orders. If you save his life, he saves yours. Besides, we are short-staffed. We need a prisoner we can trust to make our beds, serve our meals, braid our hair. Our last one died and we can't have the zombie-like immortals up here. The good news is, you will be provided a decent bed, meals of your own, and a secure environment." She scrutinizes my hideous attire. "And we will be sure to dress you correctly. A shower wouldn't go astray, either. Let me address that wound of yours."

Hoisting herself onto her knees, she leans towards the cauldron and dips her slender hand into the boiling concoction. Without so much as a flinch, she scoops up the gooey substance and nudges my hand away from my neck. She slaps the warm essence onto my flesh, holding it there for a moment.

It's uncomfortably hot, but I try not to move. When Sharnique sits back, I go to caress my wound, only to find spongy skin instead.

"Handy, isn't it?" Sharnique grins, never showing her teeth. "We can't have our maiden in poor condition. I'm not particularly fond of the blue skin either, so after your shower and meal, I will endeavor to regenerate your blood."

"The drained blood wasn't your idea?"

"No!" Offended, she tips her nose in the air. "Certainly not. Neither was the poisoned meals."

Finding comfort in her humanity, I relax enough to let my guard down. "Sharnique, I truly appreciate your hospitality and I promise to serve you well. I only ask that you let me aid my friends trapped beneath the bridge. Taylin and Rune have been good to me and might be possible contenders for serving you here. They're hard workers."

Sharnique's forehead crinkles, a displeased pout forming. "Hmm. The troublemakers. No, Malin. I'm afraid nobody from the labor camp will be joining you. I've watched the easterner and moronic guard escape with half of the laborers, luring the hybrids towards you. Thank goodness Garu knows how to handle those creatures. I witnessed the cannibals causing no end of chaos. Then your friends had the audacity to destroy the bridge you were working on. I've never been exposed to such anarchy. Now we need to construct a speedy alternative so that our guests may visit the prison."

Contemplating the best choice of dialogue, I settle on perhaps the stupidest one. "Who are the guests?"

"Friends," she says casually. "Good friends with a great purpose."

My shoulders roll forward at the thought of my good friends, possibly injured beneath the fallen bridge. I've come to the conclusion I am a terrible companion, forever abandoning my comrades or neglecting my people. I could've fought Garu or denied his request. But I didn't.

"Please, Sharnique. I can't bear to think of my friends suffering down there." Timidly, I tent my fingers, slowly bringing them together so that I'm physically pleading. "I beg of you. They've become my family. How is it fair that I'm here while they're there?"

"Life isn't fair," she says curtly. "You will soon learn, Malin, that certain circumstances are out of your control. The sooner you accept it, the better. There will be sacrifices that must be made for the greater good."

"Is there any good left in the world?" I ask quietly, the hazelnut scent no longer comforting.

"Pardon?"

"Is there any good left in the world?" I repeat, instantly regretting the rhetorical question.

Sharnique ponders this for a moment, a sly smile on her lips. "There will be good again. Once balance has been restored. At the moment, there is no north, which means no wealth to be distributed to the others. The whole land is in a recession. To add insult to injury, it's mortals versus immortals. We are in a time of great unease, but our friends can help that. Once we purge this immortal issue once and for all, we will live in harmony." She stands, her long skirt flowing by her ankles, nonchalant despite my horrified expression. "We shall discuss this no further. Not at this moment. Apologies for my forwardness, but your body odor is beginning to distress me. Follow me to the showers."

I comply, excited by the prospect of being clean, but wish I had the courage to press for details about her 'friends'. Zain said the guests planned on killing the immortals permanently. Has this woman unknowingly confirmed that? Have I misinterpreted her? Where do I stand?

Guiding me through the circular room, we reach another doorway blocked by a golden velvet curtain. She sweeps it to the side, and I duck as I follow her into the showers.

There are golden tiles in place of the stone, and one large bathtub in the center. To the side is a small table, where soaps and various candles are placed.

My eyes widen at the sight as I'm mentally teleported back home, where we were spoiled with riches. It's such an old memory that I sometimes fear I've imagined it.

"Is that...for me?" I ask in disbelief.

"Yes, you can draw it yourself. You're our servant, remember. I will, however, do the polite thing and gather your new clothes. That will be the last thing I do for you, mind."

"Didn't you say there were other superiors?" I glance around the room, searching for signs of life.

"Yes. They're busy. We have three rooms dedicated to hygiene." She reaches up to a shelf, where towels and sheets have been neatly folded. Her fingers land on a violet towel, swiftly grabbing it and handing it to me. "Please use twenty minutes to clean yourself thoroughly. The others will not be as forgiving of the stench."

With a half-hearted smile, she flounces out of the room. When she doesn't return, I sit on the edge of the bath and turn the golden tap. Water streams out of the faucet, filling the tub. I genuinely can't remember the last time I had a bath. Years, of course, but the actual number eludes me. I've only ever had quick showers, usually in the wilderness when I was certain nobody was following me.

Steam soon fills the room, pink bubbles foaming in the water from soap that was already sitting in the bottom of the tub.

Uncertainly, I strip naked and drop my robe on the floor. I feel like I'm stealing or doing something wrong. Lifting my foot, I dangle my toe in the water to test the heat, which is just right. Stepping into the bath, I slide down, immersed in the bubbly warmth.

Exhaling at the relaxing sensation, I allow grateful tears to roll down my cheek. It's remarkably easy to take something as simple as a bath for granted. Never will I do that again.

Massaging my head with the soap, I soak in the aromas. Dirt, grease, and blood slip off my skin and into the water. I'm still a dull blue, but portions of my body are regaining a healthy glow as my cells regenerate.

Twenty minutes pass far too quickly. I could've stayed in the little slice of paradise all day, and probably would've if not for Sharnique bursting through the curtain. A navy dress in a similar style to her own dangles from her index fingers and thumbs. She's holding it as if it's diseased.

"This will be your uniform. I much prefer blue cloth to blue skin, anyway. Quickly now, towel yourself off and get dressed. Do you still stink?"

"I don't think so." I reach for the towel, stealthily covering up my body while still in the bath. Fumbling to protect my modesty, I stand and step out, dripping all over the floor. I've never felt more disrespectful than I do now, as I approach a stranger in the nude. "Thank you."

She's out of the door as soon as soon as I receive the dress. I'm relieved to find that attached beneath the gown are undergarments. I've become accustomed to the lack of support, but it'll be a relief to walk without the incessant jiggling around my chest.

Drying off my hair and skin, I smile. This is too good to be true, surely.

The dress and undergarments fit perfectly, and I jump up and down to test the support. My jiggly girls are nice and secured, so I'm feeling good.

Picking up my old robe and towel, I return to the circular room where Sharnique is back in her position in front of the fire.

"Throw that robe and towel in here," she says without turning to look at me. She lazily points at the flames. "They won't be of much use anymore. Please help yourself to the food at the table. Once you are fed, you will begin your services."

It feels so wasteful to burn a towel. And suffice it to say, I'm slightly remorseful to watch my robes disintegrate into nothing. They've represented immense suffering, utter strength, and conviction. Now, they're part of the flames, reduced to ash.

Concealing my sadness, I head to the table and relish in the choice of food. Fresh fruit, pastries, cheese, salads, and sea creatures galore. This is so much better than when we stole from the guard's buffet. In the center of the table is a glass vase with three lavender flowers, their sweet scent masked by the treats. They're the first flora I've seen in a while, their vibrant color and blossomed petals oddly calming.

But enough flower admiration. There's food, and I intend to eat as much of it as possible.

Filling my mouth and my stomach, I fall into a state of pure ecstasy; flavors and textures teasing every sense. Keeping away from the fringle fruit, I hover around the table, wondering if this is an everyday luxury or if I'm being far too greedy.

Sharnique is in a meditative state, mouthing incoherent words next to the fire. Picking at the blueberry muffin, I walk towards an oval window where the violet haze drifts out.

It truly is an incredible view from here. I can see everything. The campsite, the collapsed bridge, the distant forests, tiny specks that are hybrids surrounding the grounds, Taylin...

I almost choke. Spluttering for air, I squint my eyes, focusing on the lanky prisoner who is weakly removing stone and debris from the bridge. She's hunched over, tired and sickly.

And here I am. Clothed. Fed. Bathed. I'm a *monster*...

Other immortals gather in the gully, attempting to help those trapped. Garu is at the top of the gully with two of his guards, their sudden appearance a mystery. They look unharmed but don't move much. Not that they're known for their energetic behavior anyway...

"Are you finished eating?" Sharnique asks, miraculously beside me.

I jolt, so focused on the outside world that I forgot where I was. Swallowing hard, I nod. "Yes."

"Splendid. Your first task is cleaning the bath and disposing of any food you haven't eaten. We will receive new meals this evening."

I glance at the table, mountains of food piled on top of each other. "You're asking me to dispose of that?"

"Yes." She doesn't understand my reluctance. "We're not eating it."

"But we can eat later. Or we can send leftovers to the laborers."

Confused, she tilts her head to the side. "There will always be more food. Dispose of it now. Feed the flames."

Begrudgingly, I return to the table and scoop up several servings.

I'm walking as if I'm on death row, slowly marching towards the fireplace and swaying slightly in front of it.

"Throw it in. We haven't got all day!"

I drop a pastry into the flames, the bright blaze gobbling it up immediately. I'm beginning to wonder if this is actually a fire at all. One by one, I throw perfectly edible food into the violet heat, thinking of all the immortals at the campsite who would benefit from digesting a good meal.

"The fire must always be fed," Sharnique says, her eyes reflecting the glow. "All day, every day."

I don't ask why. Instead, I do as I'm told, albeit reluctantly. When I'm finished disposing of the food, I return to the bath and dry the floors with a fresh towel, throwing it into the fire when I'm finished.

I clean the bath, the walls, and the windows, then return to the circular room where Sharnique sits on the rug, eyes closed.

Sneaking back to the window, I peer down at the campsite. Very little progress has been made as the immortals continue to clear the debris. Taylin is slumped over by the well, her skin pale. If only I could reach out to her. As far as she knows, I'm crushed beneath tons of weight.

"Malin." Sharnique has silently crept to my side once again, a sneaky talent I'm not so fond of. She smooths out the crinkle in her dress. "Please sweep the floors. There is a broom in the cupboard."

"Do I throw the broom into the fire when I'm done?" I ask somewhat facetiously, mentally branding the question as a joke.

"Yes. I appreciate your ability to learn quickly. A new broom will be brought to us tomorrow. When you have finished, wipe down the walls to ensure they are clean. Once everything is complete, you may sleep in that bed."

My head stoops forward. "The four-poster bed?"

"Yes. Our chambers are elsewhere. It is up to you to feed the fire during the night. Do not let it die. Keep it company when I am not here. Do you understand?"

I nod.

"Wonderful." She exhales with a sense of relief. "Over the next few days, you will meet the other superiors. They are extremely busy."

I nod once more and continue my tasks well into the evening. Sharnique doesn't move from her spot. She doesn't leave to use the facilities, to drink or eat. For hours she simply sits and occasionally hums to herself.

Careful not to disturb her when my duties are complete, I climb into the massive bed which overlooks the fire. I hold back a delighted moan as the satin hugs my skin, my backside sinking into the soft mattress. I had a bed like this back in the north, but I'd long forgotten the overwhelming comfort.

Within moments, I drift into a dreamless slumber, Sharnique's gentle hum like a lullaby.

*"Don't let the fire die..."*

CHAPTER 3

XV

I'm oblivious as to who I am, where I am, and what I'm doing when I wake.

It's almost pitch-black, save for a dull purple glow. The covers do nothing to stave off the bitter chill in the air.

Purple glow.

Comfortable mattress.

Oh no.

Scurrying out of bed, I trip over my feet as I hurry to the dying fire.

Don't let the fire die. Don't let the fire die.

"No! No! Sorry, sorry!" I utter, frantically rushing around the room to find objects to burn. What is acceptable? I burned the towels, the food...would bed covers do?

Desperate, I pull off the sheets, pillowcases, the flowers—absolutely anything and toss them into the fireplace. For a moment, I fear the weight of the material did the exact opposite and extinguished the fire entirely.

Anxiously tapping my fingernails onto one another, I drop to my knees and stare into the abyss of the fireplace. When tiny flames spark and feed on the fabric, I sigh.

"I'll just stay here," I speak to the fire. "I'll keep you company as Sharnique said."

Yawning, I curl into a ball on the soft rug and smile as the blaze's warmth embraces the room.

Keep the fire happy. Always keep the fire happy...

∞

THE FOLLOWINGS DAYS give me a strange sense of déjà vu. Sharnique only ever moves from her spot to sleep or change her attire, deep within her mystery chambers.

I bathe, then clean the floors. I eat, then dispose of the leftovers. I sweep, then burn the broom. I sneak to the window and get chastised by Sharnique for doing so. I scrub the walls, then throw the cleaning products into the flames. I greet the guards who arrive with several boxes. I open the packages and replace the towels, covers, brooms, and food that we've destroyed. I tend to the fire. I wake and do it all over again.

Each day I await the arrival of the other superiors, but it's only ever Sharnique and me. We barely talk, existing side by side as ghosts. I'm beginning to feel more like a prisoner than I did in even my worse circumstances.

On the fourth day, Sharnique asks me to braid her golden locks. Nervous, as I've never been much of a hairstylist, I join her on the rug and run my fingers through her hair, wondering how I'm going to pull this off.

"I am not particularly good at this," I finally admit after several failed attempts.

"Keep trying, Malin," Sharnique replies. "We have time. You may learn a new skill today. And if you would like, you can join me in a candid conversation. You have been working silently and proactively. I will reward you with answers. There must be much you want to know. This prison is a mystery to most."

Grateful and admittedly suspicious of her gesture, I mull over the various concerns. "Who is delivering all the supplies to us? The food, the towels?"

"The guards," she replies simply.

"I understand, but where are they getting it from? Isn't the prison underfunded?"

"It was until we took over. We have a lot of wealth, so we ensure that we are taken care of so that the prisoners can be taken care of. We have a storage facility beneath the prison where we stock the supplies. Chefs have recently been...*employed* to cook delicious meals for the thousands of people here."

"What about the laborers?" I ask, glancing at the window. "They only gave us stale bread."

Sharnique shrugs, disinterested in the question. "They're too far away from the prison grounds. That's Garu's area. You haven't asked about the fire. I assumed that would be your first curiosity."

"I wasn't sure you'd answer," I confess, unraveling the messy braid I styled.

Despite only seeing the back of her head, I imagine her smiling somewhat majestically. "The fire and I are united. It gives me power if I give it power. People from my land have the ability to manifest whatever we desire—clothes, premonitions, even people. This gift comes at a price."

"People from your land?" I repeat, stunned by the revelation. I wasn't aware there were lands other than ours. It was an old wives' tale. "Are you not from here?"

"I am from across the water."

I stifle a gasp. There are lands across the water? There were always farcical stories about such places, but nobody ever believed them to be true. "What's it like?"

"Very much like yours, only without the divide between immortals and mortals. Our sources tell us it was due to the corrupt northerners abusing their power. Is this true?"

"Yes, it's true." I feel like I'm betraying my people by speaking ill of them, but facts don't care about feelings. "I shared the authority with my family, but I didn't agree to sacrifice mortals annually. I knew it was just a way to keep control and power. I've always seen mortals as children; they're fragile and young. All I wanted was to protect them. Still do. I stood up to my family, opposing the murders. I was emotionally exiled, so I left soon after. The battle erupted as I watched from afar. It wasn't long until the other corners turned against immortals and built this prison. As a northerner, I stood out. Mortal or immortal, I was hated simply because of my appearance.

With the collapse of the north, the land had nobody to sell their goods to. My people singlehandedly ruined our society." Clearing my throat, I return to Sharnique's braids, realizing they've unraveled naturally. "Apologies for over-sharing."

"Don't be silly. It is vital that I understand your history. Hearing it from your perspective is remarkably helpful." She turns to the fire, checking its strength. "Tell me, Malin. If you could choose, what would you wish for the future?"

"Easy." I keep my voice low as if speaking too loudly will disrupt my unlikely dream. "I wish for mortals and immortals to live in peace. I would love for the north to be restored, but without the ego attached."

"Interesting..."

"What side are you on?" I ask with great caution. "Mortals or the immortals? I mean, I assume you're mortal, based on the fact you're running the prison."

"Assumptions are a foolish error." Sharnique's tone is chilled, her body tense. "I am neither mortal nor immortal."

My hands tremble as I tie the ribbon at the end of the completed braid. The sentence hangs in the air, leaving me terrified of what I already know. "What a-are you?"

"I am a god."

A rush of air leaves my lungs. "I wasn't sure you existed."

"There are many of us who live across the water. War is coming, and it is time for us to interfere."

My hands drop into my lap, a whirlwind of images flooding my mind's eye. Is she referring to Zain and Mitty?

"My friends proposed a revolution," I say. "They want to rise up against the mortals."

"And that is exactly what they will do. Many will die. An eye for an eye and the world goes blind."

I feel physically sick to my stomach, the same way I feel whenever Garu looks at me. That's when it hits me. "Garu is one of you, isn't he?"

"Yes."

"And the other guards he orders around? The ones that don't speak?"

"His guards are a manifestation."

If there were a staircase inside my stomach, it would've dropped several floors. For some reason, I feel violated by that information. If Garu could manifest humans, then what else was fake? Was I the only *real* being out there? When I internally compose myself, I continue.

"The chefs you said you employed. They're manifestations too, aren't they?"

"Yes. It takes great power. The fire must be fed constantly. Surprisingly, it is far easier to manifest a fraudulent copy of a human to prepare food, than to create food out of thin air. See, food is consumed, digested, and absorbed. It is far too much energy. The food must indeed be physically real."

I'm glad she isn't facing me because there is no way I could look her in the eye. "What about the blood draining? You're feeding the immortals food and helping them regain energy. Why wouldn't you cease such an archaic practice?"

"Feeding the immortals poison was grotesque. Starving them was inhumane. When we bought the prison from the mortals, the first course of action was to feed the inmates correctly. However, it was practical for us to maintain drainings. I must reiterate, however, that it was not my idea. I do not condone them, but I understand the practicality behind them. When immortals are at their strongest, they can rely heavily on their unique corner abilities. If all prisoners were strong, easterners would manipulate others into turning on one another. Central immortals would've been immensely tortured by corrupt guards and cannibals due to their ability to regenerate quicker than others. If we had more northerners, your kind would've given up their immortality and committed suicide. We cannot have that. I am not here to oversee mass death or encourage violence. Mind, I personally wish to end the drainings soon."

"Then why don't you let us go?"

"Do you honestly think releasing thousands of brain-dead immortals into a land they no longer recognize is wise? Or perhaps we should unleash the angry, vengeful cannibals. These immortals require rehabilitation, Malin. They require leaders to show them the way forward. We are in the process of building a better life for them."

"And what about the dead immortals? Surely that's not a better life."

Sharnique's shoulders raise slightly. "Sacrifices had to be made. I do not like death, but for the greater good and all."

"What does that mean?" Following Rune's obsessive habit, I repeat the question when she ignores me.

She turns to look at me, her young face so much harder than before. I never realized how striking her jawline is, or how piercing her frosty eyes are. Her glossy lips are ruby-red, her skin creamy and blemish-free. Everything about her presence is exponentially intimidating, more now that I'm privy to her origins.

"What does that mean?" Sharnique says, her voice cutting. "It means to save a life, an immortal life must be exchanged. You live because they died. I rip out the essences of a force and give it to you to ensure your survival."

I physically crawl backward off the rug as Sharnique stares me down. I can't bring myself to believe what she's saying. So the times I was poisoned or bled out...was when I was supposed to die?

"*Why?*" My voice croaks. "*Why* would you bother to save *me*? I gave up my immortality for someone else. My people are all but extinct. Why would a god bother to save me? And to k-kill *innocent* immortals for the sake of *me*? *Why?*" Sobs are peppered through my speech, as I curl my knees to my chest and rock, imagining the blood on my hands...knowing I slept on the grave of somebody whose life was sacrificed for mine...

"Why?" Sharnique rises to her feet, the violet flames growing in size and bursting out of the fireplace until they wrap around her like a vicious serpent. "Because you are Malin, Princess of the North. And the choices that are to be made over the coming week will decide the fate of the land."

I recoil at the mention of my identity, an omen I've desperately attempted to shed. "No..."

"Yes, Malin. It is imperative you stay alive until our guests arrive."

I scan the room for an escape. The window is too high to jump out of. The other doorways lead to bed chambers or showers. I curse myself for being northern, wishing more than ever I had the charisma of an easterner or the regenerative ability of a central immortal. I could talk my way out of this or jump out of the window, healing my bones immediately.

"There is no emergency exit," Sharnique continues, the now calm flames curling around her body like a coat. "It is in your best interest to relax."

I have never experienced a panic attack until this moment. It's like my lungs are compressing into one another, my vision tunneling. From one nightmare to another, I lament every decision, every path, every*thing*.

But then again...nothing has been my choice while I've been here.

What if I let the cannibal kill me?

Sharnique would've given me somebody else's life force.

What if I escaped with Zain?

Garu would've worked harder to stop it.

What if I pleaded with Taylin and Rune to not destroy the bridge?

The guests would've arrived as promised and summoned me to this point.

There are no choices in life. There is no such thing as freedom. Everything is set in stone by the decisions made by others. Our lives are controlled without our realization.

Resigning myself to my fate, I settle back onto the rug, watching as a salty tear lands and disappears into the fabric of my dress.

"Princesses do not cry," Sharnique criticizes, dismissing the flames so they return to the fireplace. "I hope you do not show such weakness when you reclaim your throne."

"There is no throne when there are no people," I say, my voice tight. "I don't know who your *friendly* guests are, but I want nothing to do with them."

"Oh, you certainly will." Sharnique glances at the window. "Garu says they are arriving late tonight."

I haven't personally seen her contact Garu and wonder if they share a telepathic link.

"How? There's no bridge!" I counter. "I was told they're too important to come via the regular, rough terrain on the other side of the prison."

"The direction in which they're coming from would add additional days to their trek if they were to arrive at the same entrance you did. You needn't worry about the lack of a bridge. Garu is devising a plan as we speak, Princess."

"Stop calling me that!" I scream, forgetting my place. Like an adolescent, I cover my ears with my hands. "It's not who I was, and it's not who I am!"

"Cease this childish behavior!" Sharnique's alto voice booms in the small space. Glaring, she waits for me to remove my hands. "I had hoped you would be ready to meet the others, but it is evident you are not. Perhaps it is time to retire to our chambers."

"It's still light out," I counter.

"Use any spare moment you can to rest. I assure you, there won't be an opportunity to do so in the near future." Tossing the messy braid over her shoulder, she strides towards the bookshelf that conceals the doorway to her chambers. She nudges it so that it swings open, disappearing into her quarters.

Forget this nonsense. Maybe I should just toss myself out of the window and end it all. Anything is better than this.

I run towards the window, watching the laborers slowly working on the collapsed bridge. Taylin moves sluggishly to and fro, and Rune is nowhere to be seen.

My gaze extends beyond the horizon, hoping for some signs of life. Did Zain and Mitty make it out alive? Did the hybrids get to them? How far did the tunnel stretch? Enough that I wouldn't see the exit from this view?

I remain by the window, staring longingly at the camp as the sun sets and twilight begins. The immortals below haven't had a break since I've been watching. They've managed to retrieve one of the trapped prisoners beneath the crumbled bridge, but it's not a pretty sight. Pulling him out by his torso, his legs are completely crushed and the side of his face is caved in. He doesn't appear to be coherent, as the few prisoners that are left crowd around and attempt to aid in some way.

Glancing at the fire, I recall Sharnique using the goo from the cauldron to help the gash on my neck. My eyes dart back to the mangled immortal and a slumped-over Taylin barely able to keep her head up.

No. I *couldn't*. I physically wouldn't make it. Could I?

There's nobody in this room. The guards have already dropped off the replacement supplies for the day. Nothing is stopping me from running downstairs and back to the camp. I know the way. I'm feeling strong and healthy. I could return without Sharnique even missing me.

Fueled by insanity, I crouch beside the cauldron and dip my hands inside, wincing at the heat. Scooping up the ooze, I conceal it in my dress and tiptoe out of the tower and down the uneven steps. I go slowly at first, careful not to allow my feet to slap against the stone. But once I see the door below, I pick up the pace until I'm outside in the cold and sprinting downhill towards the campsite.

*What am I doing? What am I doing? What. Am. I. Doing?*

I'm actively going out of my way to piss off gods who have enormous power. Between Sharnique and Garu I'm no doubt doomed, but I'd rather risk eternal damnation than see innocent people suffer. I've been a bystander for too long.

Out of breath, I pump my arms, the goo sloshing against my dress. There are no trees or shrubs to hide behind. I'm out in the open for Sharnique to see from the tower and Garu to watch from the broken bridge. There's no going back now.

The cold air burns my lungs, my heart hammering when I spy Taylin at the well fetching a drink. She's nothing more than a shell, her face gaunt and her eyes dark. She doesn't even seem to recognize me when I skid to my knees.

"Taylin?" I say. "Taylin, are you all right?"

She looks at me without really looking. "Malin?"

Her voice is unfamiliar; hoarse and weak. Her lips are a pale blue, matching her fingernails. Why isn't she regenerating?

"Yes, it's me. I have something for you!" I speak quickly, keeping an eye out for Garu. Digging into my undergarments, I pull out the goo. "Umm. I'm not sure how this works. Where do you hurt?"

"Everywhere. I'm dying."

"Impossible," I dismiss, rubbing the ooze onto her throat. "Where's Rune?"

"Under the bridge. He pushed me out of the way as it fell. I thought...I thought you were gone."

"Garu led me to the tower," I explain, placing more goo into her hands. "I can't stay, but please take this. Give it to Rune when you find him...or you could even use it on that mangled immortal. I'm trying to fix everything. I just don't know how yet..."

"You look so good." Taylin smiles weakly. "Strong. Healthy. Glowing. Your skin is dark."

"It's the goo. And they've been feeding me well. Long slumbers. I have to go, but I'll be back, all right? I'll bring food!"

"Food?"

"Be good, all right? Garu is a g—"

I duck behind the well when Garu strides towards us, his focus on Taylin. "Why aren't you working?"

"I need a break, sir."

"Breaks are not on the itinerary," he says, sparks flying out of his hand. "This collapse was your fault. We only have a handful of laborers left, so you best exert all of your energy and retrieve them."

I sink into the ground as much as I can, petrified of Garu finding me. Holding my breath, I ignore the blood rushing in my ears and zone in on the conversation.

"Aren't your guests going to kill us, anyway?" Taylin says through gritted teeth. Maybe that strange ooze is giving her some energy after all.

Garu hesitates. "What are you suggesting?"

"The guests who are meant to arrive via the bridge. They're going to permanently kill all immortals, ending the dilemma once and for all."

"Interesting. Be assured you will be privy to their intentions soon enough. They are arriving momentarily."

I freeze, but Taylin doesn't want to back down from the confrontation.

"How are they supposed to get over the bridge?"

"That is not your concern. Do not forget your place."

"I am past that!" Taylin snaps, a vein in her temple throbbing. "I don't belong here! I've never belonged here! If your guests are planning on killing us anyway, then I may as well drop now and await the grisly demise. It's over for me. It's over for Rune. I can't get to him but his tortured screams haunt me, even when I can no longer physically hear him. I don't know where Malin's gone. I couldn't escape the hybrids. I was left out when the tunnelers ran. I'm not recuperating from this blood drain. What's left for me, Garu? What's left?"

I can't see Garu, but the dead grass beneath his boots crunch as he steps closer. "Believe me when I say this, northerner. Your existence is more beneficial to this land than you know."

The bizarre revelation is enough to stun Taylin into silence and after a tense moment, his boots stomp away.

Carefully, I pull myself into a comfortable position, peering over the well to ensure Garu is gone.

"Are you all right?" I whisper.

"What did he mean by that?" Taylin asks, staring after him. "I'm a nobody."

"I don't know," I admit. "Taylin, Garu is a god. He escorted me to the tower where I've been serving another god. I know it sounds crazy, but they're real. They arrived from across the water. They're trying to prevent war, but I feel like there's more to it than that."

"Is it because you're the princess?"

It's as if I temporarily lose consciousness, unable to process her question. "What?"

"Rune told me. He said Zain recognized you from centuries ago when he worked as a messenger. You're the last hope of our people, Malin. If you rise to power, you might be able to restore the north!"

I can't believe this. Everybody knew about my lineage? "Zain knew?"

"Rune said that's one of the reasons why Zain didn't release us. Northerners ruined it for all immortals when they turned on each other. If he wants an uprising, he doesn't want us by his side. He wants us to die here. But you can change that. I wondered about Garu too. If he's a god, it makes sense. Keep him on your side. If you claim the throne with a god supporting you, the mortals will be too afraid to come after us, and any other northerners in hiding will come out. We can have a home, Malin. *You* can give us a home."

"No I can't!" I protest. "For starters, I gave up my immortality. I'm a fragile fugitive trapped in a tower in the confines of a prison. Secondly, my family kicked me out when I refused to sacrifice a mortal. I don't know anything about running a land. I only know how to run away."

"You risked everything to come down here in an attempt to heal me. Only a true leader would do that," Taylin says, her gaze pulled away from mine when the clip-clop of hooves draws near. "They're here."

Twisting my neck to see, I keep behind Taylin and gape at the sight across the gully. A white carriage adorned in golden vines is pulled by a majestic snowy creature, its mane and tail gently flowing in the breeze. It practically glows against the moonlight, the stumpy horn between its eyes glittering.

"Is that a unihorn?" Taylin breathes.

My heart flutters when I recognize the beautiful creature. "It's Nellabix! Oh, she's alive! I thought they all died in the northern war," I say. "They're large, immortal creatures with remarkable stamina. Some wild ones can allegedly fly, but I've never seen it. She's gorgeous. Oh, I adored Nellabix. We had so much fun riding around the crystal beds together." I wipe away a stray tear, wanting nothing more than to be reunited with such a pure essence.

"You're so lucky..." Taylin whispers dreamily.

Garu stands on the edge of the collapse, raising his electrical fist in the air. "Welcome, guests. Please, exit your carriage."

The few prisoners who remain climb up the gully until they're standing behind Garu and his two...oh, now *three* guards. My heart sinks at the sight of Thrillia who, albeit disheveled and sickly, is up and about.

We watch in awe as the guests step out of the carriage, a collective gasp resonating as three giant northerners stride in sync to the edge.

I can't believe it. I genuinely can't believe it. *Three* northerners? Are they mortal? They'd have to be! All the immortals gave up their immortality and died! Unless that's what they wanted us to think...

All dressed in silky, silver robes, they stand tall and proud.

I'm not sure if I recognize any of them. There are two males and one female, although we tend to all look alike, especially in those robes. They all sport auburn hair, no longer than the tip of their chins. One seems a little different from the others. Instead of a frown, he sports a worried expression, his hair slightly lighter than his counterparts. There's something about the glimmer in his eyes, but I can't figure out what it is...

"Dalin, Cheralin, and Wylin. Thank you for coming," Garu greets loudly, but I don't know which name belongs to whom, their stoic gray eyes staring at the divide. They do seem familiar though...

"Please excuse the mess. We had an accident. I do however have an alternative method to help you cross; one that doesn't involve traveling around the gully to the front entrance. I understand that would add unnecessary delays."

Fist still in the air, Garu whistles, and a sense of dread washes over me. I hold Taylin's hand, which is freezing. We wait with bated breath as the howls of the hybrids approach.

"He's not..." Taylin says under her breath. "Can't unihorns leap over a gap like that?"

"Not a gap that wide," I mutter. "And certainly not with passengers."

"Can't they, I don't know, climb down like the rest of us? It's not easy or quick, but it's doable, isn't it?"

I snort. "And risk staining their silky robes? Northerners from my time never lifted a finger. They'd sooner die than perform menial tasks. I can't believe all of this work has been for *them*. What a waste of resources."

"If Garu is a god, can't he just make a bridge?"

"He can manifest one, but it won't be real. That's why we never hear the guards speak. They're merely a projection that fades when he's weak. Even the god in the tower doesn't manifest food—she has it prepared and brought to her. It's an illusion. The only way to make it real is to exchange the energy with something real. A life for a life." I think of the hungry violet fire and what Sharnique must be manifesting for the flames to need constant stoking.

The hybrids surround us, crawling up the hill and snarling at the prisoners who instinctively hide behind Garu and the guards.

Taylin clutches onto me as we watch three hybrids slink towards the edge of the gully, leaping with such prowess that they barely falter as they cling to the rocky sides, using their great strength to lift themselves up.

The northerners remain nonchalant and silent, scrutinizing the terrifying beasts who rise before them.

"Please, get on their backs. They will escort you over. Apologies for this method, but it is better and safer than traversing around the other side," Garu's powerful voice booms.

Nodding, the northerners climb onto the back of the hybrids who growl and snap at one another. They're hating every second of the experience, and I can't understand why they're not shredding the northerners to pieces.

Clinging to their bristly neck fur, the northerners look so out of place on such horrendous beasts, their long legs dangling off the sides. Once they've settled, the hybrids step backward, then charge forward and sprint towards the edge, leaping into the air.

It's an unnerving sight, watching such vicious entities glide through the air, but the northerner's elegance adds a strange sense of beauty to the scene.

Miraculously, the hybrids land with a thud just shy of Garu as the prisoners clamber over one another to keep from the beast's checked fury.

The northerners gracefully dismount, barely a hair out of place.

"That was an interesting ride," the female says. She glances over her shoulder at the unihorn. "Nellabix. You may leave the carriage and enjoy the sights for now. We will return."

The unihorn neighs and shakes off the reigns connected to her saddle. Stretching out her legs she gallops down the valley.

"I hope it was suitable," Garu says. "Now, if you care to take a step back, I am indebted to the hybrids for agreeing to such an unprecedented favor."

The three hybrids snarl at Garu, their salivating tongues licking their bloodied teeth.

"In exchange for your services, it is only fair to give you a prisoner to feast on. Exchange is a vital part of my culture. You may take the broken immortal left in the gully below and the two cannibals." Garu points to the sacrifices.

I don't want to watch this. The spared immortals scurry back as Fello and Thrillia scream for mercy. Two hybrids lunge and pin them to the ground, their lips smacking together as they rip their muscles apart. The third hybrid dives into the gully, the immortal's screams unbearable. Other hybrids watch enviously, practically on pins and needles to join in.

Tears run down my cheeks as I squeeze Taylin's hand. "I have to go."

"I know. Thank you for coming to me."

"We will find a way out of here, all right? Just stay strong. Keep trying to get Rune out of the debris. We will make it out of here."

"Alive?"

"Alive," I promise. "The guests are just northerners. They won't know how to kill immortals."

"Are you sure about that?"

I don't answer. It seems redundant when we both know I'm going to lie, anyway. Keeping low to the ground, I bolt away from the campsite while the others are distracted by the hybrids. It would be foolish to disrupt their meal, so at the very least, they've bought me time.

Relieved that the darkness helps conceal me, I sprint uphill, frustrated by physics and gravity for slowing me down.

As I reach the tower, I hurry upstairs and draw back the curtain to find an enraged Sharnique standing in the center of the room, arms folded, fingers anxiously tapping her forearms.

Breathless, I try to think of an excuse...but I don't have one.

"You stole from me, Malin."

I expected this response. I figured she would watch my every move from the window. What I didn't expect was the tall northerner by her side, looking equally unimpressed.

What I didn't expect...was my sister.

# CHAPTER XVI

"I'm sorry." I almost choke on the words, bypassing Sharnique and staring straight at Adalin. "I was desperate to help someone."

"You betrayed my trust," Sharnique says, her usually cool exterior now flustered. "That is an offense in our culture. No wonder your kind are doomed to suffer eternal battles and horrors."

Her words fly over my head as I stare at my sister.

Adalin hasn't changed much over the years. She was only twenty years older than me and always cherished her nobility. She took her job as princess seriously, offering sage advice, choosing the annual mortal sacrifice, and bestowing false blessings upon those who asked for it.

A picture of grace, her slender neck adorned in silver jewels, her short auburn hair slicked back with a band of sapphires. All of her features are sharp and pointed, but despite this, she still manages to look remarkably pretty.

I glance down at her porcelain skin, devoid of scars, scratches, and hideous brandings. She's picture-perfect.

I run a light finger over my own wrist where the sideways 8 is tattooed onto my skin and struggling to heal. It's a constant reminder of my eternal prison.

"Ugh." Sharnique throws her hands up in the air. "I see you are far too distracted by your sister to understand the repercussions of your action. I will punish you for this!"

"She has been punished enough, don't you think?" Adalin says, her green eyes lined with a dark streak of makeup.

"No. She stole from the flames!"

"Are you feeling weak?"

"No. Just fury."

"Then let us allow her punishment to unravel on its own." Adalin has always been good at mollifying people, and clearly, her talent has improved enough over the years to be able to calm a god. "Malin, we have much to catch up on, and little time. Our guests have arrived. I should speak with you before they join us here."

Sharnique rolls her eyes and motions at the table, where mountains of fresh food await. "Let us sit."

Reluctantly, I follow them, politely pulling out their seats before I take my own. Fidgeting with my dress, I wait for somebody to speak.

"Malin, it is wonderful to see you," Adalin finally says, her voice soothing despite the situation.

"I thought you were dead," I blurt. "After I was exiled, it's all everybody could talk about. The northern royals had fallen. The recession began."

"I faked my death to survive," she says, reaching for a fringle fruit before scrunching up her nose and putting it back. "I thought I told the guard not to deliver these things."

"The fringles? I'd never heard of them until I came here," I confess.

"Nor had I. I react poorly to them. Moving on. I want to apologize for what happened the day you left. That was father, mother, and brother's persuasion. I personally did not believe you should be removed from society because of your beliefs. It was noble of you to protect the mortals."

A compliment is not something I've ever received from Adalin. We were never close—she took her duties seriously while I avoided them. Whenever she spoke with our family about how to encourage immortal worshipping, I'd be outside painting murals with the elderly.

"Thank you," I say unsurely. "Where is the rest of our family?"

"Deceased, I'm afraid. Father was impaled by that scoundrel Pegalin. He was in immense pain and could not heal with the blade wedged in important organs. He gave up his immortality and died on the spot. Mother didn't want to survive without Father, so she died right beside him. It was all very tragic, Malin. I'm relieved you didn't witness it."

"And our brother?"

"He is as good as dead. I'm not entirely sure what became of him. If he is alive, we have lost all contact. I, along with a few others, were the few left standing. Our home was reduced to ash. We attempted to rebuild, but it was hopeless. Within that time, the other corners had turned on immortals and decided we were a menace to society. If we could wipe out the north with our greed, what's to say the others weren't next? We went underground and hid for decades when the guards came for us. Some mortals allegedly survived and did the same, keeping to the shadows as they reproduced. Not many successfully integrated with other corners. How did you hide for so long?"

I smile to myself, proud of my survival skills over the years. Leave it to my sister to keep living a secret life of luxury underground. "I just kept running. From town to town, hideout to hideout. The guards who knew to chase me would retire or die and then their sons would carry the torch, so to speak. A never-ending circle. I didn't sleep much. I barely ate or drank. I considered giving up multiple times."

"Hmm. Indeed. I understand the feeling." She says that, but she wouldn't *begin* to understand the pain I've endured. Not one for emotion, Adalin continues without inflection in her voice. "I sent some of our survivors out to investigate your whereabouts. You were extremely difficult to track. They'd report back to me whenever they could. When we heard you'd been captured, we knew it was time to put our plan in place. We enlisted the help of Sharnique and used our leftover wealth to buy the prison. Eventually, I would love to redecorate all the cells so that each prisoner has a bedroom instead. We can rehabilitate them so they can rejoin the land in good mental and physical health after the torture they've endured. My heart bleeds for them."

"That's wonderful," I say. "Truly, I thank you. These prisoners don't deserve the mistreatment. We have some in the field who are nothing more than talking heads. If there is a way to heal or mend them, I would suggest we do that quickly."

"That is good to know, thank you Malin."

"But what plan are you talking about? And how did you enlist Sharnique? I didn't even know there were lands beyond ours. What is your end goal here?"

"I'm glad you ask, because the end goal, as you say, involves you. We were so relieved to have found you. See, we want our home restored to its former glory. Sharnique wants to ensure our land doesn't end up battling, as it affects their culture. As gods, they draw on elemental powers. Hence chaos and war do not bode well for them. A land in peril, deprived of care, deeply impacts the elements. She found us and explained the future she foresaw. I said we could only prevent it if she helped us."

Sharnique smirks, seemingly proud of herself.

"She has been of great assistance," Adalin continues. "As for our 'end goal', Malin. We want our home back. We want our power back. We want our wealth back. We want our throne back. If we can rule again peacefully, we can prove that northerners are not corrupt. We can show the land how we're trying to improve the prison. We can convince all corners that immortals aren't evil and that this was all a big misunderstanding."

Relaxing a little, I nod in agreement. I can't believe I've been so tense when all anybody has wanted is peace. "That sounds perfect. How do we do this?"

"Tradition states that for a princess to become queen, a northern mortal sacrifice must be made."

And it all crumbles in my face. "Again with the sacrifices? Adalin, it's a stupid tradition that doesn't mean anything!"

"It means *everything!*" Adalin slams her fists on the table, her pupils dilating. "*Everything* was spoiled when the mortals rose up against us! It was a butterfly effect that resulted in us losing *everything*! I will *not* return to my life underground!"

"The mortals were sick of being victims," I say calmly, trying to subdue her outburst. "They were my friends, all right? When they fought back, they did so to gain freedom from your corruption. If you sacrifice an innocent, you're only proving their claims about immortals being violent and malevolent."

"Not if we sacrifice you," Adalin says, her tone still tainted with anger. "I heard you gave up your immortality. You're an easy kill. If we publicly slaughter a royal northerner, it will restore trust. It's a symbol of good faith to eliminate the toxicity, the very thing that represents our downfall. We will be seen as martyrs for making such a sacrifice."

My jaw drops at the stupidity of her so-called plan. "Adalin, I'm genuinely concerned for your wellbeing. I'm worried years hidden underground has impacted your mental health. Killing me will only confirm to the people that you're a malevolent tyrant."

"No. See, like me, you're a public figure. We're in the mortal history books. But history is blurred. We will explain to the land that you initiated the northern war, and that you pushed for more mortal sacrifices. Disposing of you will be heroic. It's for the greater good."

I splutter incoherently, at a loss for words. It's bad enough that my sister is willing to murder me for personal gain, but to tarnish my name to do it? Bitter, I swipe at the food on the table and watch the plates crash and the pastries roll.

"And you agree with this, Sharnique?" I ask. "You've been nice and quiet. After exchanging two immortal lives for mine, you agree to having me publicly killed?"

Completely disconnected from the conversation, Sharnique draws imaginary patterns on the table with her finger. "According to my premonition, only one princess must survive for there to be peace in the land. On the contrary, your execution wouldn't be public. They would just need your head to parade about."

"It's a win, win," Adalin continues. "Clearly you gave up your immortality for a reason. You're finished with living, right? Your sacrifice means I am officially entitled to the throne as queen and the land will be satisfied. A northern royal executed for her crimes will only benefit us. Corners will trade with us again. We will be out of a recession. Step by step, we can release the immortals back into the world without fear."

Before I can protest, we turn to face the doorway when the three northerners enter silently. They wait patiently until Adalin greets them.

"Ah, perfect timing! Malin, do you remember the young triplets? Their father was one of the advisors."

Blurry flashes from my past alight in my mind's eye. Vaguely, I recall three young immortals occasionally seen playing in our courtyard.

"Are you three in on this?" I ask bluntly. "You're keen to murder me? Rumor has it you're here to kill *all* the immortals. That's why Mitty the guard escaped with the others."

Sharnique rolls her eyes. "What an idiot. Your species sure know how to twist words and sensationalize things. Sneaky little pest eavesdropped on everyone and everything. He was always asking the delivery guards about what they overheard. We spoke about purging the immortal issue. Clearly, he deciphered that as meaning a mass execution. Of course we were referring to the immortal situation, period. We want to abolish the imprisonments. No doubt the mention of a sacrifice was also lost in translation. Our guests are here to witness the sacrifice and to plan the next steps."

I'm too stunned to feel sorrow. Everything I've been through was for naught. I lived just so I could die at the right time, at the hands of my sociopathic sister. Frustrated, I grab the lone fringle still balancing on the edge of the table and squeeze it in my hand, imagining Adalin's head in my palm.

"You know what? Just kill me. It's not worth the hunt, the chase, the fight. If my death is the answer to all of life's problems, then just do it."

My attempt to call her bluff fails miserably.

Adalin exhales sharply, as if she's held her breath all day. "Oh, wonderful, this will make it much easier. Dalin, be a dear and restrain her."

Shoving the fringle into my undergarments, I stand and stretch out my arms to surrender as the triplets wrap their cold fingers around my body. "You don't need to hold so tightly when I'm not fighting."

They loosen their grip for a moment, then think better of it.

My heart hammers against my chest as Adalin draws a small blade from a sheath concealed in her leather belt. I recognize that blade, the way the steel spirals together until it reaches the fatal tip. It was a design favored by my father. In fact, it was this very blade that was used to sacrifice mortals all those years ago. Sapphires adorn the hilt, beauty in its malice.

"I'm truly sorry that our reunion was met with a farewell," Adalin says with only a hint of remorse. "This is for the greater good. Just remember that. Your death will bring light. We will add makeup to your face before we parade it around. We will keep you looking pretty."

"I hate you." I clench my jaw, fighting the tears. "I didn't think you would actually do this."

"When I put my mind to something, I always complete my task. Especially if that task means benefit for the majority."

Squeezing my eyes shut at her bold lie of where the benefits go, I shakily inhale my final breath. "Just do it."

Trembling in the triplets' grip, I embrace my fate. Jolting backwards, I'm too agonized to utter a single sound as the blade penetrates my flesh. A copper taste floods my mouth as my heart strains against the pressure of the foreign object in my body.

"Twist it, Adalin," one of the triplets says. "The light is still in her eyes. Stab again if need be."

Adalin takes the first piece of advice and wrenches it deeper into my heart, the excruciating sensation sending ripples of goosebumps down my arms.

"Stab her again!"

"No!" Adalin snaps. "It only takes one thrust to the heart!"

"Why didn't we just decapitate her? Don't we need her head to prove her death, anyway?"

"That's. Not. How. It's. Done!" A tense Adalin removes the blade with a grunt. "A sacrifice is *always* performed this way. Then you do what you wish with the body. We shall let her bleed out."

Sharnique scrunches up her nose. "All over the floor? Once she's dead, we're without a maid."

I watch as the crimson liquid pours out of the gaping wound in my chest and wait for the relief that is death. My knees weaken in the triplet's grip, but beyond that, nothing seems to happen.

A few minutes pass. They awkwardly wait, whispering to one another as they watch me cling to the physical realm, my flowing life force messing up the pristine white rugs.

"She's not keen on dying, is she?" Sharnique sighs. "Are you sure she's mortal?"

"Yes!" Adalin throws her hands in the air, her cool demeanor quickly diminishing. "My spies did extensive research! You even traded other lives to ensure she survives! Don't tell me you somehow passed their immortality to her?"

"Impossible. I don't possess that ability. I can merely take an immortal life to aid a dying one. That is the extent of it."

Flaring her nostrils, Adalin tosses her robes and bends over so she's at my hunched eye level. "What are you playing at, Malin? What is the big secret?"

"Nothing." I spit blood deliberately in her face. "I'm mortal now."

A mischievous grin spreads across Sharnique's face. "Interesting. Aren't northerners a funny species? They're able to give up their immortality entirely or bequeath it to another. Malin is awfully friendly with that sickly little northerner in the labor camp. Wish to share some insight?"

In my pained state, it hits me. The night our blood was drained should've killed me. Miraculously, I survived and have been thriving ever since. I've been stronger, healing quickly and feeling less troubled by dehydration and starvation.

And Taylin has been dying before my very eyes ever since.

Her paleness.

Her nausea.

Her struggle.

She gave up her immortality and returned it to me...

"Conniving little monster," Adalin says, using her blade to cut my wrist for the sake of it. "I *knew* you were up to something!"

"I didn't know!" I shout, instantly regretting it. I may be immortal, but the pain and discomfort sure sticks around.

"Then give up your immortality now! And none of this exchanging it nonsense! You were happy to sacrifice yourself a moment ago! Come on! *Do it!*"

One of the triplets, the one I assume is Dalin, releases me so that I collapse to the floor. "Why should we waste time? That sickly northerner outside looks a lot like Malin. We can sacrifice her instead, and the land will believe it's Malin. We'll just lock this one up in the meantime. We are in a prison, after all."

Adalin's eyes light up as mine widen in horror. "Oh, now that's a wonderful idea! Thank you, Dalin! All right, subdue Malin and we will kill the other one."

"No," I utter, my increased heart rate only pushing more blood through the wound. "Please don't. She's innocent!"

"There are many innocents." Sharnique picks up her panpipes from the shelf above the fire. "You are one of them. However, as I predicted...only one princess must survive for peace. Your opposing perspectives encourage too much future confrontation. Do not mince my words. Only *one* of you will live. If you are no longer needed for a sacrifice, then I shall extract your life force myself. I cannot risk my power for petty family disputes."

And there it is. Finality. No more lucky second chances. No god to replenish my life force. No Taylin to exchange immortality. Complete, eternal lack of existence.

Glancing at the vase on the table, I spring to my feet and yank the flowers out. Hoping my actions are erratic enough to confuse the others, I zigzag to the fireplace and throw the water onto the flames.

Considering the possibility that water could also potentially feed the fire, I hold my breath as the flames flicker while they fight the opposing element. Triumphant, the blaze springs back to life with more force than ever, before dulling once more. There was nowhere near enough water to extinguish the fire, but at least it's weak.

Shoulders slumping forward, I await a tackle or a sly comment. But the triplets don't budge. Neither do Adalin or Sharnique. They gape at me in horror.

"How could you?" Adalin croaks, cursing under her breath. "You never purposefully mix a god's elements!"

Perplexed, I check the fire which is slowly but certainly dying. Sharnique doesn't move from her spot, frozen in place as a gray liquid cements over her body, leaving a beautiful replica of the god's once-majestic and fierce energy.

Unable to speak, I remain in place. "What..."

"Malin." Disgust taints my sister's tongue. "A god and their ability are always connected. If they choose to manipulate and manifest reality, then they must bond with an element and nurture it relentlessly. With great power comes great sacrifice. By extinguishing her flame...you extinguished her. You murdered a god."

"I j-just w-wanted to slow her d-down!" I stammer. "I can fix it! I'll r-relight it!"

Wait. No. *Damn* it, no! I am *not* going to apologize for standing up for myself!

Lightheaded from the blood loss, I clear my head of guilty thoughts and bolt for the exit.

"Don't let her get away!" A voice yells as I trip and roll down the uneven stairs, bumping into the wall as I spiral down the steps. When

I land at the bottom of the tower battered, bruised, and with a trail of blood, I heave myself up and hobble downhill towards the campsite.

The northerners pick up the pace behind me, their breaths heavy and loud. Exhausted, I focus on the campsite ahead, ignoring the aggressive hand clinging to the back of my dress as I run, hoping to slip out of their clutches.

Fringle juice drips down my hand as I squeeze into it. I don't know if it will work. But considering this bizarre fruit was unheard of to most northerners, there's a good chance we could *all* be allergic.

Gripping onto the hexagonal fruit, I twist so that I'm facing an enraged Dalin. I shove the entire fruit into his mouth, pressing it further into his lips when he attempts to spit it out.

It's enough for him to loosen his clasp. As I back away, he bends over and spits out the fruit, his lips swelling to twice their size.

Turning away from Dalin, I overhear him dry heaving; an unpleasant sloshing sound slapping into the dirt. I dread thinking about the consequences of eating an entire fringle. The poisonous effects are instantaneous.

In the darkness ahead, the remaining immortals are preparing for sleep as Garu and the guards lift the chains and motion for the prisoners to take their place to be detained for the night.

Before Taylin's name can escape my lips, I'm catapulted forward, face planting the dirt as a mighty force pins me to the ground. My neck cracks as the delicate hands wrap around my throat, bending it unnaturally.

"You make no sense to me, Malin," the feminine voice says. "You were a useless princess then, and you're a useless princess now. Just *die* so our people can be free!"

Writhing beneath Cheralin's weight, I shift enough to elbow her bony sides. She flinches, but doesn't budge.

"I'm immortal. What are you expecting? Hoping to strangle me into annoyance?" I say, in between attempting to bite her fingers.

Wylin catches up, awkwardly towering over us. Slightly out of breath, he speaks slowly. "Adalin said to bring her back to the tower."

"Yes, yes, we will. But right now, she can suffer! Watching her as kids was an embarrassment. I'd follow her through the streets when she foolishly thought her face was concealed. She'd speak with the mortals, offering them lavish items and food that wasn't as well-prepared as ours. Traitor!" Cheralin snaps, then softens her tone. "Is Dalin all right?"

"He's throwing up. A *lot*. And his face has seen better days; he's as swollen as a tinkerbug. Come on, Cheralin. If you carry Malin, I'll take Dalin."

"Wait!" She digs her sharp nails into my skin, relishing in my discomfort. "Grab that tall mortal down there. She's the one we need to sacrifice."

"But..."

"Garu will aid you. He will understand. Gracious, we will need to inform him of Sharnique's passing. How *wonderful*. Not. Ugh! I might decapitate this *thing* and force her to watch the mortal's execution!"

Wylin's jaw drops at the harsh threat. "That's a touch extreme, don't you think?"

"Do you understand the pain this *thing* has caused us? I bet the prison wouldn't even *exist* if it weren't for her. She gave the mortals hope. She planted ideas in their heads so they thought they didn't need to worship immortals! And now look. They started an uprising. This is singlehandedly Malin's fault! I deserve to torture her!"

"I'm sure this isn't all her fault," Wylin mumbles, his tone much softer than his sibling's. "She didn't want to become a tyrant—that's all. Even Sharnique said many gods have walked down a dangerous road due to corruption. Maybe that's the way our people were heading."

"Whose side are you on?" Cheralin hisses, her delicate hands wrapped around my throat. "I hate her, I hate her, I *hate* her!"

Red spots fill my vision, but I notice Wylin staring over at the camp, no doubt straight at Taylin. Squirming in discomfort, I fret at the thought of him attacking an innocent.

"Don't," I attempt to splutter, my voice muffled.

My choked cries are stifled in the eerie silence, Wylin's conflicted gaze darting from Taylin to me. "I said I wouldn't kill anyone."

"Ugh, you don't have to." Cheralin uses all of her weight to bear down on my windpipe. "Just lure her here. Do you want our home back or not? Sharnique herself said only one princess must survive for there to be peace. Who knows; this thing might kill herself in grief if we sacrifice the mortal."

Wylin takes a knee beside me, his watery eyes wide. "You can't force peace with an act of violence. Malin only ever wanted peace. Malin, do you remember when I was a little boy, the other young immortals were throwing rocks at the mortals because they were inferior to them?"

Right now, I can't think of much. As the lack of oxygen disrupts any coherent thinking patterns, I get a mental glimpse of a young Wylin standing behind his siblings and friends, looking down at a smooth rock in his hand.

"You came up behind me and you gently slipped the rock out of my hand. You told me the mortals were fragile, delicate, temporary. They deserved to be nurtured, for they weren't blessed with a long life such as ours. They weren't gifted the same amount of time as we had to find love, learn lessons, or overcome grief. Every emotion they felt therefore, was heightened, which in a sense, made them much more powerful and even magical. You said we had a lot to learn from them. I never forgot that, Malin. Even during the uprising, I never laid a hand on any of them. And they never harmed me, either. I don't like where this is going and you shouldn't be punished for wanting peace."

"And the rest of us thought Malin was a crackpot, and we threw sticks at the mortals the next day." Cheralin throws her head back and laughs, loosening her grip just enough that I gasp for air. Using the little energy I have left, I punch her in the face, forcing her backwards. Thrown onto her side, she covers her nose once she notices the blood trickling from her nostrils, staining her perfect gown.

I scurry up, staring at Wylin who remains on his knees.

"We need peace, Malin." He swallows. "Keep surviving. I don't want any more stones thrown."

I don't have time to respond. Before Cheralin composes herself, I sprint towards the campsite, dizzy and nauseated.

"Taylin," I croak. "Taylin, run. Just run!"

I've never seen anybody look so close to the brink of death. Skinnier than I've ever seen her, Taylin's droopy eyes barely manage to stay open. Did that strange ooze not sustain her? Or is it useless since I extinguished the flames?

Garu and Taylin turn to look at me in unison, startled by my frenzied state.

"Stay there," Garu instructs the others as he strides towards me.

No. I can't deal with him. He'll ask questions and slow me down enough for Cheralin to catch up.

I change my course and run diagonally around him. "Taylin! *Run! Run, run, run!*"

Hysterical, I continue towards the crumbled bridge, watching as Taylin reluctantly follows my route, barely able to outrun Garu.

"Hey!" He shouts, raising his electric hand. "Hey, wait! What are you doing? Stop! Malin, stop!"

My every instinct wishes to believe in his decency. I want to have faith that he could be our protector in the way I thought Mitty could've been, who only ended up abandoning us like everyone else in my life. But Garu is a god, forever linked to Sharnique. If he is involved with my sister, then he is undoubtedly the enemy.

I charge towards the collapsed bridge, motioning for Taylin to hurry up. As she reaches me, I take her by the hand and slide down the gully to the bottom.

"Come on! Climb up the other side!"

"What's going on?" Taylin breathes, fumbling on the cliff wall. I give her a boost to propel her upwards as Garu slides down the gully.

"Hey," he says again. "What happened, Malin?"

Don't engage. Do. Not. Engage.

"You know what happened. They tried to sacrifice me," I yell over my shoulder as I make the steep ascent up the gully. "The guests were jilted northerners desperate to regain their wealth. They wanted me killed to prove to the land that they're not how they are perceived in history. That they'd rather dispose of a northern royal as a sign of good faith to prove that things will change. That's not how you mollify mortals or free immortals."

"Of course it isn't," Garu responds calmly, a small spark of electricity leaping from his fingers. "That is a surefire way to create chaos. Perhaps your sister isn't seeking peace. Perhaps she isn't treating the prisoners better out of the goodness of her heart. Perhaps she is preparing them for something. Perhaps she is preparing for war. *Revenge*."

I stop mid-climb, despite Taylin's panicked cries above. She offers her arm to help pull me up, but I don't accept.

"What? In the same way Zain is organizing a revolution?"

Garu inches closer, his boots sinking in the soft earth beneath him. "Do you not find it oddly suspicious his escape timed with your sister's arrival? Sharnique's premonition of one sister living in the name of peace is unfortunately an accurate depiction of the future."

"Then you can't be trusted!" I shriek. "Get away from me! If Sharnique is helping my sister, then you're in on it too!"

An eyebrow raises on his otherwise expressionless face. "Sharnique saved you on multiple occasions, Malin. Who's to say she isn't vying for your success? Who's to say *you* aren't the sister who must prevail? You're a royal who doesn't care about the longevity of anyone's life. You're who the people must turn to if this land has any chance of survival. This system isn't working. Not for you. Not for them. Not for us. The imbalance has caused turmoil amongst the elements and the gods are losing their power. We've turned to other sources to maintain our once natural abilities."

"This is all one big contradiction!" I scream, accepting Taylin's hand. As I scramble to the top, I look down at the motionless Garu. "If you wanted peace, then Sharnique wouldn't have let my sister attempt to murder me. You would've fed us better. You wouldn't have forced us to build a bridge. You wouldn't have allowed the hybrids to snack on the prisoners."

"Life is an exchange," he says. "If you were a god, you'd understand. Foreseeing events means selectively choosing which choices must be made for the best outcome. There's now a triplet who has seen the true colors of his people. Think about how that revelation will affect his future actions. Imagine how erratic your sister's decisions will be, knowing that you destroyed her partner's life force. Her advisor is no more. Her confidence is shattered. Turning Sharnique to stone was a carefully planned inevitability. As was everything else."

Blinking, I lower my voice. "You know?"

"*She* knew all. I do not. She told me if everything went to plan, then I must do this." He places his wide fingers in his mouth and whistles. "Everything else from this moment is in your hands. I trust Sharnique. I trust her future."

"What about the dead immortal?"

"The one you buried?"

"No. The first one. The corpse wasn't in the grave."

"Oh. Interesting. One may question whether the second immortal is still in his grave, too."

My response is interrupted by the howls of the nearing hybrids. Taylin tugs on my arm, her eyes swiftly darting to the trees.

"Malin. Let's go back to Garu. Only he can control them."

"He summoned them..." I whisper.

I don't know what he expects me to do. I can't trust anything he says. Is he manipulating me so I succumb and return to him? Or is he testing my smarts? My courage? I don't possess either of those.

"Nellabix..." I utter under my breath, focusing on the image of the majestic unihorn. "Nellabix!"

"What are you on about?" Taylin asks, almost running on the spot. "We need to *go!*"

Multiple hybrids stampede towards us, frothing at the mouth as they surround us. I glance at Garu who stands in the gully, forever stoic. He has no intention of intervening this time, curious as to how the scene will play out. He's unwittingly sent me straight to a grisly end, which for all I know was part of his miserable plan.

The hybrid's stench reminds me of incessant death as they communicate to one another with slow blinks. The devilish creatures are formulating an attack, circling as if to taunt us.

"Nellabix! It's Malin!" I scream, the shrillness alerting the hybrids. An eager, smaller beast springs towards us, but I shield Taylin. Even if I'm horribly mangled, at least I'll survive.

A gust of wind appears out of nowhere, a glowing white blur leaping from the trees and trampling the hybrid before us. The essence of benevolence stands proud, her thick mane constantly rippling as though it were underwater. Her hooves are the size of my head, her coat glittering in the moonlight.

"You've grown up beautifully," I say, pushing Taylin onto the unihorn's bare back.

Nellabix whinnies in response, her large form intimidating the hybrids as I heave myself onto her back. Once secured, the unihorn neighs and charges through the beasts, barreling two over as we speed towards freedom.

It's only in the distance I hear a frightened voice call my name. Struggling to look over my shoulder, I catch a glimpse of the limping, disoriented figure hobbling after us as the hybrids redirect their hungry attention to him.

It's Rune.

# CHAPTER XVII

"Nellabix! Turn back!" I cry, the rushing air instantly drying out my mouth.

"What?" Taylin cries. "No! The hybrids!"

"Rune is back there!"

Taylin hesitates. "We can't."

"He'd do the same for us!" I protest, thinking of what he gave up just to stay with me. He could've left with Zain, possibly to freedom. Instead, he ended up crushed by a bridge he spent weeks building.

Arms wrapped around Nellabix's trunk of a neck, I ask her to turn around. She seems to share Taylin's mentality, only reluctantly turning around when I dig my feet into her sides.

As we speed back into the chaos, I lament Rune's deformed body. His neck flops to one side, resting on his shoulder, his ankles bent in such a way that I cringe to think of the pain he must be in as he stumbles towards us.

It's all right. He can regenerate quicker than most. Even in an unhealthy state, he can still heal. He's not like the other immortals who have spent years malnourished and mistreated. It's just going to be a long process.

"We're not going to make it," Taylin says through gritted teeth as a hybrid swipes at Rune, who only avoids such a swing because of the luckily timed trip over his mangled ankle.

"You can do this Nellabix," I encourage. "Just keep running. I'm going to grab him. Ready, girl?"

She snorts in response, as I grip onto the unihorn with my thighs and lean over to the left, arms outstretched.

"Rune! Reach out!" I cry as we approach him. "We only have one shot at this!"

As Nellabix charges full throttle at the hybrids, I smack into Rune, clinging to his underarms as he drags through the startled creatures.

"Pull us up!" I scream as Taylin locks onto my waist, hoisting me into a better position.

Using every ounce of strength, I lift Rune off the ground until he is awkwardly draped over Nellabix's back.

"Are you all right?" I ask, in such a position that I can't tend to him personally.

He doesn't respond.

"Taylin? I can't see him. Is he all right?"

"That's a matter of perception," she grunts, clinging to his body. "He's in really bad shape."

"Don't stop, Nellabix," I instruct as the unihorn flees from the hybrids. "Don't stop until we're out of harm's way. Then we'll help Rune."

Happily obliging, Nellabix thunders through the valleys, over the mountains, and across the rivers until the sun begins to rise.

Sore and strained, we shift uncomfortably when the unihorn comes to an abrupt halt at the top of a grand hill overlooking a vast field of small lakes and clusters of trees. The sunrise's warm colors skim across the water, the mesmerizing hue dreamlike.

Carefully, I slide off Nellabix, guiding a dazed Rune and a tired Taylin to the mossy grass below.

Nellabix rewards herself by trotting downhill to the nearest body of fresh water to hydrate, her tail flicking behind her. I will treat that beautiful being to a lifetime of happiness and freedom for rescuing us.

Rune curls over onto his side, his eyes swollen and his nose crushed. He's but a shell of the immortal I've come to know and love.

I place my hand on his burning forehead, eager to heal him. "He has a fever."

"No kidding," Taylin says, shivering in contrast. "He will recover quickly. We just need water and a good meal. And plenty of rest."

"Taylin," I say after she lets out a mighty yawn. "Taylin, you gave up your immortality for me. You could've died."

She shrugs, avoiding eye contact and tending to Rune by lifting his head and gently placing it in her lap. "I only gave you back what was yours. When I realized how selflessly you sacrificed yourself to save your people...I knew I couldn't resent you. You were a hero. You *are* a hero."

"But you're dying."

She shrugs again. "That ooze took away a lot of my pain."

Exhaling heavily at her nonchalance, I put my hand to my chest and mutter incoherently. Within moments, I feel an abundance of emotion and fragility as my life force exits my body and slips into Taylin, who almost convulses at the sudden jolt of energy.

"What did you do?" she rasps.

"Exchanging my immortality," I say with a smile.

"But...but...you need it! Have you seen your reflection? You're covered in blood and blisters and bruises and—"

"Then you can give it back to me once you feel like you've overcome your ailments. Fair trade, I would say."

Taylin goes to protest, but then attempts to conceal a smirk. "Well, I suppose that makes sense. You can have it back tonight."

Relieved by her compliance, I stretch out my aching muscles and lay down next to Rune, enjoying the sunlight's warmth. Taylin remains upright, keeping guard and protecting Rune's split head.

My now mortal body sighs in relief as I settle into the grass, falling into a deep slumber surrounded by my friends.

"Rise and shine!"

Bleary-eyed, I blink several times as I struggle to make out the blurry figure. Silhouetted against the sunlight, I yawn and curl my toes.

"How long have I been out?" I ask.

"Hmm. Eight hours, maybe?"

Wait a minute. That's not Taylin's voice.

I shoot upright and laugh at the fresh-faced Rune. His neck is only slightly askew, his eyes now bright and curious.

"Rune!" I reach out and embrace him, happy tears rolling down my cheek. "Oh goodness gracious, how are you feeling?"

"Grateful that I'm a central-land boy. My ankles are still killing me, though. And don't think I'm as cute with this crushed centerpiece." He tenderly touches his broken nose, beaming despite the pain he must still be in. "Another couple of days and I'll be back to my chipper self, I'm sure. I reckon I've been healing faster since working in labor. Maybe I'm stronger. Maybe it's these weird neckbands. So, I need to ask. Um. Where *are* we? And what's that cool creature? Where is everyone else?"

I glance at Taylin who is on her side, back facing us. No doubt she is faking sleep to avoid the barrage of questions.

"That's a unihorn," I say, answering the easier questions first. I smile at my old friend who gently nudges at flying insects with her horn. She's always been a curious specimen. "Nellabix. She was my pet when I was a young immortal in the north. She's grown up beautifully."

He inhales shakily. "I get the feeling I missed a lot while I was crushed beneath that bridge."

"How did you get out?" I ask, cautiously changing the subject.

"I don't know. I heard Garu's voice often. There must've been a lot of lightning because I saw these flashes from time to time. One night, the stone I pushed on was finally loose and I crawled out."

I cringe at the thought of going through such an ordeal. "I'm so sorry."

He shrugs. "So, where are we?"

Begrudgingly, I recount the events that took place over the week, explaining the northerners, Garu, and our bizarre escape. He picks at the grass while he listens, nodding thoughtfully as I reveal my sister's intentions.

"Interesting..." Rune says, his voice husky. We could both do with a drink. "Did I ever tell you the cannibals didn't leave that threatening message in your cell? The 'you're next mortal'."

"Then who did?"

"Zain," he says matter-of-factly. "Well, to be accurate, it was Mitty who wrote it on behalf of Zain. He was trying to get the message across that you're either with him or against him. He wants the blood of all mortals."

Spluttering incoherently, I finally wrap my mouth around my words. "But Mitty is mortal!"

"And a great puppet for the time being. But who knows how long Zain feels he needs him around? It's a sad truth and an admission I only managed to dig out of him when I brought enough water to quench his delirious state. I feel like an idiot for helping him now." Rune puts his head in his hands, rocking slowly. "This is all my fault."

It's somewhat comforting seeing an innocent party blame themselves for something that wasn't their fault. It's oddly relatable. Placing a loving arm over his shoulder, I pull him close for an embrace.

"Zain is manipulative. He would've found a way out one way or another. Dehydrated, malnourished and sleep deprived, he was always going to succeed. It's in his nature."

Rune doesn't respond, and I don't feel the urge to strike up further conversation. Instead, we enjoy the view and eventually make our way towards the pools of water to drink.

"Would you look at that?" Rune says, water dripping off his chin.

"What?" I ask, instantly on edge.

"That." He motions at the sun setting on the horizon, the pinky hues complimenting the greenery. "It's freedom."

I suppose I haven't had the opportunity to appreciate it. We're free from the walls of the prison, the cannibals, the judgmental stares. Sure, I'm back in the wilderness without a home to my name. But at least now I have the company of those who matter.

"For now," I reply cynically, fearful of the inevitable chase. This picture-perfect moment is on borrowed time.

When Taylin arises, we explore the immediate area with Nellabix, finding appropriate shelter. We forage fruit from nearby trees. It's not much, but it sure beats stale bread.

As night falls, Nellabix settles in a patch of flowers, and the three of us snuggle into her perpetually warm body.

So this is what a family is.

I WAKE EARLY the next morning when the unihorn stands abruptly, gazing suspiciously at the mountains, where the prison is tucked away.

"What is it, girl?" I ask warily. "Are they coming after us? Do we need to move?"

The unihorn flicks her tail and my heart sinks at her signal for 'yes'. It figures. Of *course* we couldn't have our happy ending. Not yet.

I jostle Taylin and Rune until they stir, pointing at the mountains.

"Are they coming?" Rune mumbles, one eye still closed.

"Who?" Taylin asks.

"Probably all of them," I say without inflection. "Garu. Adalin. The prison guards. The northerners."

Sighing, Taylin gets to her feet and stretches. "All right. Back to a life of fleeing, then. Let's find a desert island somewhere."

"That sounds delightful!" Rune agrees somewhat sarcastically, slower to wake.

Disgusted with the pair's eagerness to hide, I stand my ground. "No. We're not running away to an island."

"It *is* pretty hard navigating the seas," Rune says, ignorant to the context. "Most people never come back. Unless they find paradise and don't feel the need to return? Or they die grisly deaths. Interesting. Let's take that option off the table. We might consider a cabin in the mountains. Not *those* mountains."

"No," I repeat. "I don't know if Garu is rooting for us or not, but a lot of events don't add up. The only thing I know for sure is I can't allow a revolution filled with slaughter and sacrifice to happen. Zain and my sister are about to destroy all that's good in this land. This needs to end with me."

Nellabix's tail swishes again as Rune pulls himself up and stands by my side, his head only coming up to my shoulder. "All right, Malin. I'll stand by you. What do we need to do?"

Oh, if only I knew. If only I trusted my destiny the same way Garu trusted Sharnique's premonitions.

In this utopian valley filled with picturesque views, an abundance of fruit, and warm hues, I can only feel the chill of the breeze, the darkness within, and the icy gaze of my two soldiers beside me.

Despite the external world, I'm suffocated by shadows that are screaming to be released. My inner turmoil is surfacing with every passing moment as I visualize the war to come and the people who are at the helm of it.

My people will *not* suffer anymore. My people will *not* become corrupt tyrants. My people will *not* kill mortals.

Inhaling deeply, I brace for the future path I'm setting for myself, uncertain whether I'm even the right person for the task at hand.

"First step," I say, digging my feet into the grass. "We take back the throne."

"Second step," a velvety voice says. "Introduce yourself."

My muscles tense, Nellabix whinnying at the intrusive greeting. Stepping out from behind the trees is a woman with a smug smile, her blonde hair messily pulled back into a ponytail. She is wearing my exact outfit—an expensive navy dress that reaches the ankles.

I clench my fists, ready to fight if I need to. "What do you want?"

The woman looks me up and down, nonchalant in nature. "Look at us wearing the same clothes. Would've expected more variety from someone as eccentric as Sharnique. Perhaps fashion isn't her forte."

"What do you want?" I repeat, my voice shaky. "Are you a god?"

The woman looks almost affronted by the accusation, then bursts into laughter. "A god? Honey, no. I *served* a god if that means anything. I'm the dead immortal whose life force was ripped away in order to save yours."

Nellabix's snort is the only thing that fills the silence.

"But...but you're dead," I say, unable to grasp her explanation.

"I *was* dead. Let's say, I've discovered some nifty, unique abilities. Maybe gods aren't much different from immortals, after all. Sharnique killed me. There was darkness. Then a spark of electricity. And I was suffocating underground. Now, here I am. And I am *pissed*. I'm pissed at mortals for imprisoning us. I'm pissed at a god for killing me. I'm pissed at *you* for being the reason why I died in the first place. My death was nothing more than a distraction! Nothing more than to help *you*. What makes *you* so deserving?"

I'm cautious of her shift in tone. Desperate to mollify her, I raise my hands as if to surrender and lower my voice. "I'm so sorry. Please, tell me what you want and we'll see if we can come to an arrangement. Perhaps we can help you."

"Oh, you're definitely helping me," she says, a nervous laugh escaping her lips. "I'm a little unhinged, Malin. I've come back *wrong*. I think *I'm* the *real* god now."

Her eyes roll to the back of her head, and she convulses violently, jerking her head in unnatural ways.

Then, she vanishes, leaving the three of us speechless.

I've never seen anything so inexplainable in all of my years. Lost in a sea of confusion, I stare at the blank space where the woman was and wonder if I imagined the whole scene.

Nellabix grunts, her gaze focused on the hills ahead as if warning us of imminent danger. Rune tugs on my arm, his voice tight. "Malin?

What just happened? What is going on? Are you all right? What do we do?"

I wish I knew the answer to his barrage of questions. I wish I understood what we just witnessed. I wish...I wish...

Switching back to leadership mode, I swallow the lump in my throat and force an assertive demeanor. Watching the shadows coming over the mountains, I stride towards Nellabix and direct Taylin and Rune to hop on.

"We need to run."

# About the Author

A performing arts teacher by day, writer by twilight. In the last six years, Tyrolin has had twelve novels published, many of which are internationally bestselling and award-winning.

When she's not choreographing for the stage or creating worlds on the page, she can be found writing songs, hypnotizing clients for anxiety and grief, eating chocolate and playing video games.

This has been an
Immortal Production

www.ingramcontent.com/pod-product-compliance
Lightning Source LLC
Chambersburg PA
CBHW061549210726
48287CB00006B/2129